DISCARD

Pictures of Ascent in the Fiction of Edgar Allan Poe

Pictures of Ascent in the Fiction of Edgar Allan Poe

Douglas Anderson

palgrave
macmillan

PICTURES OF ASCENT IN THE FICTION OF EDGAR ALLAN POE
Copyright © Douglas Anderson, 2009.

First published in 2009 by
PALGRAVE MACMILLAN®
in the United States—a division of St. Martin's Press LLC,
175 Fifth Avenue, New York, NY 10010.

Where this book is distributed in the UK, Europe and the rest of the world,
this is by Palgrave Macmillan, a division of Macmillan Publishers Limited,
registered in England, company number 785998, of Houndmills,
Basingstoke, Hampshire RG21 6XS.

Palgrave Macmillan is the global academic imprint of the above companies
and has companies and representatives throughout the world.

Palgrave® and Macmillan® are registered trademarks in the United States,
the United Kingdom, Europe and other countries.

ISBN: 978–0–230–61943–2

Library of Congress Cataloging-in-Publication Data

Anderson, Douglas, 1950–
    Pictures of ascent in the fiction of Edgar Allan Poe / Douglas Anderson.
        p. cm.
    Includes bibliographical references.
    ISBN 978–0–230–61943–2 (alk. paper)
        1. Poe, Edgar Allan, 1809–1849—Criticism and interpretation.
    2. Calvino, Italo, 1923–1985—Criticism and interpretation. I. Title.

PS2638.A63 2009
818'.309—dc22   2009005355

A catalogue record of the book is available from the British Library.

Design by Newgen Imaging Systems (P) Ltd., Chennai, India.

First edition: October 2009

10 9 8 7 6 5 4 3 2 1

Printed in the United States of America.

When storms rage and we fear the shipwreck of the state, there is nothing nobler for us to do than let down the anchor of our studies into the peaceful ground of eternity.

Johannes Kepler, 1628

An infinity of error makes its way into our Philosophy, through Man's habit of considering himself a citizen of a world solely—of an individual planet—instead of at least occasionally contemplating his position as cosmopolite proper—as denizen of the universe.

Poe, "Marginalia" (June 1849)

Contents

Preface

Readers of this book who are familiar with the conventions of academic prose will immediately recognize that the following pages strive to keep their extraneous professional cargo to a minimum. Poe's fiction is filled with extravagantly overfurnished rooms or badly stowed ships that reflect the mental disarray of their occupants. Mindful of the fate of many of these characters, I have tried to jettison all unavoidable encumbrances—replacing footnotes, for instance, with a succinct account of the secondary resources I have used for each chapter in an appendix to the book. Nearly fifty years ago Richard Wilbur suggested that Poe's overwrought interiors depict the visionary consciousness of a poetic soul besieged by the mundane, physical world. The warfare between these two antagonists, Wilbur believes, is Poe's "fundamental subject." Over time, this view of Poe's fascination with decor has come to strike me as too schematic. His heroes and narrators frequently find themselves surrounded by a gorgeous clutter that the poetic consciousness ultimately sheds—a tactic I propose to emulate as best I can.

These five chapters take as their point of departure the provocative conjunction between Italo Calvino's striking lecture on "Lightness," from *Six Memos for the Next Millennium*, and the trajectory of Poe's professional life. Calvino cites Poe as one of the artistic predecessors whose engagement with the "existential function of literature" most influenced what Calvino terms his own "search for lightness as a reaction to the weight of living." Poe's imagination was forced to contend with this crippling weight in a number of personal and cultural forms: a ballast of material and psychological affliction aptly symbolized by the 1832 and 1849 worldwide cholera outbreaks that almost perfectly frame Poe's career. To such challenges his fiction repeatedly responds with vivid explorations of cognitive possibility that he came to understand as the transmutation of "rudimentary" into "ultimate" life. Poe coined these terms late in his career to describe an expressive struggle that lies at the heart of his work. I hope to establish the seriousness and the coherence of that struggle through a deep excursion into the literal and figurative pictures of ascent that shape the experiential world of his tales.

Quotations from Poe's stories and reviews, identified by an abbreviation and a page number, are drawn almost entirely from the generous collections published by the Library of America: *Poetry and Tales* (PT), prepared by Patrick Quinn, and *Essays and Reviews* (ER), prepared by G. R. Thompson. In a handful of cases, I cite T. O. Mabbott's *Collected Works of Edgar Allan Poe* (Cambridge, MA: Harvard University Press, 1978) by abbreviation (CW), volume, and page number when I need to present material that Poe included in early versions of one or two stories but cut from the later reprintings that modern editors customarily follow—a trimming away of textual ballast that sometimes enhances narrative buoyancy at the expense of details that help illuminate Poe's intentions. Mabbott's volumes have been recently reissued by the University of Illinois Press and remain an indispensable guide to the editorial evolution of Poe's fiction. Without his exhaustive efforts, Poe's artistic life would have remained almost entirely inaccessible to today's reader, obscured behind the apparent stability and security of dozens of contemporary collections of his work.

I am grateful to the University of Georgia for extending to me the continued support of the Sterling-Goodman Professorship. The Research Media office at the University of Georgia, the Public Library of Cincinnati and Hamilton County, the Library and the Special Collections Department of the American Museum of Natural History, the permissions and imaging staff of the J. Paul Getty Museum, and the New York Public Library helped with obtaining and preparing illustrations. Brigitte Shull and Lee Norton at Palgrave Macmillan moved the manuscript through the evaluation and editorial process with great efficiency and care.

I cannot stress too strongly that this book is not an attempt to resituate Poe's work in literary or cultural history, to adapt a new interpretive vocabulary to his stories or his life, to engage at any length in the kind of critical friction that often characterizes literary scholarship, or to offer an original vision of Poe's meaning. The following pages may contribute, in some measure, to all of those goals, but their primary purpose is to serve as a vehicle for the reader's renewed immersion in Poe's language. Much of what I present may seem obvious to many admirers of Poe's work, but I hope it will not be the less welcome or the less refreshing for being so. I am mindful of one of Poe's own, exhilarating critical pronouncements early in "The Rationale of Verse": "In one case out of a hundred a point is excessively discussed because it is obscure; in the ninety-nine remaining it is obscure because excessively discussed. When a topic is thus circumstanced, the readiest mode of investigating it is to forget that any previous investigation has been attempted." In the following chapters, for better or for worse, I have tried to take this advice.

INTRODUCTION

Cosmos

Charles Baudelaire was so deeply impressed by the opening scenes of "William Wilson" that he quoted without interruption nine consecutive paragraphs from the beginning of Poe's story in the 1852 *Revue de Paris* essay where he first attempts to explain Poe's appeal to a growing circle of French readers. Like many critics and biographers since, Baudelaire finds himself drawn to the poignant disaster of the life. All of Poe's work is autobiographical, he explains, and offers a rich sample from "William Wilson" to illustrate his claim. But the illustration itself seduces Baudelaire from his journalistic task. "What do you think of this passage?" he demands of his reader, much as a teacher today might address a classroom filled with students, suddenly required to surrender the pleasurable distractions of twenty-first century American life for the uncanny atmosphere of a quaint old schoolhouse "in a misty-looking village of England" two hundred years ago. "For my part," Baudelaire quickly insists, "I feel that this picture of school life gives off a dark perfume."

The artist whose evocative power Baudelaire set out to praise had been dead for three years when the *Revue de Paris* essay appeared—killed by alcohol poisoning, or "congestion of the brain" (according to newspaper reports), contracted during an unruly congressional election that took place in Baltimore in October 1849. Poe was forty when he died while making a brief visit to the city where his father's family was still prominent, the city where his dream of being a poet had come to an end in 1831 and his more successful career as a master of short fiction began one year later. Philadelphia, Richmond, and New York formed the outlines of the urban vortex that ultimately consumed Poe's talents and his life. He passed through all of these places between June and October of 1849, during a whirlwind tour that he hoped would end in a second marriage, filling the emotional void caused by the death of Virginia Poe in January 1847. These cities formed the volatile human perimeter of Poe's existence: a collection of transient rooming houses, rented cottages, and cheap editorial offices, with Baltimore at its heart.

From Baltimore, Poe would send his first, neatly penned stories to a Philadelphia weekly magazine's fiction contest when he was twenty-two. Baltimore had been his refuge more than once, through his late teens, as he struggled to mend relations with his Richmond guardian John Allan, to advance his military career at West Point, or to reenter civilian life after sabotaging his future at the military academy. From Baltimore he traveled to his first important magazine job on the staff of the *Southern Literary Messenger* in Richmond in 1835. To Baltimore he would return to die fourteen years later. Poe's boyhood excursion to England between 1815 and 1820 as an anomalous member of John Allan's household—the basis of "William Wilson"—his year of study at Charlottesville, Virginia in 1826, as Thomas Jefferson lay dying at Monticello, and his two years as a soldier in Boston, Virginia, and South Carolina are the only significant intervals of time that he spent outside the mid-Atlantic zone where he hoped to make a name for himself as an editor, a critic, and a teller of tales.

It was a tightly circumscribed outer life for an imagination that tolerated no earthly limits, that exulted in the mind's extraordinary spatial mobility. This contrast partly accounts for the alluring, dark perfume that Baudelaire detects in Poe's semiautobiographical treatment of his boyhood experience in an English private school outside London. The narrator of "William Wilson" claims that the tedious confinement of his early years was linked with a "more intense excitement than my riper youth has derived from luxury, or my full manhood from crime." The schoolhouse and the surrounding village that William Wilson describes are not merely old but "excessively ancient," like those natural registers of inconceivable age, the "gigantic and gnarled trees," which fill the fictional landscape. The hours that toll from the village church bell across this vividly remembered world break "with sullen and sudden roar" upon the pervading stillness in a haunting reminder of the oceans of time and space that engulf Poe's narrator.

"Oh, outcast of all outcasts most abandoned!" Wilson exclaims, like a contemporary Robinson Crusoe preparing to unburden his soul: "to the earth art thou not forever dead? to its honors, to its flowers, to its golden aspirations?—and a cloud, dense, dismal, and limitless, does it not hang eternally between thy hopes and heaven?" Such spiritual extremity certainly springs, in some degree, from Poe's painful recollection of the acute anxiety he felt when, at eighteen years of age, he quarreled with John Allan and fled Richmond to join the army under an assumed name in Boston, the city of his birth. But Wilson is also giving voice to the sheer exhilaration of scope—the intoxication of astrophysical scale—that had begun to infuse modern astronomy and geology in Poe's lifetime, eclipsing any feelings of personal remorse or fear on Wilson's part with the sublimity of the limitless.

Baudelaire is certainly right to point to Dr. John Bransby's Manor House School at Stoke Newington as the biographical background to the paragraphs that he quotes. Between 1818 and 1820, John Allan's precocious young ward received an unforgettable taste of English educational discipline at Bransby's school, while Allan himself struggled to keep his merchant export business afloat. But language, not documentary accuracy, is the source of the strange perfume that Baudelaire detects in his long extract. No writer has ever grasped more clearly than Poe the vital importance of a story's threshold, the verbal doorway through which it ushers the reader into figurative experience. "How many good books suffer neglect through the inefficiency of their beginnings!" he once complained in his "Marginalia": "At all risks, let there be a few vivid sentences *imprimis*, by way of the electric bell to the telegraph" (*ER*, 1322). "William Wilson" has an electrical beginning:

> But the house!—how quaint an old building was this!—to me how veritably a palace of enchantment! There was really no end to its windings—to its incomprehensible subdivisions. It was difficult, at any given time to say with certainty upon which of its two stories one happened to be. From each room to every other there were sure to be found three or four steps either in ascent or descent. Then the lateral branches were innumerable—inconceivable—and so returning in upon themselves, that our most exact ideas in regard to the whole mansion were not very far different from those with which we pondered upon infinity. During the five years of my residence here, I was never able to ascertain with precision, in what remote locality lay the little sleeping apartment assigned to myself and some eighteen or twenty other scholars. (PT, 340)

The house of Poe's fiction is a blend of infinite possibility and enticing complexity—of the boundless and the tightly bound—that arouses and thwarts the human hunger for precision. It is both a single "mansion" and a labyrinthine city, like the Paris of Poe's imagination, or like the tangled byways of Philadelphia, New York, and Baltimore, where he plotted out the euphoric ascents and bitter descents of his artistic life.

The years that William Wilson spent in this palace of enchantment are (he insists) stamped upon his memory "in lines as vivid, as deep, and as durable as the *exergues* of the Carthaginian medals." Adults generally recollect very little from early childhood, Wilson believes: "An indistinct regathering of feeble pleasures and phantasmagoric pains" is all that survives from this halcyon period. But despite a lifetime of dissipation and reckless gambling throughout England and the capitals of Europe, Wilson's school memories remain vivid. They constitute, in retrospect, a Carthage of the spirit: a period of glorious but doomed independence marked by "a wilderness of sensation, a world of rich incident, an universe of varied emotion" that leaves indelible traces upon his character before yielding to the luxury and crime of his decadent Roman maturity. These words foreshadow Wilson's own dual nature, a state of being eerily prefigured in the image of his school principal, Dr. Bransby, whose officious public piety at Sunday services clashes with the private zeal that he brings to classroom discipline. "With how deep a spirit of wonder and perplexity was I wont to regard him from our remote pew in the gallery," Wilson recalls: "Oh, gigantic paradox, too utterly monstrous for solution!" (PT, 339). Strictly policed enclosure is the sign of Bransby's narrowness of mind; by contrast depth and distance, "a plenitude of mystery—a world of matter for solemn remark" comprise the unbounded mental horizon of Wilson's schoolboy universe.

For Baudelaire these evocative passages form part of Poe's "psychological dictionary," the unique vocabulary that he gradually brought to bear against the practicality, the arrogance, and the jealousy of contemporary Americans, a nation of pious hypocrites for whom Dr. Bransby in his pulpit is a comprehensive symbol. That "stray planet," Edgar Poe (as Baudelaire memorably calls him) how little his personal suffering mattered to the crude tyranny of American public opinion: "They are so proud of their youthful greatness," Baudelaire observes of Poe's unappreciative countrymen: "they have such a naive faith in the omnipotence of industry, they are so sure that it will succeed in devouring the Devil, that they feel a certain pity for all these idle dreams. Forward, they say, forward, and let us forget the dead."

Baudelaire's crass and domineering Americans in fact resemble a subtly transposed portrait of William Wilson himself: willful and unscrupulously materialistic; a victim of his own "ungovernable passions" and of a vague "constitutional malady" in his parents; a childish tyrant in his own household, who seems only too adept at forgetting the "dead," that enigmatic race of "imaginative and easily excitable" forbears whose constitutional legacy Wilson both inherits and strives to destroy. The potential for figurative contraction and expansion in such language points to what Baudelaire calls the "compact and *concatenated*" effect of Poe's style: its ability to evoke an absorbing verbal interior that, like the infinite confusion of William Wilson's schoolhouse, generates feelings of limitless possibility. "All his ideas," Baudelaire suggests, "like obedient arrows, fly to the same target"—toward the cosmic ideality and unity glimpsed at the close of *Eureka*, foretold in the ecstatic testimony of "Mesmeric Revelation," and disclosed in fragments throughout the swift trajectory of Poe's career. He was, Baudelaire concludes, one of those "rare, exotic plants" forever unsuited to the "heavy vegetables" that literary critics and biographers are so fond of grafting upon them.

Indeed, a contempt for the conventional fruits of criticism marks the earliest phases of Poe's career. The 1831 edition of his poems that Poe published in Baltimore shortly after his truncated career at West Point opens with a preface that both plagiarizes and mocks Coleridge's critical authority. Volcanic intellect though he may be, the English sage is hampered by his "very profundity," Poe declares: "It is lamentable to think that such a mind should be buried in metaphysics, and like the Nyctanthes, waste its perfume upon the night alone" (PT, 16). Poe never wavers from the implications (and the paradoxes) of this fastidiously intellectual anti-intellectualism. The night-flowering jasmine *Nyctanthes arbor tristis*, tree of sorrow, is a sensory figure for the misguided acuity of the critical establishment that both Poe and Baudelaire come to scorn. In an 1847 reassessment of Nathaniel Hawthorne's short stories, Poe reframes the same iconoclastic attitudes, repudiating the pretension of the literary quarterlies (ER, 579). A year later, *Eureka*, Poe's speculative cosmogony, heaps a final measure of ridicule on "the cuttlefish reputation for profundity" enjoyed by the critical savants of the day "with whom darkness and depth are synonymous" (PT, 1275).

As Poe's celebrated fictional detective, Auguste Dupin, affirms in one of the many procedural disquisitions that repeatedly interrupt his investigation of the grotesque double murder in the Rue Morgue: "Truth is not always in a well. In fact, as regards the more important knowledge, I do believe that she is invariably superficial. The depth lies in the valleys where we seek her, and not upon the mountain-tops where she is found.... By undue profundity we perplex and enfeeble thought; and it is possible to make even Venus herself vanish from the firmament by a scrutiny too sustained, too concentrated, or too direct" (PT, 412). Poe's youthful self-confidence anticipates this passage a decade before his memorable hero Dupin came to formulate it. "Learning has little to do with the imagination," Poe brashly declares in the 1831 preface to his collection of poems. The admiring companion who narrates Auguste Dupin's adventures agrees. The superficially unpretentious game of checkers, he suggests, offers far richer mental rewards than "the elaborate frivolity of chess." Let's call this imaginative posture the conundrum of lightness.

Baudelaire points to it, in his *Revue de Paris* essay, when he comments with undisguised satisfaction on the "dark perfume" of Poe's language, or when he mocks the "heavy vegetables" so beloved of scholarly gardeners. Poe's art (he insists) resembles an insubstantial scent or a delicate flower. It won't do to impose more weight on these stories or poems than their designs are meant to support. Yet Baudelaire almost instinctively grasps that Poe's narrator in "William Wilson" embraces the ponderous architecture of his old school building as if its weighty shell were a necessary complement for, or antagonist of, the limitless and weightless space that it contains. The age-blackened desks in William Wilson's schoolroom are deeply carved tablets of boyish despair, "piled desperately with much be-thumbed books"—testaments to the massive futility of Dr. Bransby's old learning. By contrast Wilson's volatile blend of "ardor," "enthusiasm," and "imperiousness" quickly confers upon him a potent "ascendancy" among his peers (PT, 341). This is lightness of a very suggestive kind, a close relative of the key imaginative quality to which Italo Calvino pays perceptive tribute in his undelivered and unfinished series of Charles Eliot Norton lectures, *Six Memos for the Next Millennium*.

In "Lightness," the first of the five talks that Calvino lived to complete, he describes a conjunction that he perceives between his forty years of artistic practice and the needs of a new century, a new human era. "My working method," Calvino confesses, "has more often than not involved the subtraction of weight ... sometimes from people, sometimes from heavenly bodies, sometimes from cities; above all I have tried to remove weight from the structure of stories and from language." The outcome of this process is a poetic strategy for evading what Calvino calls the "opacity" of the world, one that yolks together very ancient and very recent verbal resources. In the fable of Perseus and Medusa, in Lucretius's *De Rerum Natura*, and in Ovid's metamorphic agility, Calvino finds evidence of the kind of lightness that he prizes, a "lightness of thoughtfulness" that transmutes the intractable matter of physical existence symbolized by the Medusa's petrifying gaze. The thirteenth-century Florentine poet Guido Cavalcanti embodies Calvino's ideal of "the sudden agile leap of the poet-philosopher who raises himself above the weight of the world" through his perception of "the equality of all existing things," an insight that is implicit in the atomism of Lucretius and the corporeal mutability that Ovid's poem repeatedly celebrates.

Modern physics seems to Calvino as fertile in images of lightness as Lucretius's ancient theories. The complexity and power of DNA or the evocative significance of the term "software" tell the same story: the "iron machines" of industrial and economic history still exist, Calvino recognizes, "but they obey the orders of weightless bits." In suggesting this affinity between aesthetic and scientific perception, Calvino pays tribute, in particular, to the achievement of Cyrano de Bergerac, whose 1657 *Voyage to the Moon* represents the first fruits of a scientific and artistic synthesis that liberates human consciousness from what Calvino calls "anthropocentric parochialism." Poe too is a moon voyager, a poet philosopher who (like Cyrano) employs his serio-comic powers of invention (as well as a flair for theft) in the service of an expansive cosmology. Perhaps for this reason Calvino names Poe, along with Hoffmann, Gogol, Hawthorne, Dickens, Kipling, and Wells among others, as his creative models. These are the figures who, in Calvino's judgment, contribute most significantly to what he calls the "existential function" of literature: "the search for lightness as a reaction to the weight of living."

Poe's experience taught him a great deal about the weight of living, both as a personal and a communal burden. The deaths of his mother, his brother, and his wife are the most prominent of the emotional assaults that he endured. His bitter estrangement from John Allan, the only father he had ever known, casts a shadow over the eight years between 1826 and 1834, when Poe's adolescent ambitions were most fragile and his artistic growth had just begun. His lifelong struggle with alcoholism and with poverty is legendary. These bleak biographical materials intersect with equally disruptive public events crisscrossing his path through the first half of the nineteenth century: a multiyear depression triggered by the Panic of 1837, weakening a literary marketplace that Poe depended on for his support; the volatile class hostilities of Jacksonian politics; the rise of the abolitionist movement and the sectional conflict that it aroused; the two great cholera epidemics of 1832 and 1849, public health crises circumscribing an era in American history that saw itself as increasingly beset with cultural as well as physiological plagues and fevers. The seventeen years between 1832 and 1849 coincide perfectly with Poe's career as a writer of fiction.

Indeed, for many of the catalytic occurrences of his day, Poe's private experience provided a ringside seat. During his brief stint as an enlisted man in the United States Army, after his 1827 flight from John Allan's home, he served for thirteen months at Ft. Moultrie on Sullivan's Island, a few miles from Charleston, South Carolina. That state's key politicians had only recently begun to assert, in print and in fiery speeches, their right to defy Federal law and nullify the Tariff of 1828—a precursor to the secessionist movement that would ultimately precipitate the Civil War. "Carolina fever" was the term one observer coined to describe the state's political frenzy, a bleak allusion to the nearly annual recurrence of yellow fever that repeatedly thinned Charleston's population in these troubled years.

Poe's earliest period of residence in Baltimore, awaiting an offer of admission to West Point, coincided with William Lloyd Garrison's emergence as editor of an abolitionist newspaper in that city, and with Garrison's brief imprisonment for libel in a Baltimore jail, an experience that crystallized his radical calling and led directly to the establishment of "The Liberator" in January 1831. Many slaveholders came to hold Garrison personally accountable for Nat Turner's insurrection in August of 1831, when Poe was once more in Baltimore, having left the Army and rejoined the household of his aunt, Maria Clemm, close enough to the site of Turner's outbreak to appreciate the intense anxiety it aroused. Baltimore hosted the first national political convention in the fall of 1831, when the Anti-Masonic Party nominated William Wirt for President, effectively splitting the opposition to Andrew Jackson and ensuring his reelection. In these same months, the Baltimore and Ohio Railroad completed its first sixty miles of track, linking the city with Frederick, Maryland and making it a leader in the national transportation revolution. Poe was still living in Baltimore when cholera broke out there in the late summer of 1832, the third city on the eastern seaboard to experience a full-blown epidemic.

Like the editorials and letters inveighing against the fever of nullification or the plague of slavery in these years, Poe's stories repeatedly reflect the blend of figurative and actual contagion that marked his times. The enigmatic Mr. Bedlo in "A Tale of the Ragged Mountains" ultimately dies when a leech applied to his temple to help reduce a fever proves to be poisonous. The narrator of "The Facts in the Case of M. Valdemar" revels in the gruesome physiological progression of advanced tuberculosis. A variety of mysterious afflictions strike down a number of Poe's most memorable heroines and devastate his narrators— catastrophes that Poe parodies in still other stories that mock the body's material fragility. The effete narrator of "The Duc de L'Omelette," for instance, dies after eating a parrot and plays a game of *écarté* in Hell to retrieve his soul. "The Man That Was Used Up" makes a grotesque farce out of the improbable success of the prosthetic devices employed to rehabilitate a badly mutilated soldier. In "How to Write a Blackwood Article," Poe appears to disparage the melodramatic "intensities" of his greatest stories by offering a scatological prescription for writing them: "Take a dose of Brandreth's pills, and then give us your sensations," Mr. Blackwood cheerfully advises the story's aspiring narrator. Brandreth's pills were a potent laxative, a popular remedy at the time for a host of physical complaints.

Like the disfigured frontier veteran General John A.B.C. Smith, all of these characters and narrators—the serious and the parodic alike— are "used up," an occupational hazard of the writer who is consumed by the world of letters. But in using up one kind of body, Poe dreams of liberating another, or of at least glimpsing the possibilities for doing so that form the subject of "Mesmeric Revelation," a fantasy account of a dying man's hypnotic insights so vivid that many of its readers could not bear to take it for fiction. For Poe as for Emily Dickinson, the perceptual experience of sickness—its dual impact on witnesses and on the delirious consciousness itself—was an irresistible artistic resource, an opportunity to depict the mix of defilement and exaltation that formed the extremes of bodily life. The epidemic and endemic menace of cholera throughout Poe's lifetime exposed those extremes as few other events could, but cholera was simply one component among many that formed what Poe called, in his late poem "For Annie," "the fever called 'Living.'"

Unlike Emerson, Poe did not have the residual structure of religious tradition (and a secure inherited income) as a psychological and emotional refuge within which to nurture his literary ambitions. Hawthorne drew on three political patronage jobs to sustain him across the vicissitudes of his artistic career. Thoreau's surveying skills and a modest family business answered his slender needs. Margaret Fuller, born in 1810, a little over a year after Poe, was able to live with her family until her father's death from cholera in 1835 forced her to craft a career as a teacher and a journalist for the last fourteen years of her life. From the time that the eighteen-year-old Poe left Richmond in the spring of 1827 to join the Army, he had only his pen, his passion for reading, and a growing fascination with the metaphysical implications of modern scientific inquiry as his sole resources for survival.

As his career unfolded, he increasingly turned away from the world of anthropocentric parochialism toward the general phenomenon of consciousness itself rather than the cultural and metaphysical debris that Hawthorne, for instance, dutifully attempts to purify in "Earth's Holocaust." Poe's holocausts do not spare the words of biblical revelation, as Hawthorne is careful to do. Indeed, they do not spare the Earth, or any other earthly or celestial body, from participation in the elaborate choreography of Separation and Reunification that *Eureka* enacts on a cosmic scale and that "William Wilson" stages on its microcosmic one. This teleological dance directly reflects the degree of conscious pleasure that Poe took throughout his career in the agility of the poetic intellect, even when the energies of that intellect were incapable of breaking the deadly grip of time and space. Scientific perception could not always triumph over anthropocentric blindness, but in the hands of a gifted artist it could illuminate the depths to which that blindness often led.

Consider the brief sketch called "The Sphinx," which Poe wrote sometime late in 1845 and published in the January 1846 issue of *Arthur's Ladies Magazine*. Like "William Wilson" this brief sketch too takes up old memories from Poe's early life, though ones less deeply buried than his recollections of the Manor House School. Instead the narrator of "The Sphinx" recalls "the dread reign of the Cholera in New York" fourteen years earlier, when he had retreated from the ravaged city to a friend's "*cottage ornée*" on the Hudson to wait out the fury of the disease:

> Not a day elapsed which did not bring us news of the decease of some acquaintance. Then, as the fatality increased, we learned to expect daily the loss of some friend. At length we trembled at the approach of every messenger. The very air from the South seemed to us redolent with death. That palsying thought, indeed, took entire possession of my soul. I could neither speak, think, nor dream of anything else. My host was of a less excitable temperament, and, although greatly depressed in spirits, exerted himself to sustain my own. His richly philosophical intellect was not at any time affected by unrealities. To the substances of terror he was sufficiently alive, but of its shadows he had no apprehension. (PT, 843)

"No apprehension" suggests both bravery and blindness on the part of the host's richly philosophical intellect—a delicate ambiguity that prefigures the course of the story. War was an all too real substance of terror lurking in the political shadows cast over national life by the annexation of Texas in July 1845, shortly before Poe wrote this tale. The boarding houses and the Fordham cottage where he and his wife spent the early months of 1846 were equally redolent with death, as Virginia Poe slowly lost her long battle with tuberculosis. The opening sentences of "The Sphinx" are saturated with a mix of real and fictive dread.

Of all the means of distraction available to Poe's narrator in his friend's country retreat, he inexplicably elects to immerse himself in a gloomy course of reading on the topic of omens. Predictably enough an extraordinary vision soon appears to him in the shape of a remarkable monster traversing "the naked face" of a distant hill, cleared by a recent landslide. So grotesque is this creature—so laden with implications of "forthcoming evil"—that the narrator begins to doubt his sanity. Compared with the size of some adjacent trees, it seems larger than any contemporary warship, armed with a proboscis "as thick as the body of an ordinary elephant," with "two gleaming tusks not unlike those of a wild boar," and a pair of prism-shaped staffs on each side of its head reflecting "in the most gorgeous manner the rays of the declining sun":

> The trunk was fashioned like a wedge with the apex to the earth. From it there were outspread two pairs of wings—each wing nearly one hundred yards in length—one pair being placed above the other, and all thickly covered with metal scales; each scale apparently some ten or twelve feet in diameter. I observed that the upper and lower tiers of wings were connected by a strong chain. But the chief peculiarity of this horrible thing, was the representation of a *Death's Head*, which covered nearly the whole surface of its breast, and which was as accurately traced in glaring white, upon the dark ground of the body, as if it had been there carefully designed by an artist. (PT, 845)

As this "terrific animal" in its weighty, metallic armor disappears from view at the foot of the hill, it utters a strange cry "so expressive of wo" that the narrator immediately faints.

When he finally brings himself to describe this apparition to his host, the response is a hearty laugh followed by "an excessively grave demeanor, as if my insanity was a thing beyond suspicion." The two men are sitting near the window where the original vision had occurred when "the association of the place and the time" prompts the narrator to make his confession. Suddenly, as if on cue, the monster appears again, but still the narrator's cool-headed companion is unable to see it. After some careful questioning, however, the host explains that his terrified guest has simply confused a tiny moth, "about the sixteenth of an inch in its extreme length," crawling on a fragment of spider's web hanging from the window sash with the spectacle of a fabulous monster on a distant hillside. It is not his reason but his vision that is disordered, misinterpreting perspective and relative proportion in a fashion that confuses imperceptible lightness with ominous weight. The philosophical intellect would appear to have reestablished a healthy ascendancy over sensory delusion.

The story's own proportions, however, are suggestively skewed. The Death's-headed Sphinx moth that the narrator's mind seems to have magnified into a monster is not found in North America. It is a member of the class of hawk-moths, very large insects with wingspans of nearly five inches, native to Africa, Asia, and Europe, but nowhere in the so-called New World. Such a creature could scarcely wriggle up a strand of spider's web, as Poe's all-too-confident host insists that it does. The larva of the Death's-headed Sphinx eventually grows into a spectacular caterpillar big enough to fill the palm of one's hand before pupating into *Sphinx atropos*, the Linnæan name by which Poe's contemporaries recognized the remarkable adult moth that bears the uncanny image of a skull on the back of its thorax and possesses the unsettling ability to emit a strange cry when disturbed.

In consulting a reference book and making his identification, this knowing host brings his own eye to within "the sixteenth of an inch" of the creature that he claims to be observing, pressing his face to the windowpane in order to describe a phenomenon that only his imagination is really capable of seeing. Indeed, the host's superior powers of reason seem at once reassuringly precise and disturbingly myopic. The illusory creature itself is the story's great achievement: a half plausible concoction of natural and artificial elements, gleaming like a great metallic machine on a hillside that it seems to have stripped of timber in order to sate its hunger or fuel its uncanny grief. Its unforgettable appearance and emblematic Death's head suggest an etching out of Goya or one of the nightmarish animals that Michel Foucault associates with the Renaissance iconography of madness: the "screech owls" with toad bodies, "winged insects with cats' heads, sphinxes with beetles' wing cases" that serve as figurative equivalents for what Foucault terms "the dark rage, the sterile madness that lie in men's hearts."

Madness, Mary Oliver reminds us, is always at issue in Poe's fiction, but it is almost never sterile. The psychological fragility that characterizes the narrator of "The Sphinx" does not impair the rich descriptive gifts that permit him to relay his marvelous vision in a series of striking images, capturing even the prism-shaped structure of the creature's elaborate antennae as they split the sunlight into its spectrum of colors.

PL. XXXVII.

To my Ingenous Friend and Benefactor Mr Dru Drury
This Plate is most Humbly Dedicated by his Obliged Servant Moses Harris

Figure 1 Death's Head Sphinx Moth, or "Bee Tiger," from Moses Harris, *The Aurelian, a Natural History of English Moths and Butterflies* (London, 1840). Reproduced by courtesy of the Library, American Museum of Natural History.

Indeed, the two men in the story begin to resemble differing developmental stages of a single individual rather than entirely separate beings. The quiet retreat of the *cottage ornée* shields them from the outside world while an immature form of consciousness pupates into a mature one. But which character is which? In what direction is the mind's transformation proceeding: toward the suggestive visions of intuition, with their rich emotional power, or the overconfident conclusions of the philosophic intellect?

The story proposes a riddle more insoluble, perhaps, than the one that the ancient Sphinx of Thebes offers her human victims: a challenge framed by the mythic possibilities of natural science as well as by the symbiosis of lightness and weight with which Calvino identifies the existential triumph of literature. The chapters that follow pursue the reading tactics that this brief treatment of "The Sphinx" has begun to explore—singling out the nature of Poe's engagement with the weight of life by means of the conceptual and figurative agility of art, his imperfect and incomplete flight from the anthropocentric parochialism of his time. To some degree I try to take up the stories in chronological order of publication, especially in Chapter 1, "Problems of Disposal," which focuses on an array of Poe's earliest tales, rooted in some of the more gruesome features of the rudimental life—those that the narrator of "The Sphinx" and his affluent host hope to evade.

Beginning with the second chapter, "A Pneumatics of Mind," Poe's own metaphorical preoccupations exert considerable influence on the number and the sequence of the stories that each section addresses. His work tends to cluster into discrete groups of tales—nebular clouds, perhaps—whose individual members have a great deal in common with one another, but which also have distinctive figurative properties of their own. The chapter titles try to indicate the particular array of forces and images that each hopes to explore, though in the end the boundaries dividing the chapters will, I hope, prove to be highly permeable ones, allowing the most vivid stories to pass easily back and forth across them in the reader's mind, as I try to outline a convincing taxonomy of one of the nineteenth century's most remarkable literary imaginations.

CHAPTER 1

Problems of Disposal

In early January 1832, the British survey vessel H.M.S. *Beagle*, carrying twenty-two-year-old naturalist Charles Darwin on the first stage of a five-year circumnavigation of the globe, was turned away from the port of Santa Cruz on Tenerife out of fear that the ship might be carrying cholera. European governments had been trying for months to stem the progress of the pandemic as it moved out of Asia, across Hungary, Poland, and Germany, toward England and France. Newspapers in London and in the port cities of North America kept track of the successive outbreaks of sickness as they moved steadily and fatally to the west. In the English press, conservatives and radicals alike came to view the relentless approach of the disease as an ominous symbol for the social and political upheaval associated with months of acrimonious debate over the first Reform Bill.

No one understood the microbiological basis of cholera, though contemporary physicians were reasonably sure that it was connected, in some way, to the problem of public sanitation. Unlike tuberculosis, the other great scourge of the day, cholera killed with stunning speed. Excruciating abdominal cramps and vomiting were usually the first signs of infection. Severe diarrhea, dehydration, and death followed in quick succession, often in the space of a single day. "The symptoms" William H. McNeill observes, "were peculiarly horrible: radical dehydration meant that a victim shrank into a wizened caricature of his former self within a few hours, while ruptured capillaries discolored the skin, turning it black and blue." A nineteenth-century French physiologist, François Magendie, called this rapid deterioration of cholera patients "cadaverization": the mimicry of death by life. An Edinburgh surgeon experienced in diagnosing the disease from his service in India took note of the wrinkling of a victim's hands and feet "as if they had been long steeped in water" and the hollow, unnatural sound of the

voice. Throughout this grim metamorphosis, the mind of a cholera suf-
ferer usually remained clear, before lapsing into a coma that signaled
the final phase of the illness. Postmortem muscle contractions occasionally led to fears that bodies were being hurried into mass graves at
the height of an epidemic before the patients were dead. "Spasmodic
cholera" the disease was sometimes called, in recognition of this uncanny
galvanic phenomenon, or "blue cholera," from the deeply stained skin
of its European and Asian victims.

These frightening attacks prompted nineteenth-century ministers in
England and the United States to remind their anxious congregations of
the swift retribution visited upon sinners by an outraged Deity. "Iniquity
runs down our streets like a river," the American Tract Society warned
in a widely circulated 1832 pamphlet aimed at forestalling judgmental
plagues by encouraging reform among its readers. The catastrophic
symptoms of cholera seemed a gruesomely apt means of chastisement
for the nation's communal pollution. As if to confirm attempts to
impose religious significance on its spread, the epidemic appeared to
single out centers of urban vice, exacting a terrible price among prostitutes, drunkards, poor emigrants, the homeless. But cholera claimed
affluent victims as well, and like all gastrointestinal infections it was
particularly deadly in its effects on children.

Aboard the *Beagle*, at twenty-two, Charles Darwin was making his
third attempt at finding a suitable career. For the second son of a wealthy
Shropshire physician and grandson of Erasmus Darwin, medicine had
initially seemed the logical choice. A few months in Edinburgh attend-
ing lectures, cadaver dissections, and graphic surgical demonstrations
quickly convinced the young Darwin that he did not have the stomach
to be a doctor like his father and grandfather. Further study at
Cambridge, aimed at preparing him to enter the Church, only whetted
a longstanding childhood fascination with natural science. The invitation to sail on the *Beagle* had offered a propitious change in direction.
By the time he returned to England in October 1836, the great cholera
pandemic had burned itself out, and Darwin found himself supplied
with the specimens and the experience he needed to address the intriguing riddle of biological complexity and environmental diversity that
had confronted him at every turn on his world voyage.

Meanwhile another twenty-two-year-old was also embarking on his
third career in January 1832, without the luxury of the leisure that
Charles Darwin enjoyed. Edgar Allan Poe had taken refuge in Baltimore
the previous spring in the crowded household of his widowed aunt,
Maria Clemm, abandoning an appointment at West Point that John

Allan had secured for him, and along with it the prospect of life as an army officer. A slim collection of poems, expanded and republished twice between 1827 and 1831, had convinced Poe that being a poet was no more viable a path toward independence than being a soldier. Perhaps in Baltimore, amid his father's extended family, he would be able to make a new beginning.

Unlike Darwin, Poe had to support himself. Disowned by the wealthy Richmond tobacco merchant who had raised him, he needed a paying job, not an engrossing hobby. The American periodicals and newspapers of the day—ephemeral though they often were—would pay for prose fiction and, in due course, for the labor involved in soliciting, editing, and publishing it. Accordingly, Poe turned his attention to prose, and on January 14, 1832, five days before his twenty-third birthday, his first tale, "Metzengerstein," appeared in the Philadelphia *Saturday Courier*. He selected as a Latin epigraph for the story Martin Luther's 1526 challenge to Pope Clement VII: "Pestis eram vivus—moriens tua mors ero," "Alive I was your plague—dying I shall be your death." The first word of Poe's first work of fiction is "pestis," plague. His choice of epigraph would prove to be prophetic. Between 1832 and 1835, Poe would learn to transform his own concrete experience with the century's first cholera pandemic into a figurative resource of great flexibility and subtlety. Like Darwin, he too began to assemble the particulars of a sweeping intellectual synthesis in the laboratory of his art.

* * *

Cholera did succeed in crossing the ocean in 1832, five months after "Metzengerstein" had presented the *Saturday Courier's* readers with the tale of a dissolute Hungarian nobleman borne to a fiery death by a mysterious demonic stallion—an agent of vengeful transmission as inexplicable as the movements of disease. The epidemic first broke out in New York City in June, moving to Philadelphia by early July and to Baltimore by mid-August. No Poe letters survive from this period to suggest how carefully the residents in Maria Clemm's rented rooms on Baltimore's Mechanics Row followed the epidemic's spread. Many years later, however, Frederick Douglass recalled that the city was in a feverish state long before the infection actually arrived. Nat Turner's slave insurrection of August 1831 had deeply alarmed the white population. As Douglass's reading skills increased, he began to marvel at the mixture of rage and fear generated by the potent term "abolition" in the Baltimore newspapers. William Lloyd Garrison formed The New England

Anti-slavery Society in December 1831 and printed the new organization's constitution in *The Liberator* the following February. South Carolina's threat to nullify a Federal tariff had thrust the country into a constitutional crisis. Accompanying all this turmoil (Douglass remembered) the cholera was coming, like a divine chastisement, "armed with Death." It was a momentous time.

Poe is largely silent during these months of anticipation and dread. Indeed, between June and November of 1832, even his trickle of contributions to the Philadelphia *Saturday Courier* dries up, and with it the flow of desperate appeals for sympathy and support that had filled Poe's letters to John Allan for the past five years. August and September 1832 proved to be the most virulent months of the cholera epidemic in Baltimore. Within the city limits, 853 people died of the disease. Just outside the city proper, 125 inmates of the Baltimore almshouse also died. Mortality rates associated with cholera can vary widely, but medical historians agree that fifty percent is a reasonable figure for such epidemics in the early nineteenth century. This estimate suggests that nearly two thousand people fell ill with the disease during the height of the Baltimore outbreak—one person in forty out of a population of 80,000. In the city's poorer neighborhoods, circumstances undoubtedly magnified the density of infection.

Cholera breeds in conditions where problems of disposal are acute. Two-thirds of Baltimore households in 1832 relied on wells for their supply of drinking water. In the absence of a modern sewage system, human waste carrying the cholera bacillus readily spreads the infection, adding mounds of contaminated bedding and clothes, along with hundreds of corpses, to the already overburdened stream of public waste disposal. One would expect an experience of this nature to leave its mark on a perceptive witness, as it clearly did with Frederick Douglass. But with the exception of a passing allusion to "cholera morbus" in one of his early burlesques, Poe does not directly address the subject of the epidemic until he writes "The Sphinx" in 1846. This apparent reticence is superficial at best. Over the next seventeen years, the complex phenomenon of contagion exerts a pervasive influence on Poe's fiction, threading its way through his exotic landscapes, creating an intimate perceptual theater where an attentive observer might briefly glimpse the troubled intersection of flesh and spirit, the confrontation between a disposable body and the indefinable essence that it contained.

"William Wilson" stages this confrontation with memorable force, likening the enfeebled whispers of conscience to "a pestilence" that pursues Poe's frantic narrator from city to city across Europe, after a midnight visit to a schoolmate's bedchamber triggers an instantaneous infection:

> Having reached his closet, I noiselessly entered, leaving the lamp, with a shade over it, on the outside. I advanced a step, and listened to the sound of his tranquil breathing. Assured of his being asleep, I returned, took the light, and with it again approached the bed. Close curtains were around it, which, in the prosecution of my plan, I slowly and quietly withdrew, when the bright rays fell vividly upon the sleeper, and my eyes, at the same moment upon his countenance. I looked; —and a numbness, an iciness of feeling instantly pervaded my frame. My breast heaved, my knees tottered, my whole spirit became possessed with an objectless yet intolerable horror. Gasping for breath, I lowered the lamp in still nearer proximity to the face. Were these—*these* the lineaments of William Wilson? I saw, indeed, that they were his, but I shook as if with a fit of the ague in fancying they were not. . . . Was it, in truth, within the bounds of human possibility, that *what I now saw* was the result, merely, of the habitual practice of this sarcastic imitation? Awe-stricken, and with a creeping shudder, I extinguished the lamp, passed silently from the chamber, and left, at once, the halls of that old academy, never to enter them again. (PT, 346–347)

Cholera's dramatic impact on the "lineaments" of its victims lies behind this sickening conflation of psychological and physiological symptoms. Wilson's uncanny double is both an infected and an uninfected self.

The mysteries of transmission that lead to this celebrated scene began to infuse Poe's work in the months immediately following the 1832 epidemic, as he prepared a collection of stories called "Eleven Tales of the Arabesque," narrated by the eleven members of a literary club whose interspersed remarks Poe intended as a "burlesque upon criticism." In an effort to entice the editors of the *New England Magazine* to accept this ambitious series, Poe sent them, in May 1833, the manuscript of his first completely new story in almost two years, a sketch that he eventually titled "Four Beasts in One—The Homo-Cameleopard." Aimed at an audience with well-established biblical appetites, the narrative records a visionary excursion to Antioch during the reign of Antiochus Epiphanes, a Syrian tyrant especially notorious for the graphic account of his horrible death in 2 Maccabees.

Few of Poe's contemporaries would have been unfamiliar with the memorable fate of Antiochus, struck down by "the Lord almighty, the God of Israel" with "an incurable and invisible plague . . . a pain of the bowels that was remediless...and that most justly, for he had tormented other men's bowels with many and strange torments" (2 Maccabees 9:5–6). Enraged by the victories of Judas Maccabeus, and maddened by disease, Antiochus rushed toward Jerusalem in order to slaughter the rebellious Jews, only to be thrown from his chariot. His injuries swiftly combined with his sickness to destroy him: "the worms rose up out of the body of this wicked man...and the filthiness of his smell was noisome to all his army." Even while still clinging to life, Antiochus is reduced to a vile burden that "no man could endure to carry for his intolerable stink." Poe blandly alludes to this striking episode at the beginning of his tale before turning to earlier incidents from Antiochus's violent reign, set in his capital of Antiocha Epidaphne, two centuries before the birth of Christ.

The story's narrator introduces his "gentle reader" to the historical and geographical circumstances of this ancient place, prompting a dialogue concerning the "mass of houses" lying at their feet as they view the streets of Antioch from one of the city's battlements, very much like a modern tourist and a hired guide. At the end of a brief account of Antioch's eventual ruin and decay, the narrator abruptly inquires whether his companion does not find the city's present appearance grotesque. The reply at first is tentative and unsatisfying:

> "It is well fortified; and in this respect is as much indebted to nature as to art."
> Very true.
> "There are a prodigious number of stately palaces."
> There are.
> "And the numerous temples, sumptuous and magnificent, may bear comparison with the most lauded of antiquity."
> All this I must acknowledge. Still there is an infinity of mud huts, and abominable hovels. We cannot help perceiving abundance of filth in every kennel, and, were it not for the overpowering fumes of idolatrous incense, I have no doubt we should find a most intolerable stench. Did you ever behold streets so insufferably narrow, or houses so miraculously tall? What a gloom their shadows cast upon the ground! It is well the swinging lamps in those endless colonnades are kept burning throughout the day; we should otherwise have the darkness of Egypt in the time of her desolation. (PT, 182–183)

The conventional spectacle of wealth and power noted by the naïve tourist does not particularly interest Poe's jaded narrator. Sumptuous and magnificent palaces, he insists, are a kind of costume—the first of several that this story will address—a glittering architectural shell that encases infinite filth. The city's stench, in fact, anticipates the grim fate of its monarch; its unstable blend of abominable hovels and stately palaces, of pride and corruption, forms a shadowy link between this visionary sketch and the cholera ravaged cities of Europe and America in 1832. Iniquity runs like a river down Antioch's ancient streets.

"Come let us be off!" the narrator/guide abruptly insists, just at the point where his companion begins to show signs of being intoxicated by the "tumultuous mob of idiots and madmen" celebrating the murderous prowess of their degraded king: "Surely this is the most populous city of the East!" Poe's excitable tourist cries, "What a wilderness of people! what a jumble of all ranks and ages! what a multiplicity of sects and nations! what a variety of costumes! what a Babel of languages! what a screaming of beasts! what a tinkling of instruments! what a parcel of philosophers!" (PT, 188). Poe submitted the story to the *New England Magazine* within a few weeks of Andrew Jackson's second inauguration. The ecstatic cry of pleasure from the guide's gullible companion echoes the carnival mood of Jackson's Democratic electorate, pictured as a composite mob of human beings and wild animals in Poe's plot, staging their political euphoria in eastern cities that had only recently purged themselves of disease. America and Antioch appear to be at least two beasts in one.

Poe's interest in this sketch clearly lay in the degree of surreal satire that he was able to achieve through its elaborate network of costumes, evoking in the mind of a contemporary reader the nightmarish pageant of squalor and fear that comprise a great epidemic, cast in the identical interpretive framework that many religious pamphlets and sermons had sought to impose on the cholera outbreaks of the previous year. The glib tone of Poe's narrator/guide mocks all pious disguises—the pagan fictions of Antiochus's craven court, and by extension the judgmental fictions of the American clergy as well, each of which seeks to mask the noisome scent of urban poverty with its own idolatrous fumes. The editors of the *New England Magazine* declined to take Poe's biblically seasoned but clearly heterodox bait, the first of two early collections of his work for which he was unable to find a publisher.

A few months later, in "The Visionary," a story that he would eventually retitle "The Assignation," Poe begins to extend the range of his evocative effects, finding in contemporary Venice an equivalent for the splendid filth of Antioch, but replacing his ironic guide and gullible tourist with a single figure who combines elements of both: a neutral observer who seems inoculated against imaginative contagion but whose emotions are deeply engaged by a spectacle of romantic despair that he witnesses. Published in *The Lady's Book* for January 1834, the story is the first of several early experiments that Poe makes in probing the paradoxical bond between the luminous operations of consciousness and the defilements of flesh. The double nature of Venice itself plays a key role in this complex investigation. The city is partly a "star-beloved Elysium of the sea," Poe's narrator declares, and partly a scene of "dim visions... whose Palladian palaces look down with a deep and bitter meaning upon the secrets of her silent waters" (PT, 200). Venice's glory casts an inverse image of itself in the stagnant decay that fills its canals.

The story's opening paragraphs, in fact, construct an ornate chamber of multiple reflections, beginning with those of the city's enigmatic waters, but adding the "black mirror of marble" beneath the silvery feet of a young marchesa and the "shattered mirror" of her troubled eye as it "multiplies the images of its sorrow." The architectural shadows of an adjacent building and the murky depths of a canal likewise echo one another's secretive darkness. Venice as a whole forms an unusually apt mirror of the human body. Poe treats it as an urban organism with its own circulatory system and potentially corrupted avenues of ingestion. The story's narrator almost seems to stumble on these potent analogies:

> It was a night of unusual gloom. The great clock of the Piazza had sounded the fifth hour of the Italian evening. The square of the Campanile lay silent and deserted, and the lights in the old Ducal Palace were dying fast away. I was returning home from the Piazzetta by way of the Grand Canal. But as my gondola arrived opposite the mouth of the canal San Marco, a female voice from its recesses broke suddenly upon the night, in one wild, hysterical, and long continued shriek. Startled at the sound, I sprang upon my feet: while the gondolier, letting slip his single oar, lost it in the pitchy darkness beyond a chance of recovery, and we were consequently left to the guidance of the current which here sets from the greater into the smaller channel. Like some huge and sable-feathered condor, we were slowly drifting down towards the Bridge of Sighs, when a thousand flambeaux flashing from the windows, and down the staircases of the Ducal Palace, turned all at once that deep gloom into a livid and preternatural day. (PT, 201)

Once the mouth of the canal San Marco utters its uncanny shriek, the narrator's gondola abruptly transforms itself into a hybrid creature, part aquatic swan and part desert condor, an echo of the hybrid nature of the city itself. The scene's preternatural light suggests the interior of a great theater, as well as the bodily recesses to which the "mouth" of the canal appears to lead. The events that shortly play themselves out on this vivid blend of an artificial and a natural stage ultimately point to one of Poe's most persistent themes: the flesh for all its ethereal beauty is little more than a vessel, an elaborate Palladian palace founded upon the hidden secrets of silent waters.

When on the following day the narrator of "The Assignation" visits the palazzo of the nameless "stranger" whose dramatic rescue of a drowning child began the story, he encounters there a stunning collection of priceless art and splendid furnishings, gathered in a richly illuminated and scented room that his host refers to as "my little regal cabinet"—an elaborate cultural storehouse not unlike the city that contains it. Even sound contributes to the atmosphere of these "imperial precincts." The air is filled with "low, melancholy music, whose origin was not to be discovered," the first of many problems of assignation which this magnificent room seems designed to pose (PT, 205). Some of the surrounding paintings appear to be by famous artists, but others are masterpieces of "the unknown great," the host declares, while others are "unfinished designs by men, celebrated in their day, whose very names the perspicacity of the academies has left to silence and to me" (PT, 206).

Academic memory, perhaps, is faulty, but that of the narrator's enigmatic host is not. Considered as a challenge to assignation in his own right, he is a provocatively unstable being: perspicacious yet preoccupied, a model of exquisite taste who has lost interest in tasteful things, slight of build and yet "Herculean" in strength, with dazzling Byronic features that are, at the same time, curiously ordinary, even forgettable—a physical attribute in puzzling contrast to their beauty and to the tenacious nature of the memory that they conceal:

> With the mouth and chin of a deity—singular, wild, full, liquid eyes, whose shadows varied from pure hazel to intense and brilliant jet—and a profusion of curling, black hair, from which a forehead of unusual breadth gleamed forth at intervals all light and ivory—his were features than which I have seen none more classically regular, except, perhaps, the marble ones of the Emperor Commodus. Yet his countenance was, nevertheless, one of those which all men have seen at some period of

their lives, and have never afterwards seen again. It had no peculiar—it had no settled predominant expression to be fastened upon the memory; a countenance seen and instantly forgotten—but forgotten with a vague and never-ceasing desire of recalling it to mind. Not that the spirit of each rapid passion failed, at any time, to throw its own distinct image upon the mirror of that face—but that the mirror, mirror-like, retained no vestige of the passion, when the passion had departed. (PT, 204)

This verbal portrait is the most complex of the story's varied mirrors. The host's features suggest a dispassionate expressive medium for human feeling, a surface of light and shadow that prompts the narrator to compare its "classic regularity" to sculpture but which (like desire itself) is incapable of stillness or permanence. Despite its painterly beauty, the host's countenance escapes all tactics of artistic containment at the same time that it evokes every impetus to art. Like Venice, too, it is a hybrid image: Herculean in its nobility and strength but reminiscent of the degraded appetites that Commodus and Antiochus represent.

None of the rare paintings, ancient sculpture, delicate drapery, or rich carpets with which the palazzo's exotic cabinet is filled seems capable of holding the attention of their mercurial owner, a collector almost by reflex who scorns the historical "proprieties" of place and time that might bring order to the heterogeneous medley of his surroundings. He is, instead, repeatedly distracted by imaginary noises and preoccupied by the subject of a remarkable painting, hidden behind a drapery that he now removes: an image of the same woman whose wild cry had startled the narrator the night before, the Marchesa Aphrodite di Mentoni. Standing at an upper window of her husband's palace, in a fit of inexplicable forgetfulness, she had somehow allowed her infant to slip from her arms and disappear beneath the surface of a canal—an act of disposal signaling complete despair. As this idealized canvas suggests, however, she is also an image of the city she inhabits, and of the corporeal predicament of the soul, linked by the polluted waters and the physical extremity of birth to impermanent flesh—a juxtaposition "so completely ludicrous," the story's doomed hero implies, "that a man *must* laugh or die" (PT, 205).

In the painting, the Marchesa's countenance betrays "that fitful stain of melancholy" with which the story's narrator associates "the perfection of the beautiful." One painted arm lay across her bosom, while the other "pointed downward to a curiously fashioned vase." Otherwise her image scarcely seems to touch the earth. All the gorgeous, representational extravagance of the hero's private museum echoes one aspect of the portrait's implicit story: no work of the hand, however curiously fashioned, can succeed in containing the elusive and beautiful spirit. This metaphysical essence escapes all material vessels. The puzzling vase to which the Marchesa's image points is a surrogate both for the flesh and for the womb, a vessel within a vessel that alternately stores and releases life's secret waters. Both references invoke a portrait of the city as a figurative body and the body as a figurative city: a structure of "superhuman beauty" encompassing a labyrinth of interior channels that both sustain and undermine its life.

Words may offer a partial exemption to this vulnerable alliance. The single object in the host's remarkable collection which remains capable of moving him is not the hidden painting of the Marchesa Aphrodite but a page in an Italian verse tragedy, underscored by a reader who appears recently to have wept over its meaning while writing his own stanzas on an interleaf in response:

> Thou wast that all to me, love,
>   For which my soul did pine—
> A green isle in the sea, love,
>   A fountain and a shrine,
> All wreathed with fairy fruits and flowers;
>   And all the flowers were mine.
>
> Ah, dream too bright to last;
>   Ah, starry Hope that didst arise
> But to be overcast!
>   A voice from out the Future cries
> "Onward!"—but o'er the Past
>   (Dim gulf!) my spirit hovering lies,
> Mute, motionless, aghast!

Moments after the narrator reads this anonymous poem, his mysterious young host is dead. The poison that he takes, by prearrangement with his beautiful lover, leaves the goblet from which he quenches an apparently desperate thirst "cracked and blackened," a vivid emblem of the corrosive effects of disease on the fragile vessel of the flesh.

*   *   *

The cluster of stories that Poe wrote between the end of the 1832 cholera epidemic and his departure for Richmond in 1835 develops the thematic and figurative energy of "The Assignation" in every conceivable direction. The artistic relationships among these tales become visible when Poe publishes or republishes them in successive issues of the *Southern Literary Messenger* once he becomes a regular contributor to the magazine in March 1835, a few months before joining its staff. Unable to find an outlet for a book-length collection of his early work, he took advantage of his first editorial job to serialize his own development. The Palladian order and decadent squalor of Venice find scenic equivalents in other plots and sketches: the ruinous pest zone of London during an outbreak of plague or a surreal African swamp surrounding an enigmatic stone monolith. The desperate laughter of his mysterious Venetian hero reechoes through succeeding stories in demonic as well as burlesque forms. The baroque splendor of the regal cabinet where "The Assignation" comes to an end prefigures the stark but opulent simplicity that encloses the narrator of Poe's first explicit treatment of an epidemic's psychological terror.

Two of these early stories, "Berenice" and "Morella," pay particular attention to the rich symbolic possibilities of romantic passion as a virulent and exalting infection. In both Poe conflates the key voices of "The Assignation," the moralizing narrator and his doomed friend, tying the speaker of each tale directly to an extraordinary partner whose powers of attraction have the hallucinatory grip of an intense fever. In each tale, too, the cultural density captured in the lavish interior of a Venetian palazzo takes the still more compressed form of a library: a verbal "museum" that is partly an intellectual treasure house, partly a refuge, and partly a tomb. A book is the only remaining item in his regal cabinet that is still capable of awakening the hero's emotions at the close of "The Assignation." The printed word plays a more equivocal role in these subsequent tales, one that stresses the capacity for delusion or delirium associated with the intoxication of language.

In "Berenice," Poe links the mortal necessity of disposal to its desperate sentimental complement: the instinctive urge to preserve some incorruptible token of corruptible flesh. His title character divides into a disposable body on the one hand and a set of glistening teeth on the other, which Egæus, the story's maddened narrator, collects from his cousin's grave and stores in a little box in his ancestral library. This superficially gruesome plot is inextricably involved with what Poe's narrator refers to as the "ruminating propensity" of consciousness: the mind's restless confrontation with the existential mysteries that encompass it. Egæus is nothing if not a ruminative intelligence, though his characteristic "disease" (as he terms it) differs from the fruitful ruminations of the genuinely "ardent imagination," one drawn to meditate on some topic of true importance. His own preoccupations, Egæus insists, are frivolous, obsessive, barren, and *"never* pleasurable" (PT, 228). Sterile trivialities become his avenue of escape from the relentless physical mutations that seem to doom his beautiful young cousin.

Poe eventually excised from the earliest version of "Berenice" a vivid scene in which Egæus spends a few moments "in the strictest communion" with his cousin's body. The curtained bedroom enclosure where his servants had placed her open coffin loosely mimics a confessional booth where Egæus suddenly finds himself alone with what appears to be Berenice's corpse:

> The very atmosphere was redolent of death. The peculiar smell of the coffin sickened me; and I fancied a deleterious odor was already exhaling from the body. I would have given worlds to escape—to fly from the pernicious influence of mortality—to breathe once again the pure air of the eternal heavens. But I had no longer the power to move—my knees tottered beneath me—and I remained rooted to the spot, and gazing upon the frightful length of the rigid body as it lay outstretched in the dark coffin without a lid.
>
> God of heaven!—is it possible? Is it my brain that reels—or was it indeed the finger of the enshrouded dead that stirred in the white cerement that bound it? Frozen with unutterable awe I slowly raised my eyes to the countenance of the corpse. There had been a band around the jaws, but, I know not how, it was broken asunder. The livid lips were wreathed into a species of smile, and, through the enveloping gloom, once again there glared upon me in too palpable reality, the white and glistening, and ghastly teeth of Berenice. I sprang convulsively from the bed, and, uttering no word, rushed forth a maniac from that apartment of triple horror, and mystery, and death. (CW 2, 217)

In 1845, when Poe republished "Berenice" in the *Broadway Journal*, he deleted these paragraphs, perhaps recognizing their close resemblance to William Wilson's contemplation of his sleeping double. The unmistakable recollections of the 1832 cholera epidemic that they evoke may also have become problematic with the passage of time. The swift deterioration of Berenice's emaciated body, coupled with the alarming galvanic phenomenon of a moving corpse—a familiar feature of the "spasmodic cholera"—would have had vivid clinical significance for Poe's contemporaries.

Like Egæus the modern reader tends to focus almost obsessively on the image of the teeth alone, but Poe has gone to some trouble, in his excised paragraphs, to depict very particular social and psychological anxieties surrounding the fear of invisible sources of infection. By 1845 these excised details may have struck him as being unnecessarily specific, too circumstantial or too precise to be consistent with the story's ambitious expansive effects. Like many of Poe's most memorable plots, "Berenice" situates its portrayal of mental or physical confinement within vast psychological horizons. "Misery is manifold," Egæus moodily announces in the tale's opening sentences: "The wretchedness of earth is multiform." A sense of indefinite space and all-inclusive scope mark the beginning of what might otherwise appear to be a story of eccentric or singular human misfortune. Overwhelming disproportions of size and force entice the reader's imagination at every turn, framing in an especially memorable way the brief existence of Egæus's cousin:

> Berenice!—I call upon her name—Berenice! And from the gray ruins of memory a thousand tumultuous recollections are startled at the sound! Ah! Vividly is her image before me now, as in the early days of her lightheartedness and joy! Oh! Gorgeous yet fantastic beauty! Oh! Sylph amid the shrubberies of Arnheim!—Oh! Naiad among its fountains!—and then—then all is mystery and terror, and a tale which should not be told. Disease—a fatal disease—fell like the simoom upon her frame, and, even while I gazed upon her, the spirit of change swept over her, pervading her mind, her habits, and her character, and, in a manner the most subtle and terrible, disturbing even the identity of her person! Alas! The destroyer came and went, and the victim—where was she? I knew her not—or knew her no longer as Berenice. (PT, 226)

Like the excised passage in which Egæus communes with his cousin's body, this language too is faintly redolent with superstition. Berenice's old "habits" of mind and of dress might yield as readily to religious vows as to disease, particularly in a world as replete with Patristic influence as that of Egæus and the collection of Latin Fathers in which he has steeped his imagination. Poe is careful to itemize some of the contents of his narrator's library: Secundus Curio's de Amplitudine Beati Regni Dei, Augustine's City of God, Tertullian on the blood of Christ. Entering a convent entails a transformation of identity that might consume his cousin's former name and "person" as decisively as the physiological metamorphosis of puberty that Egæus's description of her fatal "change" faintly evokes. The lurking menace of an ambiguously sexualized Catholicism had nourished English gothic fiction for over half a century by the time Poe began his career. No market-conscious artist could afford to ignore its appeal, but none exploited the complex relation between religion and its material vehicles—its ceremonies and its books—with more ingenuity and intelligence than Poe.

Egæus's own physical condition seems at first to sympathize with the deep trances to which Berenice gradually succumbs, but it quickly takes the form of a morbid and self-hypnotic attentiveness to trivialities, presented in appropriately tedious detail:

> To muse for long unwearied hours, with my attention riveted to some frivolous device on the margin or in the typography of a book; to become absorbed, for the better part of a summer's day, in a quaint shadow falling aslant upon the tapestry or upon the floor; to lose myself for an entire night, in watching the steady flame of a lamp, or the embers of a fire; to dream away whole days over the perfume of a flower; to repeat, monotonously, some common word, until the sound by dint of frequent repetition, ceased to convey any idea whatever to the mind; to lose all sense of motion or physical existence, by means of absolute bodily quiescence long and obstinately persevered in: such were a few of the most common and least pernicious vagaries induced by a condition of the mental faculties, not, indeed, altogether unparalleled, but certainly bidding defiance to anything like analysis or explanation. (PT, 227)

Despite his own half-hearted efforts at mystification, Egæus's mental condition is not particularly difficult to assess. These vagaries are the cognitive equivalent of the physical changes that Berenice soon displays: the oddly compromised powers of vision suggested by her "lustreless" eyes, the peculiar catalepsy that reflects her deepening isolation from outward life. Any connection with nature his cousin may have once possessed dissolves. Egæus now sees her "not as the living and breathing Berenice, but as the Berenice of a dream," a purely conceptual or even ritual entity, "not as an object of love" (PT, 229). The ceremonial stillness evoked by his study lamp, his monotonous caricature of a monastic chant, his intense absorption in the appearance rather than the meaning of a printed page, his dreamy immersion in an atmosphere of natural incense—all point toward superstitious rites of veneration that culminate in the mutilation of his cousin's body in order to fill a private reliquary.

In the story's climactic scene, Egæus is musing over a book by a long-dead Persian poet when one of his servants, in "broken sentences," conveys the news of Berenice's uncanny recovery and horrible mutilation. As if in sympathy with the terrified servant's message, a little box sitting on a nearby table shatters when an agitated Egæus accidentally drops it, spilling its own unarticulated contents: "some instruments of dental surgery, intermingled with thirty-two small, white and ivory-looking substances that were scattered to and fro about the floor" (PT, 233).

These strangely denatured objects seem to have lost all connection with the body, as well as with the gross, physical struggle to remove them that had left Egæus's clothes "muddy and clotted with gore." Purity and impurity collide in this vivid confrontation with the crude "substances" of corporeal being.

Egæus's pathological fixation upon "the white and ghastly *spectrum*" of Berenice's teeth highlights the many figurative spectrums that frame Poe's plot. The story opens with his narrator's invocation of the rainbow as an emblem for the wide horizons of joy and sorrow that mark human life, an intimate blend of bliss and anguish, sunlit reason and shadowy intuition. Egæus traces the unsteady interplay between these vast conceptual extremes from the vantage point of his family library: a limitless yet profoundly limiting interior whose collection of ancient books replicates the gorgeous, imperial cabinet of "The Assignation." "The recollections of my earliest years are connected with that chamber," Egæus writes:

> and with its volumes—of which latter I will say no more. Here died my mother. Herein was I born. But it is mere idleness to say that I had not lived before—that the soul has no previous existence. You deny it?—let us not argue the matter. Convinced myself, I seek not to convince. There is, however, a remembrance of aërial forms—of spiritual and meaning eyes—of sounds, musical yet sad—a remembrance which will not be excluded; a memory like a shadow, vague, variable, indefinite, unsteady, and like a shadow, too, in the impossibility of my getting rid of it while the sunlight of my reason shall exist.
>
> In that chamber was I born. Thus awaking from the long night of what seemed, but was not, nonentity, at once into the very regions of fairy-land—into a palace of imagination—into the wild dominions of monastic thought and erudition—it is not singular that I gazed around me with a startled and ardent eye... it *is* wonderful what stagnation there fell upon the springs of my life—wonderful how total an inversion took place in the character of my commonest thought. The realities of the world affected me as visions, and as visions only, while the wild ideas of the land of dreams became, in turn,—not the material of my everyday existence—but in very deed that existence utterly and solely in itself. (PT, 225–226)

This rich passage doubles as the self-exculpatory plea of a morbid mind and as an artistic autobiography. Though Egæus's meditations ultimately deteriorate into a cultic obsession with bodily relics, they begin with a vague perception that the body itself is a shadow rather than a substance, an antechamber to cognitive palaces that lie just beyond the sensory borders of the imagination. The visionary delirium that his words evoke exerts a decisive influence over Poe's fiction in the years immediately following the great cholera epidemic.

* * *

"Berenice" focuses almost exclusively on two hermetically sealed worlds: the narcissistic consciousness of Egæus on the one hand and Berenice's impenetrable silence on the other. The story's critical characters exist in quarantine zones that overlap only briefly as the narrative unfolds, once in the excised passage where Egæus views his cousin's body, and once more in the unwritten moment when he opens her grave to remove her teeth. Their singular diseases seem incapable of crossing the barriers imposed between them. In "Morella," the second of the two early stories that extend the romantic structure of "The Assignation," the joint phenomena of transmissibility and contagion break through these barriers, extending to every feature of Poe's compact plot. The tale opens, in fact, with a mystery of romantic transmission that its narrator is never able to explain. His marriage is a bewildering blend of feverish seizure and self-centered calculation, as if his original bond with his wife were a paradoxical mixture of the medicinal and the infectious:

> With a feeling of deep yet most singular affection I regarded my friend Morella. Thrown by accident into her society many years ago, my soul, from our first meeting, burned with fires it had never before known; but the fires were not of Eros, and bitter and tormenting to my spirit was the gradual conviction that I could in no manner define their unusual meaning, or regulate their vague intensity. Yet we met; and fate bound us together at the altar; and I never spoke of passion, nor thought of love. She, however, shunned society, and, attaching herself to me alone, rendered me happy. It is a happiness to wonder;—it is a happiness to dream. (PT, 234)

This eerie coalescence of being is a completely interior bond. Indeed, Morella scarcely has a corporeal presence at all in the story that bears her name: some "wan" fingers, a crimson spot on her cheek, blue forehead veins, and a "meaning" eye. The narrator and his bride seem bound to one another not in a physical partnership but as the mind might be married to a provocative but evasive idea.

A "gigantic" intellect is in fact the most conspicuous ingredient of Morella's character. It too proves infectious. Under his wife's tutelage, the narrator consumes works of German mysticism that ultimately subject him to wild vacillations of thought and feeling aroused by the touch of Morella's cold hand, by her "low, singular words," and by a "musical language" drawn from the "ashes of a dead philosophy." This intense response to his wife's influence ultimately grows "tainted with terror" (PT, 235). Joy deteriorates into horror, beauty into hideousness, as the couple's original state of dreamy happiness slips into an obsessive hostility in which the narrator finds himself longing "with the heart of a fiend" for his wife's death.

The hypnotic influence that Morella comes to exercise over her husband's mind is closely linked to the "mystical writings" and volumes of "theological morality" that provide the basis for this peculiarly mental marriage. The riddle of personal identity engrosses both partners: Is there a "*principium individuationis,*" the narrator wonders, that survives death? The allure of this question accounts entirely for the energy of their relationship. In the first three published versions of the story, Poe includes four stanzas of "a catholic hymn" that Morella sings on the verge of her death, underscoring the intense religious longings that drive the plot:

> Sancta Maria! turn thine eyes
> Upon the sinner's sacrifice
> Of fervent prayer, and humble love
> From thy holy throne above.
>
> At morn, at noon, at twilight dim
> Maria! thou hast heard my hymn:
> In Joy and Woe—in Good and Ill
> Mother of God! be with me still.
>
> When my hours flew gently by,
> And no storms were in the sky,
> My soul—lest it should truant be—
> Thy love did guide to thine and thee.
>
> Now—when clouds of Fate oe'rcast
> All my Present, and my Past,
> Let my Future radiant shine
> With sweet hopes of thee and thine.
> (CW 2, 227–228)

Faith, knowledge, and sickness form intricate bonds with one another in both "Berenice" and "Morella," as if Poe were determined to explore, in these paired stories, the elements of a spiritual physiology in which words serve as both agents of infection and as curative drugs.

Morella's hymn, though, points toward very specific anxieties of transmission. It is an appeal to the Mother of God in the voice of a young woman, apparently on the verge of childbirth and deeply apprehensive about the oncoming trials through which Mary and her own offspring have already passed. Poe's ambivalence about retaining the hymn in the final published version of the story may reflect his desire to turn the reader's attention away from Morella's mysterious pregnancy—a condition that leaves virtually no traces in the plot itself—toward the mental pregnancy of his narrator. It is the narrator, not his wife, who grows irrationally irritable as the story progresses, becoming moody, excruciatingly sensitive to touch, ultimately nauseated in Morella's presence as her fatal decline begins: "one instant, my nature melted into pity, but, in the next, I met the glance of her meaning eyes, and then my soul sickened and became giddy with the giddiness of one who gazes downward into some dreary and unfathomable abyss" (PT, 236). The uncanny birth around which the events of the tale will pivot is a product of intense intellectual gestation, the fathering and mothering of words, to which a muse and an artist both contribute critical elements of being.

The elder Morella dies on an incomparable autumn evening, in which seasonal change serves as a conventional surrogate for bodily decay. "The winds lay still in heaven," the narrator recalls, "There was a dim mist over all the earth, and a warm glow upon the waters, and, amid the rich October leaves of the forest, a rainbow from the firmament had surely fallen" (PT, 236). In this evocative setting, Morella summons her now alienated husband to her bedside in order to deliver an ominous prophecy, along with a newborn daughter whose unexpected and unexplained arrival has all the punning significance of an afterthought. "When my spirit departs shall the child live," Morella declares, "But thy days shall be days of sorrow—that sorrow which is the most lasting of impressions, as the cypress is the most enduring of trees" (PT, 236). These words amount to a perfect inversion of the despair that leads the Marchesa Aphrodite to contemplate destroying her infant in "The Assignation." In "Morella" the child survives while the mother drowns in the glowing waters that surround her, but each tale treats birth as the transmission of a tainted legacy, a vessel of death rather than life.

At first, Morella's sober message seems simply malicious—a fruitless attempt on the part of an embittered wife to poison the future bond between a father and his surviving daughter. But soon the child's uncanny rate of growth in mind and in body unsettle the narrator's otherwise doting spirit: "ere long, the heaven of this pure affection became darkened, and gloom, and horror, and grief, swept over it in clouds," a process that duplicates almost exactly the emotional shadows of his original marriage:

> I said the child grew strangely in stature and intelligence. Strange indeed was her rapid increase in bodily size—but terrible, oh! terrible were the tumultuous thoughts which crowded upon me while watching the development of her mental being. Could it be otherwise, when I daily discovered in the conceptions of the child the adult powers and faculties of the woman?—when the lessons of experience fell from the lips of infancy? and when the wisdom or the passions of maturity I found hourly gleaming from its full and speculative eye? When, I say, all this became evident to my appalled senses—when I could no longer hide it from my soul, nor throw it off from those perceptions which trembled to receive it—is it to be wondered at that suspicions, of a nature fearful and exciting, crept in upon my spirit, or that my thoughts fell back aghast upon the wild tales and thrilling theories of the entombed Morella? I snatched from the scrutiny of the world a being whom destiny compelled me to adore, and in the rigorous seclusion of my home, watched with an agonizing anxiety over all which concerned the beloved. (PT, 237)

The "beloved" is in fact a hybrid creature, both a living child and an abstract "conception" born of its parents' peculiar mental union. After ten years spent carefully studying his daughter's "holy, and mild, and eloquent face," the narrator finally decides to baptize her. This long-postponed acknowledgment, however, produces not a body so much as a "corpus," a manuscript or a book to be titled, rather than a human being to be christened.

When the narrator draws the necronymic name "Morella" from the "recesses" of his soul and transmits it in a whisper to the officiating priest, the girl instantly collapses "on the black slabs of our ancestral vault," colored with the "hues of death" (PT, 238). Unlike her mother's autumnal transfiguration, this second disease suddenly and brutally destroys its victim, searing the brain of the child's stricken father with her last, compliant words, "I am here," a response that "like molten lead, ran hissingly into my ears." The polychromatic mists of the story's first death scene give way to a much darker setting. The narrator's family vault resembles a nightmarish press room: the black slab of a funereal composing stone, the heat of freshly cast lead type, a precisely duplicated and fatal name. The curse attached to our desire for permanence, for the survival of individuality, would appear to be a species of textual entombment: a static form of being to which the narrator's only response is the "long and bitter laugh" that for Poe is the universal signal of human futility.

*   *   *

"Berenice" and "Morella" are the first two in a series of four early tales that gradually blend the transmissible powers of language and of disease in a formidable and mysterious partnership. They appear in successive issues of the *Southern Literary Messenger* in the spring of 1835, a few months before Poe moved to Richmond to help edit the magazine. Over the summer and fall of that year, he published or republished nine of his most important early stories in issues of the *Messenger*, including a revised version of "The Assignation" in July and three pieces in the magazine's September 1835 issue alone, the largest sample of Poe's fiction to appear between two covers before *Tales of the Grotesque and Arabesque* in 1840. One of these September contributions, "Shadow—A Parable," is part of a pair of sketches that complement "Berenice" and "Morella." Its partner, which Poe would eventually title "Silence—A Fable" to stress the resemblance between them, does not appear until 1838, but together they suggest Poe's relentless concentration on the symbiosis of disease, insight, and expression around which these early stories persistently hover.

Revisiting the ancient landscape of "Four Beasts in One," "Shadow" begins with an account of a devastating plague that strikes "a dim city called Ptolemais" at some point in remote antiquity. The transmissible properties of this disease too are entangled with the mixed vehicles of speech and script. The story's narrator, "the Greek Oinos," or "One," is a human integer writing from the "region of shadows." He begins his address to "the living" by describing the intense burden of anticipation as the plague approaches, a condition almost as deadly as the "black wings of the Pestilence" itself: "The year had been a year of terror," Oinos recalls, "and of feelings more intense than terror for which there is no name upon the earth":

> There were things around us and about of which I can render no distinct account—things material and spiritual—heaviness in the atmosphere—a sense of suffocation—anxiety—and, above all, that terrible state of

existence which the nervous experience when the senses are keenly living and awake, and meanwhile the powers of thought lie dormant. A dead weight hung upon us. It hung upon our limbs—upon the household furniture—upon the goblets from which we drank; and all things were depressed, and borne down thereby—all things save only the flames of the seven iron lamps which illumined our revel. Uprearing themselves in tall slender lines of light, they thus remained burning all pallid and motionless, and in the mirror which their lustre formed upon the round table of ebony at which we sat, each of us there assembled beheld the pallor of his own countenance, and the unquiet glare in the downcast eyes of his companions. (PT, 218)

These words introduce a company of seven mourners with seven totemic candles, surrounding the body of an eighth companion who has already succumbed to the plague. Though purportedly conducting a revel, Oinos and his friends are actually awaiting their own grim fate as they watch over the corpse, attempting in vain to bolster their spirits by singing as loudly as possible "the songs of the son of Teios," Anacreontic hymns to pleasure and to resignation. Oinos himself almost perversely directs his voice toward the table's glossy surface, producing a crowd of weakening echoes to which only his dead friend appears to be listening, until a shadow "such as the moon, when low in heaven, might fashion from the figure of a man" emerges from the same draperies which consumed his last notes. This intruder at first is completely speechless—a "vague, formless, and indefinite" presence meticulously framed by "the arch of the entablature of the door" until Oinos finally summons the courage to demand its name.

None of the seven living figures in the room are able to look steadily in the shadow's direction, though the reply which it finally makes to Oinos's question does not, at first, seem openly menacing: "I am SHADOW, and my dwelling is near to the Catacombs of Ptolemais, and hard by those dim plains of Helusion which border upon the foul Charonian canal." What breaks their narcissistic reverie in the reflected depths of the ebony table is the extraordinary, compound voice with which the Shadow's words are spoken:

And then did we, the seven, start from our seats in horror, and stand trembling, and shuddering, and aghast: for the tones in the voice of the shadow were not the tones of any one being, but of a multitude of beings, and, varying in their cadences from syllable to syllable, fell duskily upon our ears in the well remembered and familiar accents of many thousand departed friends. (PT, 220)

Shadow's composite speech resembles the plural echoes that had accompanied Oinos's desperate song, as well as the composite group of early stories in which Poe originally intended it to appear: the eleven arabesques he had offered to the *New England Magazine* in the spring of 1833 or the proposed collection that he called "Tales of the Folio Club." Its "cadences" are not the instrument of a single speaker—like Oinos's name would appear to commemorate—but the aggregate utterance of a human multitude: an audible census of the dead that gives voice to the "dead weight" of sensory life, bearing down thought's dormant powers in a dramatic reenactment of the psychological "heaviness" Oinos had described in the parable's opening sentences. The grave is a repository of the "familiar accents of many thousand departed friends," a foul canal against which the only effectual defense is not a quarantine chamber and lofty brass doors, like those that enclose these seven mourners, but a stylus of iron and written "memorials" like the pages in which Oinos preserves his ceremonial setting. The parable itself, however, remains a blend of potency and futility—a shadow addressing shadows, in words that both nullify and amplify the ravages of the ancient plague.

The last of Poe's four early studies in medicinal and infected language, "Silence—A Fable," is set in yet another exotic landscape at some remote era signaled by the vaguely biblical style in which Poe casts it, employing mannerisms that subtly insist on the oral tactics of its chief character. The story is largely a Demonic monologue, taken down by a nameless narrator just outside the "cavity" of a tomb that the original version of the text locates at Balbec. When Poe published "Silence" for the first time, under the title "Siope" in an 1838 Christmas collection called the *Baltimore Book*, he made the place of the telling indeterminate. The incidents that the Demon describes, however, occur in Libya, "by the borders of the river Zaire," a dreary setting filled with troubling sounds: sighs and murmurs from a bed of "gigantic water lilies . . . that stretch toward the heaven their long and ghastly necks," a windless agitation in the sky that ravages the surrounding forest, "poisonous flowers" that "lie writhing in perturbed slumber," and an "indistinct murmur" that resembles "the rushing of subterrene water." An uncanny rain drenches these already disquieting surroundings in blood (PT, 221).

By the light of a crimson moon, the Demon detects in the midst of this turbulent morass a huge rock, "gray, and ghastly, and tall," with mysterious characters cut into its base and a man standing on its summit. At first the inscription in the stone is indecipherable, but after closer scrutiny the Demon discovers that the letters spell "Desolation."

By the end of the night-long vigil kept by the man on the rock, the word on its base miraculously changes to "Silence," and the mysterious man himself disappears. Meanwhile the Demon observes him closely, describing what appear to be the growing anxieties of this strangely godlike figure:

> And I looked upwards, and there stood a man upon the summit of the rock; and I hid myself among the water-lilies that I might discover the actions of the man. And the man was tall and stately in form, and was wrapped up from his shoulders to his feet in the toga of old Rome. And the outlines of his figure were indistinct—but his features were the features of a deity; for the mantle of the night, and of the mist, and of the moon, and of the dew, had left uncovered the features of his face. And his brow was lofty with thought, and his eye wild with care; and, in the few furrows upon his cheek I read the fables of sorrow, and weariness, and disgust with mankind, and a longing after solitude. (PT, 222)

Like the narrator of "William Wilson," the Demon is a deft reader of facial lineaments, though the complex record of weariness and disgust that he purports to find in these "few furrows" seems suggestively out of proportion to its living script.

Readers of the 1838 *Baltimore Book*, however, might have taken a particular interest in the lofty watchman of "Silence." The story is actually a pastiche of familiar and fabulous elements. In November 1829, while Poe was living in Baltimore waiting to hear about his admission to West Point, the city celebrated the completion of the nation's first Washington Monument, a Doric column of white marble 160 feet high topped with an eighteen-foot statue of George Washington in his Continental Army uniform—an impressive memorial that had taken over fourteen years to complete. Its original design called for Washington to be dressed as a Roman general driving a triumphal chariot, but the rising costs of construction eventually made a simpler arrangement necessary. The base of the column was engraved with the names of Washington's victories in the Revolutionary War.

The man on the rock in the Demon's story seems clearly intended as an hallucinatory version of this spectacular monument, transformed into an emblem of profound cultural anxiety. In place of a vibrant city or a prosperous nation surrounding the foundations of his stone tower, the noble figure that the Demon depicts finds himself trapped in a putrescent world, saturated with waters "of a saffron and sickly hue" that "palpate forever and forever beneath the red eye of the sun." Unlike the urban squalor of Antiocha Epidaphne in "Four Beasts in One," this setting seems only loosely linked to the social circumstances of its

WASHINGTON'S MONUMENT, BALTIMORE.

Figure 2 "Washington's Monument, Baltimore" from N. P. Willis, *American Scenery, or, Land, Lake, and River Illustrations of Transatlantic Nature from Drawings by W. H. Bartlett* (London, George Virtue, 1840).

reader. A subscriber to the *Baltimore Book* might detect any number of contemporary threats lying behind the feelings that the enigmatic watcher on this all-too-familiar rock displays, including the same sources of emotional turmoil that Frederick Douglass recalls as

Baltimore's white and black citizens alike awaited the onslaught of cholera or confronted the talismanic word "Abolition" in their newspapers. The Demon who presents the vision is quite ready to accommodate just such implicit, apocalyptic fables. But through the carefully measured tones of his narrator, Poe imposes indistinct scales of time and distance upon the story, thwarting interpretive certainty.

Allegories of nationhood are less pertinent to this haunting sketch than allegories of utterance or expression: the hybrid entity that is human speech in its spoken and written forms. "Listen to me," the Demon had abruptly begun in the opening words of the tale, announcing an intention to fill his listener's ears and dominate his mind by placing a priestly hand on the narrator's head as he commands his attention. These indications of authority and abasement, however, prove to be misleading. In fact, the relationship between the Demon and the narrator in "Silence" inverts the one that had existed between the magical guide of "Four Beasts in One" and his democratically intoxicated pupil. At the last minute, the narrator discloses important skeptical reserves, emerging in the final paragraph of the sketch from behind the Demon's cryptic narrative veil to address the reader directly:

> Now there are fine tales in the volumes of the Magi—in the iron-bound, melancholy volumes of the Magi. Therein, I say, are glorious histories of the Heaven, and of the Earth, and of the mighty sea—and of the Genii that over-ruled the sea, and the earth, and the lofty heaven. There was much lore too in the sayings which were said by the Sybils; and holy, holy things were heard of old by the dim leaves that trembled around Dodona—but, as Allah liveth, that fable which the demon told me as he sat by my side in the shadow of the tomb, I hold to be the most wonderful of all! And as the Demon made an end of his story, he fell back within the cavity of the tomb and laughed. And I could not laugh with the Demon, and he cursed me because I could not laugh. And the lynx which dwelleth forever in the tomb, came out therefrom, and lay down at the feet of the Demon, and looked at him steadily in the face. (PT, 224)

Laughter and curses alike seem to be interchangeable elements in the Demon's arsenal of sound—tactics that he uses to manipulate both the narrator and the watchman of his fable. In each instance, however, the manipulation appears to fail. The "rock rocked" beneath the trembling watchman during a terrible storm that the Demon's curse inflicts, but the watchman does not leave his post. An equally surreal stillness, without "any shadow of sound," finally succeeds in driving him away, but not before the word "Silence" replaces "Desolation" on the rock itself, a new inscription resembling the graven memorial that Oinos bequeaths to his reader in "Shadow." The "vast illimitable desert" of the story falls voiceless in response to the Demon's fury, but the message on the stone tower seems as mysterious as its former occupant: a sign of stoic self command in the face of a speechless void.

The Demon-teller of "Silence" is a denizen of cavities, an inhabitant of "the recesses of the morass" in which his tale begins, a reservoir of corruption rather than creation or instruction, much like the foul Charonian canal that is the home of "Shadow" or the filth-infested streets of ancient Antioch from "Four Beasts in One." The tale's resilient narrator, by contrast, is an inhabitant of more complex verbal worlds, capable of discerning wonder where the Demon finds only curses. He is a connoisseur of stories: a writer, a listener, and a consumer of the melancholy volumes and glorious histories of countless generations. Unlike the seductive powers of the voice alone, these iron-bound volumes of wisdom require a reader with the acuity and steadiness of the lynx to probe their message—an intelligence capable of dwelling in the shadow of tombs without succumbing to their grim paralysis. In the evocative conclusion that Poe has crafted for these pages, silence is both a form of defeat and a precondition for the sensitive, textual exchange that links living beings with the long stream of ancient testimony.

* * *

Two burlesques that Poe wrote between 1832 and 1835 touch directly on images of transmission to which he will return, later in his career, in more ambitious stories. The first, "Bon-Bon," is an expanded version of "The Bargain Lost," a brief sketch Poe had submitted to the Philadelphia *Saturday Courier* late in 1831. The tale's hero, Pierre Bon-Bon, a celebrated *restaurateur* of Rouen, is both an intellectual and a gastronome who embraces a spurious Chinese belief "that the soul lies in the abdomen." Bon-Bon himself is virtually all abdomen, "the rotundity of his stomach" conveying a sense of "magnificence nearly bordering on the sublime." A secondary taste for colorful clothes enhances his fleshly magnificence. One stormy winter evening as he sets to work on a "voluminous manuscript" that replicates the grotesque bulk of his body, Bon-Bon is interrupted by a mysterious speaker hidden in a shadowy corner of the room. The Devil has come to strike a bargain for Bon-Bon's soul.

As he rises from the bed and approaches the fire where Bon-Bon has arranged his writing materials, Satan's physique proves to be as elongated as that of his host is rotund. He is tall and "exceedingly lean," dressed in a skin-tight black suit that is too short for his protruding limbs. Although he appears not to be wearing a shirt, his throat is encircled by a "filthy" white cravat, "tied with extreme precision." A pair of dark green spectacles with side glasses prevents any inspection of his eyes. A set of brilliant shoe buckles and a long queue of hair growing from the back of his otherwise bald head complete the contrast with Bon-Bon's compact anatomy and ridiculously gaudy dress.

Like Bon-Bon, however, the Devil is an epicure: an eater of souls. His senses of taste and smell appear to be well developed—Bon-Bon politely offers him a pinch of snuff for his "proboscis"—but despite the conspicuous presence of the green spectacles, he has no eyes at all, "simply a dead level of flesh" across his forehead. Eyes, the Devil rather cryptically scoffs in response to Bon-Bon's surprise, might prove useful in the head of a worm: "*my* vision," he portentously declares, "is the soul." In fact, Bon-Bon's visitor is both "worm" and the worm transformed: the eyeless maggot and the mature fly that his green glasses, prominent proboscis, and tight black suit suggest. Bon-Bon too seems a weird conflation of adult and larval forms: his polychromatic dress suggesting the beauty of a butterfly or a moth, while his belly calls to mind an engorged caterpillar on the verge of metamorphosis. The Devil fondly reminisces with his host over the flavors of various famous meals that he has eaten throughout history, expressing particular pleasure in the souls of philosophers. The mention of physicians, however, makes him retch. The soul of Hippocrates, he bitterly complains, even after a thorough washing in the Styx, "gave me the cholera morbus."

The Devil likes his souls fresh, rather than pickled or putrefied, and it is finally Bon-Bon's disgusting state of intoxication, not his piety or his purity, that saves him from becoming another entry on the Devil's books. In the 1831 version of this story, the Devil wears a Roman toga and sandals and displays none of the familiar clerical mannerisms that Poe adds to the expanded text of 1835. In its revised form, after the ebb and flow of the 1832 epidemic, "Bon-Bon" mocks the conviction of contemporary ministers who pointed to intemperance as one of cholera's chief causes. The story's comic devices barely conceal the iconoclastic bitterness at its core: piety is a fly that breeds on death. Bon-Bon triumphs not in spite of his belly but because of it—a comic convention that Poe applies directly to the theme of epidemic disease in "King Pest," the second of his two plague burlesques. Published alongside "Shadow—A Parable" in the September 1835 *Southern Literary Messenger,* "King Pest" recounts the adventures of Legs and Hugh

Tarpaulin, two sailors on a drunken spree in London who flee into a quarantined zone of the city to escape an alehouse bill that they are unable to pay, preferring to face down the "Demon of Disease" rather than a wrathful tavern landlady.

This "worthy couple" (as Poe describes them) repeat the physical contrasts of "Bon-Bon." Legs, the older of the two sailors, is "exceedingly thin" and enormously tall with "huge protruding white eyes" and an "utterly solemn and serious" manner. His companion, Hugh Tarpaulin, is grotesquely short, with correspondingly thick arms and fists that "swung off dangling from his sides like the fins of a sea-turtle":

> Small eyes of no particular color, twinkled far back in his head. His nose remained buried in the mass of flesh which enveloped his round, full, and purple face; and his thick upper-lip rested upon the still thicker one beneath with an air of complacent self-satisfaction, much heightened by the owner's habit of licking them at intervals. He evidently regarded his tall shipmate with a feeling half-wondrous, half-quizzical; and stared up occasionally in his face as the red setting sun stares up at the crags of Ben Nevis. (PT, 241)

This larval creature and his morose companion, contemplating "the portentous words 'No Chalk'" above the alehouse doorway, recognize the no-credit policy of their hostess from a peculiar twist to letters that they cannot read. Finishing off a final drink, the two sailors make their escape, rushing deeper and deeper into the plague-infested regions of the city to escape the tavern keeper's pursuit, "ripe for mischief and running for life."

Indifferent to the superstitious terrors of the plague zone, they scale one of the "terrific barriers" intended to enforce the royal Pest-ban and wind their way into the "noisome and intricate recesses" of the city—an intestinal place, full of "fetid and poisonous smells" and rotting corpses. Problems of disposal have been left to resolve themselves in this forbidden region, while buildings and streets lapse into an improbably accelerated state of ruin. Before long the two sailors find themselves in the "strong hold of the pestilence," the shop of an undertaker built over a well-stocked wine cellar from which "the occasional sound of bursting bottles" inexplicably emerges, spontaneous explosions that suggest the gaseous pressures of decomposition. Like the enigmatic portrait vase or the cracked and blackened goblet in "The Assignation," these exploding vessels too depict the problems of corporeal containment and disposal that every feature of "King Pest" seems calculated to elicit. A new version of "The Assignation" had appeared in the *Messenger*'s July 1835 issue, two months before the appearance of "King Pest," as if to expose the imaginative links between the tales.

The six occupants whom Legs and Hugh Tarpaulin encounter at the undertaker's shop extend the grotesque allegory of "Bon-Bon." Sitting on coffin trestles around the undertaker's table is a collection of peculiar figures "rigged off like the foul fiends" and drinking the owner's supply of cheap gin, "blue ruin," as Legs fondly calls it, a nickname eerily suggestive of the symptoms of cholera. King Pest himself is a variation of "Bon-Bon's" satanic fly: tall and gaunt, with a face "as yellow as saffron" and a forehead so "hideously lofty" that it resembles a "crown of flesh superadded upon the natural head." His mouth is "puckered and dimpled" as if adapted only to draw nourishment through a straw, and although he does have eyes, they are "glazed" with intoxication. A feathery head-crest of "sable hearse plumes" moves like a set of antennae when he nods, and he is completely clothed in an embroidered, black velvet cloak.

Queen Pest sits across the table from her spouse wrapped entirely in a newly starched shroud with a cambric neck ruffle. She is a corpulent figure—a bloated maggot—as tall as her husband but garbed in white and resembling "the huge puncheon of October beer" that stands in one corner of the room. Her face is "round, red, and full," with a capacious mouth that sweeps like a "terrific chasm" from ear to ear. One delicate young lady to the right of the queen, the Arch Duchess Ana-Pest, boasts a nose that is "extremely long, thin, sinuous, flexible, and pimpled," like the Devil's prominent proboscis in "Bon-Bon," a characteristic feature of the family of flies. Three men complete the party in the undertaker's chambers, each afflicted with some peculiar symptom or equipped with a prop that identifies them with their dead and festering world.

The two sailors ultimately provoke a brawl with this strange assortment of beings, flooding the room in a deluge of October ale and fleeing in triumph to their vessel, the *Free and Easy*, carrying the two women with them as prizes. Autumn rains and cooling temperatures brought an end to the cholera outbreaks of 1832, as well, much as the upended cask of October ale concludes the revels of King Pest. If Poe intended to elicit this reflection, then he may also have meant the escape of the sailors to signal the mobility and the fecundity of disease: the elusive vitality of infection that led the port officials of Santa Cruz to close their harbor to Charles Darwin and the *Beagle*. Legs and Hugh Tarpaulin bring a sense of giddy immunity into the plague zone, but they leave it with sexual partners capable of regenerating its fecal ruin wherever the *Free and Easy* makes port. The cartoonish nature of Poe's story appears to resist such sober meanings, but "King Pest" offers at the same time a burlesque disguise for the grimly mixed conclusions that mark many of these first tales: a desperate appeal to laughter in the face of decay with which the enigmatic hero of "The Assignation" had first declared his scorn for the body's sordid fate.

CHAPTER 2

A Pneumatics of Mind

The September 1835 issue of the *Southern Literary Messenger* includes three of Poe's early tales that address, in strikingly different ways, the psychological and cultural experience of disease that came to dominate his imaginative life after the autumn of 1832. Two of these, "Shadow—A Parable" and "King Pest," take epidemics as their settings, the first offering an eerie tableau of death's impersonal scope—its indiscriminate absorption of individual voices in the general sweep of contagion—while the second presents a burlesque of the fly's grim dominion. The third story in the September issue is Poe's revision and expansion of "A Decided Loss," written over four years earlier, for the Philadelphia *Saturday Courier* in 1831, but now nearly doubled in length and retitled "Loss of Breath."

The original sketch begins when its nameless narrator awakens on the morning after his wedding in a towering rage with his bride. The reasons for his anger do not immediately emerge, for as he is hurling a series of bombastic insults in her direction—"thou hag!—thou whipper-snapper!—thou sink of iniquity!—thou fiery-faced quintessence of all that is abominable!"—he abruptly discovers that he has lost his breath. The first change a reader notices in the revised text of 1835 is Poe's decision to move a handful of sentences from the end of the story's first version to the beginning of its second one, where they appear as a preamble to the narrative, rather than an afterthought:

> The most notorious ill-fortune must, in the end, yield to the untiring courage of philosophy—as the most stubborn city to the ceaseless vigilance of an enemy. Salmanezer, as we have it in the holy writings, lay three years before Samaria; yet it fell. Sardanapalus—see Diodorus—maintained himself seven in Nineveh; but to no purpose. Troy expired at the close of the second lustrum; and Azoth, as Aristæus declares upon his

> honor as a gentleman, opened at last her gates to Psammitticus, after having barred them for the fifth part of a century. (PT, 151)

This passage forms a peculiar introduction to the ludicrous domestic melodrama that immediately breaks out after Poe's display of ancient learning. Like its two companions in the *Messenger* issue, "Loss of Breath" announces an initial, though in this case pedantic, interest in the predicament of besieged cities. The attack of breathlessness that cuts short the narrator's opening diatribe is a comically innocuous ailment—a far cry from the foul Shadow that stalks the doomed residents of Ptolemais or London's loathsome plague—and the narrator's fantastic adventures throughout the rest of the story, violent though they prove to be, are even more cartoonish in nature than those of the drunken couple in "King Pest." Mr. Lackobreath (as Poe names him in the 1835 revision) seems to be little more than a buffoon.

At one point in the tale, however, events take a remarkable turn that directly reflects Poe's intensifying artistic focus on the transformative impact of sickness. "Loss of Breath" contains his earliest attempt to depict a disembodied state of consciousness, the semidelirious experience of existence "on the verge," as Paul John Eakin terms it, poised at the border between life and death. Over the course of his career, Poe repeatedly addresses this theme, sometimes through dialogues involving transcendent speakers attempting to reconstruct the transition from embodied to disembodied life—Eiros and Charmion, Monos and Una, Oinos and Agathos—sometimes through the hypnotic deathbed monologues of less exotic beings, hoping for a glimpse of conscious possibility beyond the remorseless encroachments of disease. This experimental narrative interest originates in the surprising additions that Poe makes to an otherwise undistinguished sketch from 1831, recast in the aftermath of the epidemic year.

* * *

Many incidents from "A Decided Loss" remain unchanged in its successor: Mr. Lackobreath's impetuous decision to become an actor once he discovers that he can, in fact, still produce a few guttural sounds; his being mistaken for a suffocated corpse on a crowded stage coach; his accidental execution in place of a condemned mail robber. As the tale's increasingly silly events unfold, Poe's narrator poses an ongoing problem of disposal for various characters who do not know what to make of his breathless passivity. The 1835 "Loss of Breath," however, includes two long episodes that touch on a suggestive range of ideas and sensations. Only one of these remains in the 1846 version of the story, the last reprinting in Poe's lifetime, a scene in a burial vault, where the narrator has been prematurely deposited after his execution. He breaks out of his coffin and immediately begins to amuse himself by ridiculing the corpses that surround him, including one in particular that "struck me with a sense of unwelcome familiarity." Pulling the corpse to a sitting position by its nose, Lackobreath muses on the dead man's accomplishments:

> He was the originator of tall monuments—shot-towers—lightning rods—lombardy-poplars. His treatise upon "Shades and Shadows" has immortalized him. He edited with distinguished ability the last edition of "South, on the Bones." He went early to college and studied pneumatics. He then came home, talked eternally, and played upon the French-horn. He patronized the bag-pipes. Captain Barclay, who walked against Time, would not walk against *him*. Windham and Allbreath were his favorite writers—his favorite artist, Phiz. He died gloriously while inhaling gas—*levique flatu corrumpitur*, like the *fama pudicitiæ* in Hieronymus. He was indubitably a——. (PT, 160)

This fatuous litany seems capable of endless expansion, but Lackobreath breaks off abruptly when the "corpse" interrupts him, identifying itself as Mr. Windenough, the lover of Lackobreath's bride, who has also been prematurely entombed after an apparently fatal attack of epilepsy. Together the two succeed in making enough noise to attract rescuers and bring the story to an end, but not before the disturbance that they cause prompts a newspaper controversy "upon 'the nature and origin of subterranean noises.'"

Lackobreath's facetious eulogy for his rival reads like a corrupted table of contents for recent numbers of the *Southern Literary Messenger*. "Shades and Shadows" echoes the title of Poe's eerie parable on the plague in ancient Ptolemais that appears in the same issue of the magazine as "Loss of Breath." The possibility of achieving a glorious death by the inhalation of gas alludes to the scientific preoccupations of Hans Pfaall, the hero of a fantastic tale that Poe had contributed to the June issue of the *Messenger* three months earlier. Pfaall's "Unparalleled Adventure" describes in considerable technical detail a balloon voyage to the moon in which the hero must master enough pneumatic engineering to carry himself, his cargo, and his breathing apparatus on a nineteen-day journey through the perfect vacuum of space. At no point in his trip, Pfaall's physical calculations assure him, will the weight of his balloon approach the weight of the atmospheric volume that it displaces. Against all pneumatic principles and common logic, it will continue to rise through emptiness.

Hans Pfaall applies himself to the study of lightness with far greater zeal and attention to scientific detail than any of the other literary moon-voyagers whom Poe ridicules in the story's long endnote. But pneumatics is a complex and extremely suggestive term, one that resists confinement within the purely fanciful boundaries of Hans Pfaall's adventurous flight or the slapstick circumstances recorded in "Loss of Breath." Along with denoting the study of gases, it is etymologically linked to the study of souls, to *pneuma*, and to "pneumatology," the study of spiritual beings, neither of which appears to engage the interests of either Hans Pfaall or Mr. Lackobreath. The puns provide a whimsical bridge between the superficially engaging verbal energies of Mr. Lackobreath and the extraordinary attempt that Poe himself makes, in his longest major addition to the 1835 version of "Loss of Breath," to capture the spiritual experience of his narrator on the boundaries of consciousness.

The original design of "A Decided Loss," then, expands through the process of revision in more senses than one. Poe attempts (however improbably) to trap within its simple burlesque framework a cognitive pneumatics capable of lifting the characters and events of the story toward an ambitious monologue of the soul as it witnesses, but does not really suffer, the bodily insults that afflict the narrator. This effort takes place in the longest of the additions that Poe made to the original text, twenty-six new paragraphs that he would eventually cut from the tale eleven years later. At first this elaborate interlude simply amplifies one implication of the story's preposterous plot: a living man without the ability to breathe may very well seem dead to others, but he certainly cannot be strangled, as Mr. Lackobreath's fellow citizens attempt to do when they confuse him with a condemned robber and hustle him to the gallows. The only inconvenience he initially observes during his execution comes from the chafing of the hangman's rope around his neck and the throbbing of blood in his temples. But these sensations quickly prove to be a prelude to immense vistas of thought and experience, producing passages that resemble nothing else in the story:

> There were noises in my ears—first like the tolling of huge bells—then like the beating of a thousand drums—then, lastly like the low, sullen murmurs of the sea. But these noises were very far from disagreeable.

Although, too, the powers of my mind were confused and distorted, yet I was—strange to say!—well aware of such confusion and distortion. I could, with unerring promptitude determine at will in what particulars my sensations were correct—and in what particulars I wandered from the path. I could even feel with accuracy *how far*—to *what very point*, such wanderings had misguided me, but still without the power of correcting my deviations. I took besides, at the same time, a wild delight in my conceptions.

Memory, which, of all other faculties, should have first taken its departure, seemed on the contrary to have been endowed with quadrupled power. Each incident of my past life flitted before me like a shadow. There was not a brick in the building where I was born—not a dog-leaf in the primer I had thumbed over when a child—not a tree in the forest where I hunted when boy—not a street in the cities I had traversed when a man—that I did not at that time more palpably behold. I could repeat to myself entire lines, passages, chapters, books, from the studies of my earlier days; and while, I dare say, the crowd around me were blind with horror, or aghast with awe, I was alternately with Aeschylus, a demi-god, or with Aristophanes, a frog. (CW 2, 78)

These sentences depict pneumatics of a very different kind from the pseudoscientific practices of Hans Pfaall's voyage to the moon. They recount an enigmatic mental shipwreck in which consciousness resembles both the shattered vessel of individual identity and its bewildered survivor, stranded on some uncharted interior shore. Like Crusoe's literal shipwreck, this one proves to have engrossing consequences.

Stunned at first by the oceanic "murmurs" that engulf him, Poe's narrator quickly finds himself on an uncontrollable course of mental wandering. His powers of memory and perception become both tenaciously specific and inconceivably vast in scope, ranging across all states of being and all times. He is carried away by visions that he compares to the effects of opium, or "the hashish of the old assassins," mixed with "glimpses of pure, unadulterated reason." The crowd around the gallows begins to resemble a "sea of waving heads" whose "haggard" expressions the narrator pities from "the superior benignity of *my* proper stars." His intellectual powers likewise seem to expand, like the rarefied gases in Hans Pfaall's balloon, to the point where he can review and dismiss with great speed a bewildering landscape of old principles and philosophical dogmas from his childhood studies: "A storm—a tempest of ideas, vast, novel, and soul-stirring bore my spirit like a feather afar off. Confusion crowded upon confusion like a wave upon a wave. In a very short time, Schelling himself would have been satisfied with my entire loss of self-identity" (CW 2, 79).

Some features of this passage echo the ancient literary trope of spiritual ascent through the heavenly spheres, a journey that permits the liberated soul to contemplate, from a vast distance, the trivial nature of earthly experience or to instruct a pupil on the proper measure of importance to attach to bodily life: Cicero's "Dream of Scipio," the journey of Pompey's spirit at the end of Lucan's *Pharsalia*, or Troilus's vision of the wretchedness and vanity of the world at the conclusion of Chaucer's poem. Poe's interest in "Loss of Breath," however, has very little in common with this *contemptus mundi* tradition. His narrator's attention is directed inward and outward, toward indeterminate vistas of memory and sensation, rather than downward through an inherited celestial cosmography.

As the story's narrator is laid out for burial, he is dimly aware that the surrounding chamber in which he finds himself is small and crowded with furniture, yet he feels overwhelmed by the idea of "abstract magnitude—of infinity." His appendages begin to seem gigantic, and his entire body correspondingly enormous, yet he has no sense of weight but rather of buoyancy, "that tantalizing *difficulty of keeping down* which is felt by the swimmer in deep water": "I laughed with a hearty internal laugh to think what incongruity there would be—could I arise and walk—between the elasticity of my motion and the mountain of my form." But this giddy interval is short-lived. As night falls a terrible despair succeeds the narrator's brief period of elation. The unique experience that he has been describing at some length is, he suddenly realizes, tantamount to death, but this state too is utterly unlike traditional models of cessation. It is neither an entryway into a mythical afterlife nor a complete release from consciousness, but an immersion in palpable darkness and inchoate desire, an "awful void... a hideous, vague, and unmeaning anomaly—motionless, yet wishing for motion—powerless, yet longing for power—forever, forever, and forever!" (CW 2, 80).

As morning approaches, a faint perception of his physical surroundings returns. The movements of the undertaker and his attendants, the gentle friction of a shroud passing over his face, an errant screw from the coffin lid that penetrates "deep—deep—down into my shoulder"— all give a dreamy but vivid reality to the liminal state in which he finds himself. The movements of the hearse, too, awaken his dormant awareness of physical being:

> I could distinctly hear the rustling of the plumes—the whispers of the
> attendants—the solemn breathings of the horses of death. Confined as

I was in that narrow and strict embrace, I could feel the quicker or slower movement of the procession—the restlessness of the driver—the windings of the road as it led us to the right or to the left. I could distinguish the peculiar odor of the coffin—the sharp acid smell of the steel screws. I could see the texture of the shroud as it lay close against my face; and was even conscious of the rapid variations in light and shade which the flapping to and fro of the sable hangings occasioned within the body of the vehicle. (CW 2, 81)

A few sentences later, the entombed narrator emerges from his coffin, resumes the manic voice of Mr. Lackobreath, and begins the provocative monologue on the corpses with which the story draws to a close.

Poe retained this striking series of episodes and sensations when he reprinted "Loss of Breath" in *Tales of the Grotesque and Arabesque* (1840) but cut it from the final version that appeared in the 1846 *Broadway Journal*. Like his earlier excisions from "Berenice," this decision may reflect his recognition that similar passages in "The Colloquy of Monos and Una" (1841) or "Mesmeric Revelation" (1844) made this anomalous digression in a trivial early sketch expendable. But no other artistic treatment of similar material in Poe's work succeeds in capturing the rich experience of semiconscious perception with the same precision and variety that he displays in these excised paragraphs. The ability to distinctly hear and distinctly see fragments of a surrounding world with which one is powerless to interact, the hallucinatory awareness of great physical distance and great intellectual powers, the intuitive grasp of space evoked by movement, the startling pungency of odors or the hypnotic fascination of flickering light and shadow, the successive waves of disorderly thought that the mind is able to observe almost with pleasure while it submits to their illogical energy—these details convey an impressive measure of psychological authority. Poe is exploring the experience of abandonment as an inner condition rather than an outward figure of despair.

The dark gondola carrying the narrator of "The Assignation" passively drifts toward a similar spiritual shipwreck, but the nature of that disaster remains largely inaccessible to a spectator who does not directly participate in the extremities of feeling that he observes. The romantic couple at the heart of Poe's earlier story abandon very different forms of precious cargo to the sullen waters that engulf them, casting off the ballast that impedes their spiritual buoyancy just as Hans Pfaall's pneumatic analysis of his voyage through emptiness requires. On the long, agonizing night before his burial, the narrator of the 1835 "Loss of Breath" finds himself laid out in a tiny chamber "encumbered with furniture," burdened with a material excess that cripples his powers of flight, much as the contents of his regal Venetian cabinet briefly delay the escape of their volatile owner in the closing paragraphs of "The Assignation." This elaborate engagement with the figurative interrelations of matter and spirit, with the encumbered and the liberated soul, branches out from this suggestive configuration of early tales through the balance of Poe's career—a pneumatic expansion in its own right that helps explain Poe's interest in stories that might seem at first to be eccentric failures of sensibility or execution.

The most important of these elaborate pneumatic studies is "The Mystery of Marie Rogêt," a topical examination of a stalled murder investigation that Poe almost perversely chooses as the basis for his second great detective story. Few of Poe's tales would seem less hospitable to Mr. Lackobreath's cognitive buoyancy than this series of interminable reflections on the fate of a Parisian shop girl whose corpse suddenly appears floating in the Seine. Published in three installments between December 1842 and February 1843 in Snowdon's *Ladies Companion*, it is among the longest pieces of fiction that Poe wrote, weighed down both by its unusual length and by Poe's stubborn decision to tether his Parisian plot to the events of an actual crime: the murder of a New York cigar salesgirl named Mary Cecilia Rogers in July 1841. Ultimately this spurious coincidence represents an ambitious blend of empirical ballast and cognitive expansion that echoes the fabulous technology of Hans Pfaall. Though less celebrated than other exploits in the career of Poe's detective genius, C. Auguste Dupin, the story of Marie Rogêt is an instructive storehouse of key images and themes that inform Poe's fictional vision.

* * *

Charles Baudelaire had no difficulty identifying the half accommodating, half fumbling, Prefect "G——" who is the beneficiary of Auguste Dupin's investigative acumen in all three of Poe's famous detective stories. He is Joseph-Henri Gisquet, the Prefect of Police in Paris between 1831 and 1836, whose career became closely identified with the city's efforts first to prevent and then to combat the cholera onslaught that began shortly after Gisquet assumed his post. The disease reached Paris in late March 1832 and remained throughout the summer, eventually infecting one in nineteen of the city's inhabitants and killing over eighteen thousand people. Gisquet's responsibilities during these months included appointing the members of the city's Central Board of Health and supervising makeshift clinics for the poor during the height of the epidemic. His office played a role in planning improvements to public sanitation that were set in motion just before cholera arrived in Paris but which became the focus of bitter resentment on the part of the city's rag-pickers, its *chiffonniers*, who objected to the smaller refuse carts circulating through narrow streets and alleys in an attempt to remove the filth that many contemporary observers intuitively identified with the source of the disease.

The rag-pickers of Paris eked out a meager living by collecting and reselling bits of rubbish, mostly rags and bones that could be used in the manufacture of fertilizer, glue, or paper. They lived by a peculiar clock, according to one contemporary observer, "neither a working nor an astronomical day," roaming the streets by night, selling what they found in the early morning hours, and withdrawing from sight by day. When the new, compact refuse carts designed to improve the city's sanitation system seemed to menace their traditional way of life, they lodged a formal protest with Prefect Gisquet. His officers arrested hundreds of rioters who burned some of the new carts and hurled them into the Seine.

The anger of the *chiffonniers* was not the only breakdown in public order that occurred during the epidemic. Rumors circulated that the disease was actually the work of officially sanctioned poisoners, intent on reducing the numbers of the city's poor. The swift and dramatic symptoms of cholera lent themselves to the delusion. Riots took place outside hospitals, which citizen mobs had come to view with suspicion as centers of a macabre class conspiracy. During the June 1832 funeral of one of Napoleon's old generals, Maximilien Lamarque, radical insurgents fought with the troops of Louis Philippe's new monarchy, itself recently installed in power by an urban uprising in 1830. Cobblestone barricades briefly reappeared in some of the city's poorest and most disease-ravaged quarters before a period of repression began which the editors of *The North American Review*, at least, attributed in part to the authoritarian efficiency of Gisquet. "Despotism never used a more effective tool than Louis Philippe found in his prefect of police, Gisquet," the *Review* observed in April 1835: "Deceitful, cowardly, vindictive, he was the proper person to persecute the vanquished, to render their imprisonment wretched, to trample the populace still lower."

Neither of the first two Auguste Dupin detective stories directly addresses the subject of cholera. But each depicts a contest between the human intellect and an invisible, seemingly preternatural scourge preying on the inhabitants of Paris, and each casts the details of its plot against the shadowy social and political background evoked by Gisquet's role in the events of 1832. "The Murders in the Rue Morgue" opens with a scornful preamble on the aristocratic pretensions of chess, dismissing its bishops, knights, queens, and pawns as frivolous: "what is only complex," Poe's narrator complains, is mistaken for "what is profound." He favors instead the simplicity of draughts, or checkers, which reduces the role of accident in the outcome of a game. Contestants at draughts gradually reduce a board of uniform pieces, through a series of "*unique*" but geometrically parallel moves, into an array of opposed but perfectly equal "kings" that then struggle directly for victory. The individual player's ability to identify himself with his opponent's "spirit" and detect his weaknesses determines the winner.

Whist is a still more impressive game, the narrator suggests, because of the diagnostic intensity it requires on the part of the successful player, carefully studying his antagonists for any external sign that might shed light on the state of their emotions or hopes:

> He notes every variation of face as the play progresses, gathering a fund of thought from the differences in the expression of certainty, of surprise, of triumph, or of chagrin. From the manner of gathering up a trick he judges whether the person taking it can make another in the suit. He recognises what is played through feint, by the air with which it is thrown upon the table. A casual or inadvertent word; the accidental dropping or turning of a card, with the accompanying anxiety or carelessness in regard to its concealment; the counting of the tricks, with the order of their arrangement; embarrassment, hesitation, eagerness or trepidation—all afford, to his apparently intuitive perception, indications of the true state of affairs. (PT, 399)

An elaborate, inferential theatrics lies behind the card play that Poe's narrator admires: a charade aimed both at concealing and assessing "the true state of affairs." Whist is a perfect school for the agents of despotism or revolution.

An epilogue that Poe attaches to "The Mystery of Marie Rogêt" one year later offers some equally provocative observations on the Calculus of Probabilities and dice. The same narrator who had introduced readers of *Graham's Magazine* to the Rue Morgue case in 1841 now perversely insists that two throws of the dice lying "absolutely in the Past" can influence the random probabilities of a third throw. The "merely general reader" who defers to mathematical reason cannot be made to accept "that the fact of sixes having been thrown twice in succession by a player at dice, is sufficient cause for betting the largest odds that sixes will not be thrown in the third attempt" (PT, 554). But the failure to make that very bet, Poe's narrator claims, is "a gross error redolent of mischief." The laws of probability dictate that the odds are identical on all three throws, but the laws of mystery (he implies) address more comprehensive truths.

Together these set pieces on games form a pair of bookends that point to an underlying consistency of purpose in the first two Dupin narratives. Poe's decision to identify the second story as a sequel to the first immediately calls attention to the verbal interchanges that their titles invite. No murder as such actually takes place in the Rue Morgue, despite the violent fate of the two women who die there, since no human agent, no murderer, is involved. By contrast, though the killer of Marie Rogêt is never explicitly named and never caught, he is unambiguously human. Dupin ends his long discussion of the crime by suggesting that the mystery of the girl's death is as good as solved, but the solution itself remains hypothetical and incomplete: a murder without a clear-cut murderer. The two titles seem to have exchanged their most critical verbal pieces—murder and mystery—as competitors frequently exchange pieces in checkers or in chess, urging the reader to consider the stories as an asymmetrical narrative pair, a bi-part design to complement what Poe's narrator terms the bi-part soul of Auguste Dupin. In this suggestive arrangement, the more expansive and superficially tedious tale proves to have an elasticity of motion that its cumbersome form initially appears to preclude.

Dupin and the nameless figure who will record his adventures first meet at the beginning of "The Murders in the Rue Morgue" in "an obscure library" in Rue Montmartre, where both men are looking for "the same very rare and very remarkable volume." Each is a seeker after arcane knowledge, but once the narrator attaches himself to Dupin, his own search is at least partly over: "I felt my soul enkindled within me by the wild fervor, and the vivid freshness of his imagination," the narrator confesses of his new companion. Dupin's society alone is "a treasure beyond price" (PT, 400). The two men eventually decide to share living quarters, at the narrator's expense, in "a time-eaten and grotesque mansion, long deserted through superstitions into which we did not inquire"—a peculiar lapse in curiosity for two such inquisitive minds. Despite Dupin's fallen financial circumstances, his "illustrious" family connections remain sufficiently influential to secure credentials from Prefect G—— when in due course he wishes to examine a bizarre crime scene in the Rue Morgue.

From their obscure center of operations, Dupin and the narrator lead a secretive, nocturnal existence, much like that of the Paris *chiffonniers* whose furtive world had so recently been invaded by cholera and by Gisquet's sanitation carts. "We existed within ourselves alone," the narrator notes, a social quarantine that links them with the women whose deaths they will shortly decide to investigate. Dupin in particular is "enamored of the Night," and the narrator permits himself to be carried along in his new friend's eccentric habits:

> The sable divinity would not herself dwell with us always; but we could counterfeit her presence. At the first dawn of the morning we closed all the massy shutters of our old building, lighting a couple of tapers which, strongly perfumed, threw out only the ghastliest and feeblest of rays. By the aid of these we then busied our souls in dreams—reading, writing, or conversing, until warned by the clock of the advent of the true Darkness. Then we sallied forth into the streets, arm in arm, continuing the topics of the day, or roaming far and wide until a late hour, seeking, amid the wild lights and shadows of the populous city, that infinity of mental excitement which quiet observation can afford. (PT, 401)

Unlike the claustrophobic meditations of Egæus in "Berenice," this isolation is an outgrowth of, rather than a substitute for, intense verbal life. Reading and writing, along with the social communion of souls, requires a counterfeit night. The "advent of the true Darkness" announced by the clock is both a birth and a death, but night is not an apocalyptic state of nullity to these dreamy companions. It is an avenue to infinity—an expansion of mental space made possible when the wild lights and shadows of nightfall disclose hidden similarities between a populous city and the vast panorama of the stars.

As the two men are walking together one night, lost in thought, "down a long dirty street, in the vicinity of the Palais Royale," Dupin abruptly breaks the silence with a startling remark that suggests he is able to read the narrator's mind. The explanation of the psychic feat demonstrates that this aspect of Dupin's mental powers, at least, is purely material. By linking together a series of incidents during their stroll with a few mutual experiences that he remembers, Dupin is able to deduce the reason behind a slight smile on the narrator's face as he gazes toward the great nebula in Orion. Far from fathoming his friend's soul, he has simply predicted the nature of a passing thought concerning the activity of a stage-mad Parisian cobbler who had recently made himself ridiculous by abandoning his trade and taking on the role of Xerxes in a Crebillon tragedy.

Dupin's deductive "chain" begins with a minor pedestrian collision earlier in the night that had knocked the narrator down on a pile of paving stones. This incident subsequently leads both men to pay special attention to the way "the little alley called Lamartine" had recently been repaved with "overlapping and riveted blocks," a detail that contemporary readers familiar with events in Paris would readily associate with official attempts to discourage the building of street barricades. "Stereotomy," the peculiar technical name for the city's new paving design, crosses the narrator's mind as he glances at the repaired alley, and he silently mouths the word. Dupin reads his lips and follows a trail of associations that these roommates and night wanderers share, leading him to a newspaper's recent "immolation" of Chantilly's attempt to make the leap from humble cobbler to Crebillon's Persian king. The narrator offers this anecdote as an example of Dupin's "diseased" intelligence: the peculiar intuitive trances in which his voice and appearance actually change as he penetrates the intimate secrets of others. "Observing him in these moods," the narrator reports, "I often dwelt meditatively upon the old philosophy of the Bi-Part Soul, and amused myself with the fancy of a double Dupin—the creative and the resolvent." (PT, 402) Though Dupin himself exults in these gifts with a disquieting "low chuckle," his deductive ingenuity demonstrates not a pathological exception to normal thought but a general aptitude of consciousness: a cognitive agility that the narrator too displays as his thoughts move rapidly upward and outward from a pile of cast-off paving stones through the atomic theories of Lucretius to a facetious theater review.

Cognition itself is a bi-part entity, half afloat in the distant realms of infinite space and half bound to the physical ballast of its immediate surroundings. Our intelligence is constantly engaged in bridging the gap between the brute density of terrestrial fact and the celestial voyages of the imagination—just as Xerxes links Persia and Greece with his floating bridge of boats in the story that the stage-struck cobbler Chantilly longs to enact. Dupin's vocal oscillations between a low chuckle and a "treble" tenor during his deductive trances signals his own passage across a similar cognitive divide. Poe's plot offers a series of variations on this theme. The killer in the Rue Morgue case will ultimately prove to be an ape captured during an excursion on Borneo by two sailors who are eager to profit from the European market for exotic animals. Carried on yet another variety of floating bridge half way around the world, this terrified creature enacts its own brutal and ridiculous version of Hans Pfaall's unparalleled pneumatic adventure—a bi-part role several times over.

Like Chantilly and Xerxes, or Dupin and his companion, the terrified ape and his horrified keeper are emblems of the restless mobility of awareness and understanding, traveling back and forth between opposite poles on the mind's expansive, pneumatic continuum. To read the riddle of events in the Rue Morgue completely, as Dupin longs to do, requires more than the meticulous examination of physical spaces and mutilated bodies—a process that can produce, at best, only an educated guess at the sequence of events leading to the violent deaths of Madame L'Espanaye and her daughter. Complete knowledge requires an intuitive grasp of the vertiginous world of consciousness, of its extraordinary capacity for ascent and its propensity to fall. "The Murders in the Rue Morgue" ultimately follows the narrator's course of reflections on an eerie downward trajectory. Two lovers of high ideality and rarefied learning ultimately find themselves waiting in their ruined Paris mansion, armed and apprehensive, for a mysterious sailor to arrive and claim a lost ape. The flights of mental excitement with which their acquaintance had begun have made an unexpected descent toward a menacing trio of disorderly images: a wild animal wielding a razor, a sailor with a huge oaken cudgel, and two semi-invalid dreamers trusting to pistols rather than reason for their safety.

"The Mystery of Marie Rogêt" sets out to reverse this engrossing fall by means of yet another gruesome problem of disposal—that of a Parisian shop girl's battered body found floating in the Seine, where her killer had sought to hide the evidence of his crime. Much like the violent events that occur in the Rue Morgue, this discovery excites a frenzy of speculation in the Paris newspapers, completely eclipsing "the political topics of the day" (PT, 509). Each paper offers its own disposition of the circumstances surrounding Marie Rogêt's disappearance and death, and each in turn is exposed to Dupin's witheringly skeptical critique. Most of the story revolves around this extended and excruciatingly detailed critique of the press. Dupin becomes a singularly relentless spectator of a terrible human shipwreck, absorbing testimony and evidence largely at second or third hand from behind a pair of green eyeglasses that are a disquieting reminder of the satanic fly in "Bon-Bon."

Once again Prefect G—— and his officers are at a loss. The police offer an extravagant reward for the capture of the girl's killers, supplemented by private money from a "committee of citizens." The combined sum amounts to thirty thousand francs, the narrator notes, a remarkable demonstration of public interest "when we consider the humble condition of the girl, and the great frequency, in large cities, of such atrocities as the one described." Behind this essential disproportion lies a pneumatic mystery of its own: what accounts for such an unpredictable and improbable expansion of mental interest and energy so far in excess of the demonstrable weight of events? The double murder in the Rue Morgue posed a spectacular and peculiar riddle, but Marie Rogêt's grim fate is all too commonplace. Its ordinary nature, however, proves the source of its importance. The reward alone does not move Dupin to take up the case, but a private visit from G——, coupled with a "liberal proposition" that may or may not be monetary sets him on a course of energetic reading in search of the killer.

In this second Dupin mystery, reading and talking are the only activities in which Poe's hero engages. He never troubles himself to examine the body of the victim directly, as he does to memorable effect in "The Murders in the Rue Morgue." Over the course of the story he meticulously constructs a mental picture of a thicket near the banks of the Seine that could well have been the scene of Marie Rogêt's murder—itemizing each piece of fabric found ripped from her clothing, tied about her body, or left to rot in the woods—but he never visits the place itself, preferring to draw the details that he needs from newspaper accounts, though these sources frequently introduce confusion into the investigation. Indeed, for much of the story, Dupin conducts his inquiry as if he were blind, sifting his way through the facts by means of a type of cognitive Braille: "I have before observed," he reminds the narrator, "that it is by prominences above the plane of the ordinary that reason feels her way, if at all, in her search for the true" (PT, 520). The blind can now read, Dupin's words suggest, but reading entails its own sort of blindness. The "myrmidons" of the Paris police have been bewildered by the profusion of plausible "fancies" surrounding Marie Rogêt's fate. Dupin practices his sightless analysis on these false leads first, in part so that Poe can replace the immediacy of vision with the cumulative experience of perception, immersing his reader not in images but in time.

This process begins with Dupin's inexplicable insistence, at the very beginning of the story, on treating the mechanics of drowning and decay. One Paris paper in particular asserts that victims of drowning or murder whose bodies disappear into the Seine "require from six to ten days for sufficient decomposition to take place to bring them to the top of the water." Dupin goes to some lengths to discredit this claim, considering in detail the physical factors that determine how and when "the specific gravity of the human body" comes to exceed or to fall short of "the bulk of fresh water that it displaces." The first mystery that the story directly undertakes to address, in other words, is a mystery of pneumatics. Does the body's presence, at this moment, floating on the river's surface confirm or preclude its being that of a girl who had only been missing for four days? Dupin seizes on this question as an opportunity to survey a number of physical mysteries that pertain to mortality.

All human bodies do not have an equal propensity to sink, Dupin announces at the beginning of his analysis, nor is all water alike in its flotational properties. A tidal flow from the sea will make a body more buoyant than in fresh water. Lean, large-boned men will sink more readily than fat or fleshy people and far more readily than women in any sort of water. An inexperienced swimmer who falls into the river and struggles for life will only drown that much more quickly, Dupin observes: "The proper position for one who cannot swim," he declares, sounding a bit like a Red Cross instructor, "is the upright position of the walker on land, with the head thrown fully back, and immersed; the mouth and nostrils alone remaining above the surface. Thus circumstanced, we shall find that we float without difficulty and without exertion" (PT, 524). Even in this posture, however, the balance between what Dupin calls "the gravities" is very delicate. The equilibrium between the human body and the weight of the water that it displaces can be disturbed by a "trifle."

Once water gets into the stomach and lungs, a drowning victim may well sink, Dupin concedes, but probably not far and not for long. People with a great deal of fat may not sink at all. The gases of decomposition "distending the cellular tissues" into a fleshy balloon resembling the grotesque hallucination from "Loss of Breath" will bring a corpse to the surface as its specific gravity falls below that of the growing volume of displaced water—a process affected by a number of factors that Dupin cheerfully cites: heat or cold, depth or shallowness, the "mineral impregnation or purity of the water," the presence or absence of a current, the presence or absence of disease at the time of the victim's death. Sometimes a corpse will return to the surface in as little as an hour, he suggests. Sometimes it will never rise at all. A body preserved with "the Bi-chloride of Mercury," Dupin observes, would never decompose and hence never generate the gaseous buoyancy to float. Like Dupin himself, mercury bi-chloride is a bi-part entity, a pneumatic anomaly blending one of nature's densest metals with chlorine gas to form a compound that, among many medicinal uses in Poe's day, was capable of completely thwarting the shift in "gravities" that Dupin so carefully describes.

The concussion of a cannon shot might loosen a corpse from the thick mud of a riverbed or accelerate the filling of "the cellular tissues" with buoyant gas, Dupin concludes, but the natural processes of decay alone are the true agents that bring all submerged bodies to the surface. This protracted exploration of biophysical matter begins the second of the story's three installments in the December 1842 issue of Snowden's *Ladies Companion*. No vestiges of redeeming sentiment or overarching piety mingle with Dupin's purely forensic discussion of gaseous decay. Indeed, the most prominent feature of his analysis is its preoccupation with time. How long was the murdered girl's corpse hidden on shore? When could it have been thrown into the river? Will a dead body necessarily sink and, if so, how long before the gravities shift sufficiently to allow the corpse to float? "The Mystery of Marie Rogêt" is awash in calculations that seek to synchronize or separate events along time's stream—all of which Dupin seems to imbibe in his sleep, through the seven or eight "leaden footed" hours that Prefect G—— requires to explain the intricacies of the case to the narrator.

Three years before her murder, Marie had mysteriously disappeared from the perfumery shop where she worked, only to reappear just as mysteriously one week later, "with a somewhat saddened air." Are the two separate disappearances a mere coincidence? How might they relate to the customary intervals of a naval officer's cruise—to the departure and reappearance of a secret lover? Do the affidavits of Marie's distraught fiancé adequately account for all his hours on the day of her murder? Is Dupin's preposterous claim that grass will grow, during damp and warm weather, "as much as two or three inches in a single day" at all pertinent to the condition of the murdered girl's clothing, when it finally appears in a woodland thicket? Or does Poe offer us a startling sample of preternatural time, in the course of the story, in order to ensure that we will pay close attention to time in its myriad natural forms, including that of the reader's internal sense of duration as Dupin's long monologues unfold?

The latent enormity of minutia lies behind the durable appeal of virtually all detective fiction. Dupin's meticulous "divisions of the theme" as he recapitulates the circumstances surrounding Marie Rogêt's death—his calculations of the actual and probable lapses of time that mark the stages of her disappearance—aim at increasingly fine differentiations of testimony that draw Dupin into an intimate communion with the invisible parties to the crime. When two small boys belatedly discover some articles of mildewed clothing belonging to the dead girl in a dense riverside thicket, Dupin's skepticism regarding this disclosure has a psychological rather than analytical basis. The thicket was close to the boys' home and contained "three extraordinary stones" configured into a natural throne that would have exerted an irresistible attraction for the mind of a child: "Would it be a rash wager," Dupin asks, "that *a day* never passed over the heads of these boys without finding at least one of them ensconced in the umbrageous hall, and enthroned upon its natural throne? Those who would hesitate at such a wager, have either never been boys themselves, or have forgotten the boyish nature" (PT, 543). An uncanny woodland "ruin" (Dupin recognizes) is a natural site for childish fantasy, a mythical refuge from the tedium of the ordinary. Surely these boys would have discovered the girl's clothes within hours of the recovery of her body, rather than days later. Dupin has not forgotten the timeless gravities of childhood.

During his exhaustive consideration of the potential murder scene, he is surprisingly appreciative of the natural beauty that surrounds the city and sympathizes with the poetical wanderer in search of solitude who is forced to flee back to "polluted Paris" in order to escape the overflow of urban vice that seeps into the countryside. Even on ordinary working days, the rural suburbs are a desecrated temple, Dupin claims, but they are particularly so on the Sabbath, the day of the week when both the laboring and criminal classes seek to trade "the restraints and conventionalities of society" for "the utter *license* of the country" (PT, 542). Sunday is also the day that Marie Rogêt disappears—not in late July, like the unfortunate Mary Rogers, but on the twenty-second of June, a day after the Summer Solstice and the beginning of a six-month descent into the lengthening darkness of winter. Poe does not stress this celestial "clock" in his plot, but Dupin is explicit in his scorn for the Paris underworld and its appetite for consuming the innocent: an echo of the Proserpina fable that Marie's fate appears to invoke and that the Solstice purports to reflect. A small boy enthroned in an "umbrageous hall" on the banks of the Seine repeats, on a diminutive scale, this mythic geography: a miniature Hades separated from the upper world by its Stygian boundary. Dupin's digressive analysis of the crime slowly discloses a provocative truth: polluted Paris, the violated sanctity of the Sabbath, and the dead girl's brutalized body are all desecrated temples. Together they comprise a figurative "coincidence" that underlies the story's venal urban world.

As the long narrative draws to a close, it becomes progressively evident that this broader figurative pathway is the one that Poe hopes to develop. Analytical tactics alone will never succeed in reading the riddle of Marie Rogêt's death. A more penetrating exercise of soul is required. In the course of mentally sifting the debris of the potential murder scene, Dupin and the narrator briefly reduce the dead girl to a disposable construction of rags—an anonymous *chiffonnier*, like those that bitterly opposed Gisquet's refuse carts. The final stages of the investigation, however, substitute a form of intuitive communion for this icy inhumanity. First Dupin adopts the consciousness of Marie herself as she carefully plans a rendezvous with a secret lover in such a way as to allow herself the maximum amount of time, on one of the longest days of the year, for avoiding the pursuit of her disappointed fiancé:

> I am to meet a certain person for the purpose of elopement, or for certain other purposes known only to myself. It is necessary that there be no chance of interruption—there must be sufficient time given us to elude pursuit—I will give it to be understood that I shall visit and spend the day with my aunt at the Rue des Drômes . . . in this way, my absence from home for the longest possible period, without causing suspicion or anxiety, will be accounted for, and I shall gain more time than in any other manner . . . the gaining of time is the only point about which I need give myself any concern. (PT, 538)

In this hypothetical account of Marie's motives, Dupin insists on the utter centrality of time to the nature of human (and fictional) experience. When he turns his attention to the consciousness of the murderer, however, matter is his chief preoccupation:

> An individual has committed the murder. He is alone with the ghost of the departed. He is appalled by what lies motionless before him. The fury of his passion is over, and there is abundant room in his heart for the natural awe of the deed. His is none of that confidence which the presence of numbers inevitably inspires. He is *alone* with the dead. He trembles and is bewildered. Yet there is a necessity for disposing of the corpse. He bears it to the river, but leaves behind him the other evidences of guilt; for it is difficult, if not impossible to carry all the burthen at once, and it will be easy to return for what is left. But in his toilsome journey to the water his fears redouble within him. The sounds of life encompass his path. A dozen times he hears or fancies the step of an observer. Even the very lights from the city bewilder him. Yet, in time, and by long and frequent pauses of deep agony, he reaches the river's brink, and disposes of his ghastly charge—perhaps through the medium of a boat. But *now* what treasure does the world hold—what threat of vengeance could it hold out—which would have power to urge the return of that lonely murderer over that toilsome and perilous path, to the thicket and its blood-chilling recollections? . . . He turns his back forever upon those dreadful shrubberies, and flees as from the wrath to come. (PT 546)

This engrossing passage stresses the perceptual impact of magnification and of mass that propels a guilt-ridden conscience through an exponential expansion of its moral landscape. Fears redouble and the sounds of life inexplicably multiply almost from the instant that the murderer finds himself "appalled by what lies motionless before him." His isolation deprives him of support from the "presence of numbers," in Dupin's recreation of the crime, but the power of numbers in several forms accelerates the development of his dread.

Dupin enters completely into the volatile compound of awe and fear that imperceptibly converts the bank of the river into the "brink" of an abyss but cannot drive Marie Rogêt's killer back along the perilous route that he has traveled, once he has shed his "ghastly" ballast, even in the interests of collecting and destroying any remaining evidence of her murder. The pneumatics of flight are irresistible; a desperate desire to escape the vigilance of a punitive universe overwhelms all transient passions, as well as the trivial instincts of self-preservation. Poe's exquisitely subtle manipulation of cognitive space mixes the opposed perceptions of abundant and of stifling "room," the compact locality of the crime with the psychological immensity of judgmental wrath to which the crime gives rise. Even the simplicity and the restraint of Dupin's words, the repeated expansion of very brief sentences into very elaborate ones, enhance the complex pneumatics of the passage.

The two concluding paragraphs of the extended monologue that brings "The Mystery of Marie Rogêt" to an end are filled with Dupin's elaborate recapitulation of the "fruits of our long analysis," now "multiplying and gathering distinctness as we proceed." The effect of reading through this circumstantial list is that of a tightening verbal vortex, a swift aggregation of the flotsam and jetsam of the tale, until Dupin arrives at the intriguing image of an empty boat found floating in the Seine the day after Marie Rogêt's disappearance. This wayward craft is originally towed for safekeeping to the Paris barge office, where its rudder is removed, in anticipation of an owner appearing to claim it. A day later it mysteriously disappears. "Now where is that rudderless boat?" Dupin asks, "Let it be one of our first purposes to discover." This final, and apparently minor, coincidence is the key to the conjunction of human shipwrecks comprising the entire story. "With the first glimpse we obtain of it," Dupin declares, "the dawn of our success shall begin. This boat shall guide us, with a rapidity which will surprise even ourselves, to him who employed it in the midnight of the fatal Sabbath. Corroboration will rise upon corroboration, and the murderer will be traced" (PT, 552).

* * *

Poe breaks off "The Mystery of Marie Rogêt" just at this point, on the brink of the steepest pitch in Dupin's deductive plunge. The story's close connection to the circumstances of an actual murder made it awkward for him to pursue the plot to its natural conclusion, but he also clearly intended to leave the reader in a condition of imaginative vertigo, eagerly awaiting a fourth installment to the story that would never appear. An anonymous editor apparently intervenes to cut the narrative short, assure the reader that Prefect G—— was completely satisfied by Dupin's performance, and print a conclusion to "Mr. Poe's article" which gently rebukes our hunger for the delusive details of closure.

The emblematic image of the rudderless boat, however, is an arresting figure, one that recurs throughout Poe's work as a metaphor of submission, not to the aimless drift of chance, but to the purposeful currents of hidden design. In the closing weeks of 1841, between the publication of the first two Dupin mysteries, Poe's brief sketch "Eleonora" created a popular stir, in part perhaps because of the evocative portrait of the rudderless consciousness in the story's opening sentences—a passage that recapitulates elements of Auguste Dupin's intellectual devotion to the sable divinity of the night:

> I am come of a race noted for vigor of fancy and ardor of passion. Men have called me mad; but the question is not yet settled, whether madness is or is not the loftiest intelligence—whether much that is glorious—whether all that is profound—does not spring from disease of thought—from *moods* of mind exalted at the expense of the general intellect. They who dream by day are cognizant of many things which escape those who dream only by night. In their grey visions they obtain glimpses of eternity, and thrill, in awaking, to find that they have been upon the verge of the great secret. In snatches, they learn something of the wisdom which is of good, and more of the mere knowledge which is of evil. They penetrate, however rudderless or compassless, into the vast ocean of the "light ineffable" and again, like the adventurers of the Nubian geographer, "*agressi sunt mare tenebrarum, quid in eo esse exploraturi.*" (PT, 468)

"Eleonora" immediately sets out to dramatize the contrast between exalted "moods of mind" and the "general intellect" by identifying these mental states with the two distinct "epochs" of the narrator's life that divide the story's asymmetrical worlds. The first of these the narrator identifies with "lucid reason," the second with the present realm of "shadow and doubt" from which he writes. The author of these pages, too, is plainly gifted with a bi-part soul, but unlike Auguste Dupin he is the victim rather than the master of his unusual cognitive powers, inviting the reader to play "the Oedipus" to the riddle of his life. Poised on the verge of a great secret—a mental chart to the sea of shades, the *mare tenebrarum*, and its paradoxical atmosphere of ineffable light—he is uncertain of the meaning of the "grey visions" that define his existence and prompt his story.

Two antithetical landscapes divide the plot of "Eleonora" between them. The first is an isolated and idyllic world where the narrator and his lovely young cousin pass their childhood: "the Valley of the Many-Colored Grass." This baroque setting is a hybrid of artificial and natural elements: full of brilliantly colored, delicately perfumed vegetation, irrigated by an enigmatic River of Silence "winding stealthily" between lush green banks and groves of trees whose bark is speckled with ebony and silver and so smooth that it resembles the skin of "giant serpents of Syria doing homage to their Sovereign the Sun." The valley itself is a completely girdled enclosure. Only the river passes through the barrier of dim mountains that surrounds it, much as the Seine passes through the encirclement of Paris with its burden of death in "The Mystery of Marie Rogêt." This uncanny valley refashions the circumstantial urban setting of Poe's Dupin stories as a dream-idyll, dominated by a sinuous river that prefigures the wandering journeys of consciousness in each tale.

No sunlight penetrates through the shadow of gigantic mountains and fantastic trees to illuminate the "sweetest recesses" in the Valley of the Many-Colored Grass, but despite this disquieting note, and the river's ominous silence, Eleonora and the narrator spend fifteen blissful years in a state of childlike wonder "before Love entered within our hearts." As the two of them gaze one evening at their reflected images in the River of Silence, a mysterious form of transmission takes place. Eros instills within them both "the fiery souls of our forefathers"—a potent legacy of feelings and ideas that seems to have remained dormant in the river's waters like a form of insidious pollution until the young couple are capable of harboring its infection. Under the influence of this highly communicable mental change, the valley immediately becomes prolific: birds and fish suddenly appear, the color of the grass intensifies, the River of Silence emits "a lulling melody," and a brilliant cloud settles over the surrounding mountains, converting the valley into "a magic prison-house of grandeur and of glory" (PT, 470).

Like the extraordinary royal cabinet of paintings and sculpture where the final scene of "The Assignation" unfolds, this gorgeous enclosure proves to be a tomb in disguise. The dramatic changes in the landscape are an index of "the last sad change which must befall Humanity," a signal of morbidity that Eleonora herself recognizes and insists upon "interweaving... into all our converse." As the narrator quickly realizes, his cousin is doomed to an existence as brief as that of the ephemeron, the mayfly that lives only for a day. The valley itself is little more than a perfumed vestibule to the darker city of decay, where the narrator ultimately flees years after his cousin's death. The plot almost perfectly prefigures the tabloid fate of Marie Rogêt that will engross Poe's attention through the closing months of 1842. Marie too enjoys a brief period of blissful notoriety working in a perfume shop beneath the Palais Royale before the first of the two disappearances that eventually lead to a gruesome end in another river of silence.

"Eleonora" itself had a kind of tabloid life unusual among Poe's stories. It was reprinted four times, in a variety of papers and magazines, during the month of September 1841, shortly after its original publication in a Christmas giftbook. These are the same weeks in which many New York newspapers were busily speculating about the death of the beautiful salesgirl, Mary Rogers, whose mutilated body had been discovered in the Hudson River the previous July. Two more reprintings of "Eleonora" took place in the *Literary Souvenir* before July 1842, a journalistic vitality loosely resembling the role of the Paris press in the fictional variation on the Rogers murder that Poe begins to write in the autumn of 1842. This enthusiastic commercial reception derives in part from the success of the story's sentimental appeal. Poe's plot, superficially at least, sanctifies the psychological complexities of remarriage after the loss of a beloved spouse—an experience common to many nineteenth century readers. But as it does so it intensifies the feelings of guilt and betrayal associated with survival. Before dying, Eleonora extracts a terrible oath from her lover that he will never "transfer" his devotion to a maiden of the "outer" world after her death:

> And then and there, I threw myself hurriedly at the feet of Eleonora, and offered up a vow, to herself and to Heaven that I would never bind myself in marriage to any daughter of Earth—that I would in no manner prove recreant to her dear memory, or to the memory of the devout affection with which she had blessed me. And I called the Mighty Ruler of the Universe to witness the pious solemnity of my vow. And the curse which I invoked of *Him* and of her, a saint in Helusion, should I prove traitorous to that promise, involved a penalty the exceeding great horror of which will not permit me to make record of it here. (PT, 471)

This fierce pledge of undeviating loyalty to the dead involves consequences so frightening that the narrator cannot bear to write them down. Eleonora's command of the "inner" world derives from her potent alliance with the retributive power of memory.

Once the narrator finds himself adrift in the "strange city" of human passion, however, the spiritual manifestations of Eleonora's lingering influence suddenly cease: "The pomps and pageantries of a stately court, and the mad clangor of arms, and the radiant loveliness of woman, bewildered and intoxicated my brain." A mysterious wanderer "from some far, far distant and unknown land," the maiden Ermengarde, fills him with a new, acutely physical delirium. This unabashedly erotic devotion is tied, as well, to a sense of pneumatic liberation from grief—a "spirit-lifting ecstasy of adoration" eclipsing the burdensome vow that the narrator had made to his dead cousin. Unlike Eleonora, however, who shares a genealogy as well as a childhood with the narrator, Ermengarde's family origins are obscure; she is a grey vision as well as a luminous one, beckoning the narrator into an unmapped fabric of human intimacy that suggests the unexplored ocean of ineffable light at the beginning of his tale.

On the night of his wedding to this wholly captivating partner, a disembodied but familiar voice, speaking for the Spirit of Love, absolves him of his youthful pledge with its horrifying penalty and endorses his new marriage, a consolatory resolution completely at odds with the narrator's opening vision of a rudderless voyage to unknown reaches of consciousness. But incompatibility has proven to be the essence of his experience. The two distinct conditions of madness and lofty intelligence that divide the narrator's mind at the beginning of his tale correspond to the clashing outcomes of "exceeding great horror" and romantic fulfillment that collide at its end. The narrator's opening allusion to Oedipus proves only too applicable to the riddle of his story. But Poe's plot also doubles as a parable of surrender in which the dazzling but ultimately endogamous claims of lucid reason, in the Valley of the Many-Colored Grass, give way to a marriage with the darker energies of wisdom and knowledge, the cumulative products of time that can offer only glimpses of the elemental conflict between profundity and disease that compose the story's mental voyage.

Poe's most extensive treatment of the rudderless boat as a figure for consciousness is also his first exploration of the pneumatic instability of the soul—its division into separate spheres of awareness or activity that permit only occasional, imperfect glimpses across the mental and spiritual boundary that divides them. "MS. Found in a Bottle," his prize-winning story from 1833, offers two emblematic voyages rather than one—three if one counts the bottle itself as another rudderless vessel—each conditioned by a distinctive interplay between some form of cultural ballast and the extraordinary combination of external and internal forces that displace this material weight, carrying the narrator's mind to the verge of destinations which resist the ordinary descriptive resources of language.

Like "Eleonora," the story introduces another of Poe's enigmatic seekers, a narrator who withholds his name and nationality but who confesses to "hereditary" burdens of wealth, education, and "a contemplative turn of mind" that relishes exposing the products of "eloquent madness" to the discipline of "rigid thought." A restless connoisseur of antiquities and student of the "German moralists," he nevertheless appears to place exclusive confidence in the aridity of reason. Over the course of his life, he claims to have accumulated a generous cargo of mental "stores," arranging them according to the dictates of his acute analytical skills. But the "reveries of fancy" have remained for him "a dead letter and a nullity" (PT, 189). A "strong relish for physical philosophy," the narrator concedes, has impoverished his imagination, but it has also rendered him immune to superstitious delusions—a combination of traits that, he hopes, will secure a hearing for his incredible tale.

The trading vessel on which he sails at the outset of his adventure, much like the narrator himself, is curiously laden: "freighted with cotton-wool and oil" in a disturbingly explosive mix that suggests the design of a vast lamp awaiting ignition. Coir, jaggeree, ghee, cocoanuts, and "a few cases of opium" fill out this volatile and badly stowed cargo. The monotonous calm that initially greets the ship as it heads to sea quickly begins to take on ominous pneumatic properties that the narrator deftly calibrates, constructing (as any devotee of physical philosophy should) simple instruments to measure the scene's uncanny stagnation. A "narrow strip of vapor" gradually circles the horizon: "I watched it attentively until sunset," the narrator reports, as it expands from a "very singular, isolated cloud" into a perfect ring. He takes note too of the moon's strange "dusky red appearance." The ocean grows mysteriously transparent, not unlike the clarified butter, the ghee, in the ship's hold, and for a moment the scene begins to resemble a vast griddle in which the ship and its contents are a kind of grotesque meal:

The air now became intolerably hot, and was loaded with spiral exhalations similar to those arising from heated iron. As night came on, every breath of wind died away, and a more entire calm it is impossible to conceive. The flame of a candle burned upon the poop without the least perceptible motion, and a long hair, held between the finger and thumb, hung without the possibility of detecting a vibration. (PT, 190)

The storm that shortly strikes out of this portentous stillness begins as a curious humming sound, emanating from within the ship itself, just before a "wilderness of foam" sweeps its decks clear under "the immense pressure of the tempest."

The forces of compression and expansion, of stillness and of incalculable speed, are the central ingredients of these opening passages, coupled with the circular and spiral forms that anticipate the story's closing scene. The narrator's passion for reason and for measurement deeply conditions his language, making him the ideal imaginative register for the profound, elemental voyage that follows. An old Swede who had mysteriously joined the ship just as it was about to sail is the only other survivor of the blast. Indeed, the storm appears to summon him into existence to fill out the narrator's truncated self-portrait, adding a country of origin to supplement the "length of years" that the two men apparently share. Together they cling to the shattered hulk as it rushes southward, through an environment that grows progressively more strange. Even after the original storm dissipates, the sun never recovers its natural energy. As the Antarctic cold increases, its light fades to a "dull and sullen glow . . . as if its rays were polarized" (PT, 192). Reduced to "a dim, silver-like rim, alone," a cool lens rather than a radiant star, the sun at last disappears into the ocean.

Enveloped in total darkness, the old Swede quickly surrenders to "superstitious terror," despite his earlier faith that the "lightness" of the wreck's cargo will keep them afloat. The narrator, by contrast, is "wrapped in silent wonder" by the fury of the ocean and the "sweltering desert of ebony" surrounding them. This separation of mental states—a narrative echo of the division between reason and the reveries of fancy with which the story had begun—immediately precedes the separation of bodies that occurs when a huge vessel looms over the crest of a gigantic wave and destroys the wreck, obliterating the Swede and flinging the narrator into the strange vessel's rigging:

> Casting my eyes upwards, I beheld a spectacle which froze the current of my blood. At a terrific height directly above us, and upon the very verge of the precipitous descent, hovered a gigantic ship, of perhaps four thousand tons. Although upreared upon the summit of a wave more than a hundred times her own altitude, her apparent size still exceeded that of any ship of the line or East Indiaman in existence. Her huge hull was of a deep dingy black, unrelieved by any of the customary carvings of a ship. A single row of brass cannon protruded from her open ports, and dashed from their polished surfaces the fires of innumerable battle-lanterns, which swung to and fro about her rigging. But what mainly

inspired us with horror and astonishment, was that she bore up under a press of sail in the very teeth of that supernatural sea, and of that ungovernable hurricane. When we first discovered her, her bows were alone to be seen, as she rose slowly from the dim and horrible gulf beyond her. For a moment of intense terror she paused upon the giddy pinnacle, as if in contemplation of her own sublimity, then trembled and tottered, and—came down. (PT, 193–194)

"See! See!" the old Swede cries as this monstrous ship looms above them—not "Look! Look!" as one might expect in a normative physical world. A vessel ten times the bulk of the narrator's original merchant ship, a wave a hundred times the height of a tall ship's mast, a "press" of sail in a supernatural storm—these exponential details depict the sublime paradox of mountainous form united to elasticity of motion that Poe will introduce into the 1835 version of "Loss of Breath" a few months later, combined with an additional pneumatic property that the narrator of "MS. Found in a Bottle" dimly begins to detect after he has spent some time roaming the decks of the mysterious vessel.

Her timbers resemble Spanish oak of an unusual character. It is strangely porous wood, he reports, "distended" not as if the ship were a growing body, as an old Dutch proverb suggests, but as if it were decaying, like the buoyant corpse of Marie Rogêt, or ballooning like the hallucinatory narrator in "Loss of Breath," preparing for a desperate ascent, not the desperate descent into the vortex that actually awaits it. This second rudderless ship is an expansive successor to the original teak and copper-bound merchant vessel with which the tale begins, ballasted not with the volatile commercial cargo of the first but with long-forgotten charts, "iron-clasped folios," "mouldering instruments of science," and with time itself. The original lading of cotton-wool and oil appears to have generated a strange incandescence in the phantom ship: the "fires of innumerable battle-lanterns" strung in its rigging glint off the brass cannon in her open gun ports. The crew and the captain are burdened with a "length of years" that both resembles and trivializes that of the narrator. Their own, formidable physical knowledge appears no longer necessary to guide the remarkable vehicle that they appear to have built, much as Hans Pfaall built the remarkable balloon that carries him to the Moon. The ship skims away effortlessly from the most massive waves "with the facility of the arrowy sea-gull," drawn forward and downward by an "impetuous under-tow" but achieving a miraculous variety of flight at the same time.

The narrator's sensations are an equally tumultuous blend of antagonistic forces. The "terrible ship" on which he finds himself is both inexplicable and familiar: a completely novel entity that baffles his reason at the same time that it awakens peculiar memories. "I know not how it is," he confesses, "but in scrutinizing her strange model and singular cast of spars, her huge size and overgrown suits of canvass, her severely simple bow and antiquated stern, there will occasionally flash across my mind a sensation of familiar things, and there is always mixed up with such indistinct shadows of recollection, an unaccountable memory of old foreign chronicles and ages long ago" (PT, 196).

This bi-part state of mind generates the blend of curiosity and awe with which the narrator anticipates his own destruction in the "chaos of foamless water" that surrounds the phantom ship. He appears eager, at least at first, to encounter the exciting secret toward which the current seems to be carrying them: a confrontation with the "walls of the universe" itself. By contrast, the ancient captain and his crew seem to be merely peevish and confused. Great age has conferred on them a peculiar bearing that combines the "solemn dignity of a God" with the petty passions of a "second childhood," a crippling division of aptitudes in which the pneumatic laws of ascent would seem to be crippled by human limitation. As the climax of the tale approaches, however, the unreadable countenances of the phantom crew display a subtle change. They finally face the howling amphitheater at the end of the story with "eagerness of hope" rather than senile apathy or despair, displaying none of the narrator's swiftly escalating fear. Lifelong habits of rigid thought prove unequal to the sublime antagonism of attraction and repulsion with which the first of Poe's rudderless voyages draws to a close.

CHAPTER 3

The Gravity of Things

When unquestioning faith in the principles of science finally deserts the narrator of "MS. Found in a Bottle," he is thrust into a world of inexplicable and ominous sensations. The last illustration of conventional mechanics that he is able to describe is the catapult effect created when the great mass of the rapidly descending phantom ship strikes one end of the wreckage to which he is clinging and hurls him into the stranger's rigging—a result that any child can visualize. More difficult conceptual challenges quickly follow as the narrator slips through the main hatchway of his phantom host and conceals himself in "a convenient retreat between the huge timbers of the ship," the first carefully calibrated sign of the decisive pneumatic frontier that he has crossed.

The moment that he foresaw the collision, he moved to the far end of his original vessel in anticipation of this miraculous and disconcerting transfer. Once safely on board his host, however, he is immediately seized by "an indefinite sense of awe." As the story moves to its conclusion, this initial reaction gives way to a mixture of feelings that defies analysis even as the narrator's psychological horizons expand in every direction. Though the feeble members of the phantom ship's crew have no difficulty maintaining their footing on the wildly tossing deck, the narrator cannot trust his balance. The heights, depths, and speeds that he experiences are dizzying. The ancient captain and his companions are unable to see him, even when he thrusts himself into their midst, but he in turn can scarcely hear them speak. Their low and peevish voices seem to reach him only from a great distance, as if he were existing in a semiconscious state of delirium:

> The ship and all in it are imbued with the spirit of Eld. The crew glide to and fro like the ghosts of buried centuries; their eyes have an eager and uneasy meaning; and when their figures fall athwart my path in the wild

glare of the battle-lanterns, I feel as I have never felt before, although I have been all my life a dealer in antiquities, and have imbibed the shadows of fallen columns at Balbec, and Tadmor, and Persepolis, until my very soul has become a ruin. (PT, 198)

The uneasiness of the crew, like the narrator's feverish anxiety, reflects the gradual progression of some mysterious array of spiritual symptoms, a paradoxical blend of sickness and exaltation that culminates with a quivering and deafening descent into a gigantic whirlpool near the bottom of the globe.

The intimate relationship between corporeal pathology and an exhilarating (or catastrophic) expansion of consciousness is central to the pneumatics of mind that shapes Poe's long additions to the original version of "Loss of Breath" in the months that followed the cholera outbreak of 1832. With "MS. Found in a Bottle" he immediately seizes the opportunity to link these cognitive preoccupations to two artistic vehicles that reappear throughout his work: the rudderless vessel and its necessary complement, the irresistible circles or currents of gravity depicted in the figure of the vortex. The narrator of Poe's early masterpiece succumbs to this immeasurable field of force, despite the ballast provided by his mental discipline and a deep knowledge of antiquities. Poe himself proves far more buoyant. His short fiction returns repeatedly to this hypnotic blend of mental energies, particularly after 1841 when Poe's own creative vortex draws him into an ever tightening circle, eventually finding release in the alternating states of expansion and contraction that comprise the plot of *Eureka*.

* * *

"A Descent into the Maelström," published in the May 1841 issue of *Graham's Magazine*, is Poe's most elaborate imaginative response to the geophysical forces that he first addresses in "MS. Found in a Bottle." The applied pneumatics and physics that fill much of Hans Pfaall's moon voyage or the popular fascination with comets that Poe exploits in "The Conversation of Eiros and Charmion" suggest his sustained interest in the figurative possibilities of science through the earliest years of his career. But "A Descent into the Maelström" is the first of Poe's stories to take as its central subject the intersections of terrestrial and celestial space implicit in the kinetic geometry of the funnel. Poe's growing appreciation for the imaginative potential of this shape coincides with the years in which the rotational design of spiral galaxies first became visible from Earth, encouraging the application of geometrical and geographical analogies to the structure of the universe.

In *Vestiges of the Natural History of Creation* (1844), Robert Chambers opens his provocative synthesis of contemporary scientific thought by comparing the behavior of "nebulous matter" in the cosmological theories of Laplace to the movement of water "sinking through the aperture of a funnel." Clusters of stars gradually coalescing in a vast astronomical system "would all become involved in a common revolutionary motion":

> We have seen that the law which causes rotation in the single solar masses, is exactly the same which produces the familiar phenomenon of a small whirlpool or dimple in the surface of a stream. Such dimples are not always single. Upon the face of a river where there are various contending currents, it may often be observed that two or more dimples are formed near each other with more or less regularity. These fantastic eddies, which the musing poet will sometimes watch abstractedly for an hour, little thinking of the law which produces and connects them, are an illustration of the wonders of binary and ternary solar systems.

Chambers takes this account of what he calls "the celestial scenery" and its miniature earthly replica virtually word for word from *Views of the Architecture of the Heavens* (1837), a popular collection of letters on astronomy by John Pringle Nichol that Poe too eagerly ransacked in these years. Nichol, in turn, drew heavily on the work of the Herschels and Laplace to frame his extended scientific sermon on cosmic wonders, an "astral system" that he and Chambers compare to the stages of growth from infant, to boy, to man as well as to insect metamorphosis and to plant development.

Earth, a "child of the Sun" as Chambers terms it, is older than its planetary siblings Mercury or Venus but much younger than Saturn or Jupiter. The entire solar system is younger still, by an inconceivable order of magnitude, than the most distant visible stars. Long before Poe dedicated *Eureka* to Alexander von Humboldt in 1848, his fiction began to respond to the conceptual excitement prompted by the most advanced cosmological thinking of his day, as Nichol and Chambers had begun to popularize it. Like the fantastic eddies and contending currents that dimple the surface of a stream, "A Descent into the Maelström" is a scale model of , as well as a metaphor for, these astral forces.

The story begins with a bracing abruptness that is unusual even for Poe: "We had now reached the summit of the loftiest crag," his narrator declares in the tale's first words, "For some minutes the old man seemed too much exhausted to speak" (PT, 432). This stark, two-sentence opening paragraph is a verbal crag of sorts, a narrative extremity evoking the pinnacle of time that "now" implicitly represents by skipping over the customary preliminaries of fiction: who "we" are, and how we have arrived at the apex of the present. The old man who soon begins to speak explains that his apparent age is an illusion; decades have been reduced to hours by the experience that he is about to relate. Poe's narrator has deliberately sought out a bleak stretch of rocky Norwegian coast in order to see for himself a phenomenon that he only knows about from an entry in the *Encyclopedia Britannica*. His curiosity and his naiveté do not prepare him for the vertigo that quickly seizes him on the summit to which his local guide has conducted him. This mythical mountain, Helseggen the Cloudy, proves to be a "sheer unobstructed precipice of black shining rock," a great gnomon rising "some fifteen or sixteen hundred feet from the world of crags beneath us" (PT, 432).

While the old Norwegian guide perches unconcernedly on the edge of the abyss, like George Washington's serene statue on his Baltimore column, the narrator falls flat on the ground and struggles to control his fears. A complex of antagonistic energies immediately collects around this bleak pinnacle, an intersection of horizontal and vertical forces that shape the story's psychological universe and inscribe themselves on the landscape. Poe inserts his reader directly into a three-dimensional geophysical grid that the narrator's words quickly set into motion as he views the mix of ocean and rock at his feet:

> I looked dizzily, and beheld a wide expanse of ocean, whose waters wore so inky a hue as to bring at once to mind the Nubian geographer's account of the *Mare Tenebrarum*. A panorama more deplorably desolate no human imagination can conceive. To the right and left, as far as the eye could reach, there lay outstretched, like ramparts of the world, lines of horridly black and beetling cliff, whose character of gloom was but the more forcibly illustrated by the surf which reared high up against it its white and ghastly crest, howling and shrieking for ever. Just opposite the promontory upon whose apex we were placed, and at a distance of some five or six miles out at sea, there was visible a small, bleak-looking island; or, more properly, its position was discernible through the wilderness of surge in which it was enveloped. About two miles nearer the land, arose another of smaller size, hideously craggy and barren, and encompassed at various intervals by a cluster of dark rocks.
>
> The appearance of the ocean, in the space between the more distant island and the shore, had something very unusual about it...there was

here nothing like a regular swell, but only a short, quick, angry cross dashing of water in every direction—as well in the teeth of the wind as otherwise. Of foam there was little except in the immediate vicinity of the rocks. (PT, 433)

The guide in his cool "particularizing manner" fixes their exact location on the coast by degree of latitude—the cross dashing lines of navigational science—and identifies the main islands below by their Norwegian names, but such meticulous geographical detail is a ludicrous counterweight to the cosmic panorama that the narrator describes. Minute by minute the ocean surface begins to change, a transformation that requires comparatively fine units of linear and temporal measurement (minutes and moments) to depict. On this day at least, Helseggen the Cloudy seems the ideal place from which to observe the formation of the great maelstrom and to hear an exceptional story from his days as a fisherman that the guide proposes to tell.

Poe's setting immediately appeals to the two, imperfectly integrated forms of "vision" that his reader must now prepare to exercise, a blend of mental currents that resembles the unearthly churning of the sea. The story's narrator is already gripped by the tremendous spectacle beneath him even before the change of the tide begins to transform the ocean's appearance. The complete panorama of coastline and ocean overwhelms the imagination. The surf is already shrieking with fury when the two men arrive at their lofty vantage point. Once the mouth of the "terrific funnel" finally takes shape out of the "phrensied convulsion" of the sea, it reproduces in liquid form the mountains around it, "a smooth, shining, and jet-black wall of water" rotating and swaying beneath them, "and sending forth to the winds an appalling voice, half shriek, half roar, such as not even the mighty cataract of Niagara ever lifts up in its agony to Heaven" (PT, 435).

Like the old Swede and the narrator of "MS. Found in a Bottle"—or like Auguste Dupin and his secretarial companion strolling through the infinite Paris night—the narrator of "A Descent into the Maelström" and his loquacious guide embody the capacities of the bi-part soul. In this instance, the guide proves to be the more analytic mind. The bookish learning of the story's narrator deserts him, as he observes the raw force of nature at his feet and listens to the old fisherman's harrowing adventure. That adventure in turn contains a second, overlapping pair of complementary souls: the guide himself and his older brother, whose terror mirrors the narrator's psychosomatic collapse when he first finds himself stretched at full length on the summit of Helseggen, gripping some meager shrubs for security. For some minutes he is unable to persuade himself that the mountain can withstand the force of the ocean winds. Poe depicts him as a suggestive emblem of modern consciousness: clinging desperately to an unstable and rocky planet, surrounded by the bewildering inhumanities of space.

The fanciful, but nevertheless real, symptoms of vertigo with which the story begins are a prelude to several sorts of illness that appear in its pages. The convulsions of the ocean itself resemble the agony of a great animal. The strange physical condition of the "old" guide is (he insists) not a consequence of age but of "six hours of deadly terror" that blanched his hair, weakened his limbs, and shattered his nerves. When the realization first dawns on him, in the course of the long tale he tells, that he and his one surviving brother are caught in the maelstrom's grip, he remembers shaking "from head to foot as if I had had the most violent fit of the ague" (PT, 441). The steep plunge of his dismasted fishing boat down the sides of the ocean's huge waves "made me feel sick and dizzy," the guide recalls, "as if I was falling from some lofty mountain-top in a dream." At the whirlpool's edge, his eyelids "clenched themselves together as if in a spasm." Many of the hallucinatory symptoms that Poe compresses into the excised paragraphs from "Loss of Breath" recur in "A Descent into the Maelström" as a kind of narrative morphology: a sickness of the flesh, systematically preparing the mind to see as it has never seen before.

According to the guide's recollection, the "belt of surf" at the maelstrom's rim marks an uncanny physical boundary, like the ring of cloud surrounding the narrator of "MS. Found in a Bottle" at the outset of his adventure. Once across this belt, instead of plunging immediately down the "writhing wall" of the funnel, the two brothers on their shattered hull shoot off "like an air-bubble upon the surface of the surge," orbiting the core of the vortex. At this juncture, the guide's own feelings undergo a similar, startling transformation. The debilitating physical horror that he had felt as the hurricane drove them toward the whirlpool gives way to a mental buoyancy corresponding to the change in the array of physical forces guiding the boat's course:

> "It may look like boasting—but what I tell you is truth—I began to reflect how magnificent a thing it was to die in such a manner, and how foolish it was in me to think of so paltry a consideration as my own individual life, in view of so wonderful a manifestation of God's power. I do believe that I blushed with shame when this idea crossed my mind. After a little while I became possessed with the keenest curiosity about the

whirl itself. I positively felt a *wish* to explore its depths, even at the sacrifice I was going to make; and my principal grief was that I should never be able to tell my old companions on shore about the mysteries I should see. These, no doubt, were singular fancies to occupy a man's mind in such extremity—and I have often thought since, that the revolutions of the boat around the pool might have rendered me a little light-headed. (PT, 443)

Once he is out of reach of the deafening surface winds, a pneumatics of mind gradually compensates the old fisherman for the burden of personal fear.

As the guide and his brother slowly descend the funnel's sides, moonlight floods its ebony interior through a "circular rift" in the storm clouds, forming a "magnificent rainbow" in the thick mist below. An indescribable yell emerges from the maelstrom's throat, rising "to the Heavens from out of that mist," but the fear that this terrible noise might ordinarily incite is neutralized both by the rich visual spectacle and by the implication that this unearthly cry is directed not toward the whirlpool's human prey but toward the impassive, "deep bright blue" opening in the sky through which the full moon is visible. Poe has cast his old guide down a glistening tube of water that suggests the body of a vast telescope, as if to urge the reader's mind toward a provocative entanglement of celestial and earthly space. The setting has outgrown the conventional associations of a seascape to become a kind of expressionist canvas: a depiction of force rather than place. The old guide's receptivity to the complex play of energies surrounding him proves ultimately responsible for his survival.

Unlike his fear-crazed brother, he recognizes the implicit harmony of his circumstances: the interlocking circles of moon, sky, and swirling vortex that even find a diminutive echo in the ring bolt on the boat's deck which saves him when the hurricane first strikes. This last and smallest ring, however, is a fatal temptation—a sign of the constricting boundaries of paltry individuality. In order to avoid descending with it to the bottom of the maelstrom, the guide concludes that he must leave the deceptive security of the wrecked hull and lash himself to a cylindrical water cask, the buoyant "bottle" by means of which this particular narrative will be preserved. Memory and careful observation suggest that this is the only shape capable of resisting the fatal suction of the great funnel. "Unnatural curiosity" and speculative amusement—the chief mental equipment of Auguste Dupin, among other Poe characters—permit him to see a reason for hope where his brother can only descend into madness.

Poe stages another triumph of the analytical intelligence in these pages, a familiar preoccupation of his fiction, but at the end of "A Descent into the Maelström" he seems willing to dismiss the importance of the old guide's narrative. The "merry fishermen of Lofoden" who finally rescue him once the whirlpool subsides plainly regard the whole tale with skepticism—a response that Poe appears to endorse in the opening pages of the story, where the guide's words seem suspiciously polished and his choice of setting a kind of naturalistic theater. The fisherman's local acquaintances are no longer interested in his spectacular yarn, but tourists are another matter, particularly when the performer is able to relate his adventure to the accompaniment of the maelstrom's unearthly noise, on Helseggen's windy peak.

Unlike the stories involving Auguste Dupin, however, "A Descent into the Maelström" does not depend on the magnetic intelligence of a central character or on earthly plausibility for its attractive force. Poe's interest focuses instead on the conceptual scope with which he is able to fill the physical scene. He is experimenting with the verbal challenge of framing and then of setting in motion a picture of the laws that govern terrestrial and extraterrestrial space, as his scientific contemporaries were beginning to describe them. The new science posed an unprecedented challenge to the imagination—one to which Poe responded with the same selfless exhilaration that the old guide attributes to his own pneumatic epiphany on the maelstrom's writhing wall. Over the next five years Poe proposes a number of narrative solutions to the problem of situating human consciousness within the sublime operations of celestial mechanics.

* * *

"The Pit and the Pendulum" is Poe's next major experiment in constructing this joint model of consciousness and space. Written a year after "A Descent into the Maelström" and published in *The Gift* for 1843, this celebrated tale would seem at first a peculiar vehicle to propose as a treatment of vast celestial challenges to the imagination. Poe confines the narrative almost entirely within a dungeon in the city of Toledo, where a victim of the Catholic Inquisition seems doomed to an agonizing death. The story's opening sentences, however, provide a remarkable, inward projection of the Norway maelstrom, experienced through a perceptual mist of physiological distress: dizziness, nausea, galvanic spasms, euphoria, and delirium. The story's initial scenes impose the narrator's cognitive experience of illness upon what will prove to be an ambitious portrayal of cultural transformation. The reactionary terrors of the Catholic Inquisition are a perennial favorite of sensational popular fiction, but Poe's object in this tale is not popular sensation but the irrational crosscurrents of human delusion that both guide and thwart great conceptual change.

Unlike its vortex predecessors in Poe's career, "The Pit and the Pendulum" opens directly on the verge of its dizzying descent. The pervasive physical symptoms from which the narrator suffers during his imprisonment and sentencing make it difficult for him to reproduce the scene of his original trial with any clarity. "I was sick—sick unto death with that long agony," his opening words explain. The voices of his judges merged "in one dreamy indeterminate hum" like "the burr of a mill-wheel," filling his soul with "the idea of revolution," of whirling, but he could still manage to read their lips as they condemned him to death:

> I saw, too, for a few moments of delirious horror, the soft and nearly imperceptible waving of the sable draperies which enwrapped the walls of the apartment. And then my vision fell upon the seven tall candles upon the table. At first they wore the aspect of charity, and seemed white slender angels who would save me; but then, all at once, there came a most deadly nausea over my spirit, and I felt every fibre in my frame thrill as if I had touched the wire of a galvanic battery, while the angel forms became meaningless spectres, with heads of flame, and I saw that from them there would be no help. And then there stole into my fancy, like a rich musical note, the thought of what sweet rest there must be in the grave. The thought came gently and stealthily, and it seemed long before it attained full appreciation; but just as my spirit came at length properly to feel and entertain it, the figures of the judges vanished, as if magically, from before me; the tall candles sank into nothingness; their flames went out utterly; the blackness of darkness supervened; all sensations appeared swallowed up in a mad rushing descent as of the soul into Hades. Then silence, and stillness, and night were the universe. (PT, 491–492)

This passage blends a rushing descent toward impenetrable darkness with the narrator's vague perception of limitless space—recalling the bridge between Time and Eternity that the old guide seems to glimpse in the rainbow at the bottom of the Norway maelstrom, or the looming walls of the Universe toward which the great ghost vessel of "MS. Found in a Bottle" madly sails, as well as the haunting coffin visions that Poe had first introduced in the excised paragraphs from "Loss of Breath."

In reconstructing much later what had happened to him, the narrator of "The Pit and the Pendulum" carefully distinguishes the erratic progression of stages through which the mind passes as it recovers consciousness, retrieving from "the shadows of memory" a much slower version of events as he is carried steadily downward by a group of mysteriously silent "figures," beyond "the limits of the limitless" (PT, 493). This calculus of descent to infinite depths—a counting "down" to the most remote conceptual extremes—awakens a "hideous dizziness" in the narrator's mind, followed by a kind of madness: not the pure hysteria of "A Descent into the Maelström" but "the madness of a memory which busies itself among forbidden things." The cognitive pneumatics of his experience appear to reverse those of the earlier vortex stories. A vastly expanded consciousness awakens to find itself thrust into a state of mental confinement from which it slowly struggles to escape:

> Very suddenly there came back to my soul motion and sound—the tumultuous motion of the heart, and, in my ears, the sound of its beating. Then a pause in which all is blank. Then again sound, and motion, and touch—a tingling sensation pervading my frame. Then the mere consciousness of existence, without thought—a condition which lasted long. Then, very suddenly, *thought*, and shuddering terror, and earnest endeavor to comprehend my true state. Then a strong desire to lapse into insensibility. Then a rushing revival of soul and a successful effort to move. And now a full memory of the trial, of the judges, of the sable draperies, of the sentence, of the sickness, of the swoon. Then entire forgetfulness of all that followed; of all that a later day and much earnestness of endeavor have enabled me vaguely to recall. (PT, 493)

A rich sensory and reflective network lies behind the "rushing revival of soul" that gradually reintroduces the story's narrator to motion, thought, and time. These alternating perceptions of emptiness and tumultuous repletion form the nucleus around which memory is gradually able to stabilize the inchoate flow of perception.

The elaborate clinical details with which "The Pit and the Pendulum" begins reformulate portions from a number of earlier stories in order to stress the experience of the reviving and observing intelligence. Poe's prisoner/narrator, like the old guide on the top of Helseggen, the Cloudy, has a particularizing manner—an ingrained scientific curiosity and mental discipline that prompt him to analyze even the most extreme experiences. He is an eager student of the forbidden realms of physical philosophy that inquisitorial ignorance wishes to remain sealed. The elaborate punitive theater of his prison, in fact, proves to be a picture of ignorance: a clumsy apparatus that impugns the intelligence of its makers. The first and crudest portion of the narrator's ordeal is marked by profound darkness. Groping about his dungeon, he accidentally discovers a deep chasm in its floor into which his persecutors had intended him to fall—the fatal consummation of the inquisition's artificial vortex. Mentally envisioning numbers of these wells concealed in the surrounding darkness, he retreats to the dungeon wall where he finally falls into a drugged sleep.

During a second wakeful phase, a "sulphurous lustre" discloses the design and the curious decorations of his prison: a square chamber formed by huge metallic plates "rudely" painted with fiends, skeletons, and other superstitious monstrosities of the religious imagination. The narrator is in fact surrounded by pictures, though of a far less exalting kind than the splendid expressionist images that form the Norway maelstrom. Slowly regaining consciousness, he finds himself in the center of a macabre gallery, strapped by a continuous, coiled bandage—a spring or a spiraling vortex of its own—to a "low framework of wood" that recalls the remnants of the fishing smack on which the old guide had descended into the whirlpool. This platform is positioned directly beneath a figure of Time painted on the dungeon ceiling, holding a huge scythe that proves to be a moveable pendulum "such as we see on antique clocks."

In Poe's day (as in our own) the pendulum was by no means antique technology. It remained a powerful scientific tool throughout the nineteenth century, closely associated with Galileo, a celebrated victim of Catholic persecution, but adapted over the centuries to a wide range of experimental ends. Alexander von Humboldt admiringly termed the pendulum a "geognostical instrument," an earth-knower, that a skilled investigator could use to probe the planet's crust "like a sounding line," determining the unequal densities of geological strata, disclosing subtle local variations in the globe's curvature and gravitational force. "When the Earth had been measured," von Humboldt would write in *Cosmos*, summarizing the scientific role that the pendulum had played over the last half century of inquiry, "it still had to be weighed":

> The oscillations of the pendulum and the plummet have here likewise served to determine the mean density of the Earth, either in connection with astronomical and geodetic operations, with the view of finding the deflection of the plummet from a vertical line in the vicinity of a mountain, or by a comparison of the length of the pendulum in a plain and on the summit of an elevation, or, finally, by the employment of a torsion

balance, which may be considered as a horizontally vibrating pendulum for the measurement of the relative density of neighboring strata.

Different investigators drew different conclusions from the data that their instruments had obtained, von Humboldt continued, but contemporary scientists were able to agree on a mean density for the Earth 5.44 times greater than that of pure water, and had put to rest a century and a half of persistent delusions concerning the presence of a subterranean world within the Earth's hollow core.

This fantasy realm had grown ridiculously elaborate, since Edmund Halley had first suggested the possibility of its existence at the end of the seventeenth century: becoming "peopled with plants and animals" and even illuminated by its own small revolving planets, "so powerful is the morbid inclination of men" von Humboldt observes, "to fill unknown spaces with shapes of wonder, totally unmindful of the counter evidence furnished by well-attested facts and universally acknowledged natural laws." Those facts and laws actually depict a planetary core of molten metal under enormous pressure but still sufficiently fluid to respond, in faint and mysterious ways, to the gravitational fields of the Moon and the Sun—a sublime interior in its own right, and one that soon exerts its influence over the shifting physical conditions that prevail in Poe's fictional dungeon. The ability to determine Earth's density and weight is among the first fruits of modern scientific analysis applied to the study of terrestrial and celestial gravity. The pendulum is the tool that analyzes and measures them.

It is also the instrument chosen by the invisible inquisitors of Poe's story to carry out the vengeance of the Church, in a subterranean chamber decorated with pictures of an archaic and perverse underworld. Two forms of "inquisition," the scientific and the superstitious, find expression in the same object and the same scene—a figurative dissonance that the narrator repeatedly echoes in the scientific terminology that he applies to the pendulum's ominous "vibration," or in the "frenzied pleasure" with which he contrasts "its downward with its lateral velocity." He helplessly but nevertheless meticulously counts "the rushing oscillations" of the slowly descending blade. As it draws nearer, he takes note of "the odor of the sharp steel," and anticipates the moment when the scythe will reach his chest (PT, 500–501). Reduced nearly to idiocy by his plight, he begins to resemble a chaotic blend of the two brothers who are drawn into the Norway maelstrom on their wrecked fishing boat: the one driven mad by fear, the other retaining his powers of mind, along with his analytic vocabulary, and contriving an ingenious escape.

The narrator of "The Pit and the Pendulum," like the old guide in "A Descent into the Maelström," ultimately recovers his self-possession, cleverly luring the voracious rats that live in the dungeon's deep well to eat through the leather strap that ties him to the platform beneath the blade. In a handful of vivid sentences, Poe describes these creatures pouring over the narrator's body, busying themselves with the bandage that he has smeared with oily meat residue, much as his own memory had busied itself with the investigation of "forbidden things" in the delirium with which the story begins. Ultimately this second escape too proves to be no more than a postponement. The iron walls of the dungeon soon begin to glow with heat, heightening the lurid colors of their fantastic paintings and inadvertently mimicking the molten underworld of von Humboldt's modern science.

Slowly, and in a geometrically precise manner, they begin to change shape as well, forming two acute and two obtuse angles, steadily tightening with "a low rumbling or moaning sound" into a narrow parallelogram that gradually forces the narrator toward the mouth of the pit in the center of the floor. Poe's artificial vortex evolves, as it collapses, into the suggestive shape of a prism or a lens—themselves precisely calibrated tools employed to analyze the refractive properties of light or to focus the faint rays from distant stars on the eyepiece of a telescope. The lurid glare emanating from the fiendish pictures on the dungeon walls, as their temperature increases, represents the spurious triumph of unreason, but the investigative instruments mimicked by the angular design of the dungeon and its carefully constructed pendulum foretell the end of monkish ingenuity and ignorance.

The story's final sentence—"The Inquisition was in the hands of its enemies"—celebrates the narrator's dramatic rescue when soldiers of the French General Lasalle seize the city and open its prisons. A mysterious savior prevents him, at the last second, from falling into the well at the center of his dungeon. But Poe's words also point toward the substitution of one kind of inquisition for another: a transfer of tools to a new and enlightened set of hands. "The Pit and the Pendulum" is a verbal torsion balance in its own right, oscillating between the scientific and the religious spheres of cultural consciousness that would increasingly vie for dominance as nineteenth-century science extended its scope.

* * *

In all three of his vortex stories, Poe projects the instrumentation of modern science onto a colossal scale. The great ship of "MS. Found in a Bottle" is a fantastic expansion of an actual exploration vessel. Ancient books and scientific devices litter the floor of the captain's cabin, but the phantom ship as a whole is both a triumphant and a terrifying achievement—an unprecedented geognostical tool. The Norway maelstrom is sublime even in its near-animate fury, directing the eye upward like the black cylinder of an immense and powerful telescope toward the gravitational origin of its energy, the tidal influence of the Moon. At the end of Poe's inquisitorial nightmare in the dungeons of Toledo, the pendulum, the prism, and the lens shed the gothic costumes in which monkish ignorance has clothed them, linking that story too with an elaborate cognitive masquerade. In each plot, knowledge has a medicinal effect on the pervasive sickness that precedes the process of discovery.

In only one instance, however, does the medicine of physical philosophy work a complete cure, and even so it requires a powerful spiritual catalyst. The old guide who describes his descent into the whirlpool manages to avoid madness and destruction because his analytical powers are, for a brief period, almost completely free of anxiety over his personal fate. The experimental calculations that ultimately save him are bathed in the moon's golden light as it penetrates the maelstrom's core, an emblem of the serenity that frees him from the self's paltry claims. By contrast, the narrator of "MS. Found in a Bottle" leaves behind only a few sheets of writing that break off at a point of acute emotional crisis. His bodily descent into the bellowing whirlpool is preceded by an even more precipitous mental fall from wonder into horror. "The Pit and the Pendulum" too might easily have disappeared, along with its author, into the Inquisition's dungeon without the last second interposition of a rescuer, whose outstretched arm snatches the story's fainting narrator from the brink of the abyss.

Feats of analysis, in and of themselves, are not the keys to salvation. In Poe's portrait of the interaction between consciousness and a menacing universe, feats of surrender play an equally vital role. Searching for a way to picture surrender, Poe almost immediately found himself drawn to the rudderless boat. The rudderless vessel decisively reasserts its artistic significance in Poe's imaginative world through a two-stage story that he composes over a period of four years, beginning with the publication of a sketch called "The Landscape Garden" in Snowdon's *Ladies Companion* for October 1842—the same period in which he finished "The Pit and the Pendulum" and just one month before "The Mystery of Marie Rogêt" began its three-part serialization in the same magazine.

No actual landscape garden appears in this initial version of the story that would become "The Domain of Arnheim" four years later. Instead another of Poe's unnamed narrators, like Auguste Dupin's faithful secretary, describes the character and opinions of an unusual companion, the fortunate Mr. Ellison, whose extraordinary wealth permits him to create "an intermediate or secondary Nature," imitating "the handiwork of the angels that hover between man and God" (CW, 711).

Unlike the many prominent victims of emotional "shipwreck" in Poe's fiction, Ellison is the beneficiary of what his admirer terms "a gale of prosperity." He is blessed with personal beauty, a lovely wife, and an instinctive philosophy of life that neutralizes the slight tinge of materialism in his makeup with a determination to seek happiness in some object of unceasing, spiritual pursuit. These circumstances and attributes all combine to shield Ellison from what the story's narrator calls "the common vortex of unhappiness." The present world, he asserts, is marked by the "darkness and madness of all thought on the great question of the social condition." Ellison's example holds out some hope that happiness may still be possible for a few, very lucky individuals. In particular, it is Ellison's extraordinary good luck to inherit four hundred and fifty million dollars, a sum that the narrator calculates will produce an interest income, around the clock, of twenty-six dollars a minute "for every minute that flew." This giddy equation of time and money turns gain and loss into convertible terms. Ellison decides to use his rapidly proliferating wealth to shape an environment of unsurpassed physical loveliness out of some portion of the Earth.

Most of "The Landscape Garden" consists of presenting Ellison's conviction that a mix of natural and artificial elements produces the most successful landscape design, one capable of uniting "beauty, magnificence, and *strangeness*" with the idea of superintendence by an order of superior beings. In 1842, for whatever reason, Poe was unprepared to move beyond these preliminaries and describe the result of Ellison's labors. He had just left his editorial job at *Graham's Magazine* that spring and was moving his wife and mother-in-law from one set of cheap rooms to another in the Philadelphia vicinity, trying to interest various supporters in funding a new magazine of his own. The first signs of Virginia Poe's advancing tuberculosis were beginning to appear. Her husband coped with these stresses by selling bits of writing here and there, and drinking heavily. It was not a time in which he was able to envision tangible prospects for human happiness, though the calculation of Ellison's fabulous interest income may reflect Poe's own fantasy of financial emancipation.

Circumstances briefly improved after the family moved to New York City in 1844. Over the next year and a half, with the support of Horace Greeley among others, Poe published a new collection of his fiction, followed by *The Raven and Other Poems*, and became (briefly) the owner-editor of the *Broadway Journal*—a gale of very imperfect prosperity that quickly blew itself out, but which may have played some role in drawing Poe back over the course of the closing months of 1846 to Mr. Ellison's world of relentless good fortune. "The Domain of Arnheim," which Poe submitted to the *Columbian Lady's and Gentleman's Magazine* in late 1846, completes the truncated account of Ellison's story. The nameless narrator and his wealthy friend apparently spent four years searching for precisely the right geographical location in which to execute Ellison's ambitious landscape design—exactly the interval of time separating the publication of "The Landscape Garden" from the appearance of its successor. "Arnheim" is the name that Ellison gives to his finished work, an expansive estate now open to "certain classes of visitors," since the owner's death, but accessible exclusively by water.

Poe's narrator offers an elaborate account of a visit to this magical artifact, beginning somewhat mysteriously in the past tense, despite the contemporary celebrity that Arnheim apparently enjoys:

> The usual approach to Arnheim was by the river. The visitor left the city in the early morning. During the forenoon he passed between shores of a tranquil and domestic beauty, on which grazed innumerable sheep, their white fleeces spotting the vivid green of rolling meadows. By degrees the idea of cultivation subsided into that of merely pastoral care. This slowly became merged in a sense of retirement—this again in a consciousness of solitude. As the evening approached, the channel grew more narrow; the banks more and more precipitous; and these latter were clothed in richer, more profuse and more sombre foliage. The water increased in transparency. The stream took a thousand turns, so that at no moment could its gleaming surface be seen for a greater distance than a furlong. At every instant the vessel seemed imprisoned within an enchanted circle, having insuperable and impenetrable walls of foliage, a roof of ultra-marine satin, and *no* floor—the keel balancing itself with admirable nicety on that of a phantom bark which, by some accident having been turned upside down, floated in constant company with the substantial one, for the purpose of sustaining it. (PT, 865–866)

Every minute that flies, through the course of this trip, accrues its own kind of interest, deriving in part from the odd sense of chronological regression that corresponds to the enchanted circle of the landscape. Is the narrator describing a past, a present, or a prospective visit to Ellison's creation? A luxurious but increasingly gloomy vegetation covers the steadily narrowing riverbanks, as if the thousand turns that the channel takes disguise a downward or a backward journey: a descent into an enchanted vortex which reverses the stages of cultural evolution, from urban modernity to the absolute solitude of unpeopled space.

Aspects of this uncanny voyage invite comparison to the elaborate ceremonial garden constructed by the Marquis de Giradin around Rousseau's tomb at Ermenonville. Like Arnheim, Ermenonville was conceived as a therapeutic zone, administering to the diseased modernity of nearby Paris. Visitors passed through bucolic landscapes and lonely forests on an extended walking tour that ended on the banks of a small lake surrounding the Isle of Poplars where Rousseau was buried. Inscriptions, memorial benches, and a little temple reminded the pilgrim, at every turn, that Ermenonville celebrated the legacy of a particular individual. Poe knew enough about this elaborate tribute to Rousseau's life to allude to it in his 1844 "Marginalia." By contrast, Arnheim is dedicated to the escape from individuality. Though conceived and built by a Rousseau-like mind—one born both to foreshadow and exemplify "the doctrines of Turgôt, Price, Priestly and Condorcêt," as the narrator originally describes his deceased friend—Arnheim preserves no trace of its creator. Moreover, Poe is careful to strip the tale of any indication that the narrator is guiding actual corporeal visitors through this incorporeal space.

As the journey to Arnheim unfolds, the modern city recedes from view, along with its agricultural and pastoral predecessors, leaving the senses suspended in a timeless transparency: an artificial zone of roof and walls, rather than sky and stream, perfectly balanced on and sustained by its own reflection. The narrow gorge through which the traveler appears to be moving closes overhead into a vast tunnel so intricate in its windings (the narrator insists) that one loses all sense of direction. "The thought of nature still remained," Poe's narrator remarks, but it was a nature infused with "a weird symmetry, a thrilling uniformity, a wizard propriety in these her works" (PT, 866). The water over which Arnheim's visitor floats is uncannily clear and pure. Nothing is marred or misplaced; not a dead leaf or withered branch is visible. Arnheim is the domain of inorganic organicism, a nature without waste or decay.

At what appears to be the center of Ellison's vast design, the voyager emerges into a great, circular basin surrounded by flowery hills and lined with "a thick mass of small round alabaster pebbles," visible through the transparent depths. The "drapery" of blossoms covering the hillsides forms "a sea of odorous and fluctuating color," a kind of botanical fabric completely free of trees or shrubs:

> The impressions wrought on the observer were those of richness, warmth, color, quietude, uniformity, softness, delicacy, daintiness, voluptuousness, and a miraculous extremeness of culture that suggested dreams of a new race of fairies, laborious, tasteful, magnificent and fastidious; but as the eye traced upward the myriad-tinted slope, from its sharp junction with the water to its vague termination amid the folds of overhanging cloud, it became, indeed, difficult not to fancy a panoramic cataract of rubies, sapphires, opals and golden onyxes, rolling silently out of the sky. (PT, 867)

Ellison's predilection for mixing the natural with the artificial, the beautiful with the strange, shapes this description. Arnheim is an external version of the internal riches that are on display in the regal cabinet where "The Assignation" concludes. It is an anti-Venice, irrigated by waters of miraculous clarity and sheathed in a drapery of natural color that mimics the lavish interior of the young nobleman's personal museum, as well as the uncanny spiritual ecology of the Valley of the Many-Colored Grass in "Eleonora."

The atmosphere of mortality and disease infusing these early stories recedes into the background of the incorporeal landscape that Ellison has built. The final stage of this dream voyage involves a transfer from one vessel to another that coincides with the narrator's shift from past to present tense. Poe repeatedly employs the motif of two "vessels" in his vortex tales to signal the passing of a pneumatic frontier: the Batavian trading ship and its phantom successor in "MS. Found in a Bottle," the fishing smack and its buoyant water cask in "A Descent into the Maelström." Here the boundary is grammatical as well, a scarcely noticeable shift from "then" to "now" that coincides with a movement from one touring vehicle to another. To complete the survey of Ellison's estate the narrator introduces the reader to a light ivory canoe, "stained with Arabesque devices in vivid scarlet, both within and without," a fabulous gondola poised in the very center of the watery basin, like a needle in the center of a compass. A "feathery" paddle lies in the bottom of the canoe—a compass arrow within a compass needle, perhaps—but no steersman appears to take it up. "The guest is bidden to be of good cheer—that the fates will take care of him," the narrator cryptically observes, hinting at mysterious parallels between the voyage to Arnheim and the ferry that carries souls to the underworld. The canoe pivots on its axis until its prow faces directly into the setting sun and then moves with "gradually accelerated velocity" toward the "rocky gate of the vista."

Unlike Poe's earlier rudderless voyages, this last one proves to be quite brief. The canoe approaches a continuous wall of "chiseled stone" lining a river that flows out of the first basin toward a great gate of "burnished gold":

> Its ponderous wings are slowly and musically expanded. The boat glides between them, and commences a rapid descent into a vast amphitheatre entirely begirt with purple mountains whose bases are laved by a gleaming river throughout the full extent of their circuit. Meantime the whole Paradise of Arnheim bursts upon the view. There is a gush of entrancing melody; there is an oppressive sense of strange sweet odor;—there is a dream-like intermingling to the eye of tall slender Eastern trees—bosky shrubberies—flocks of golden and crimson birds—lily-fringed lakes—meadows of violets, tulips, poppies, hyacinths, and tuberoses—long intertangled lines of silver streamlets—and, upspringing confusedly from amid all, a mass of semi-Gothic, semi-Saracenic architecture, sustaining itself as if by miracle in mid air; glittering in the red sunlight with a hundred oriels, minarets, and pinnacles; and seeming the phantom handiwork, conjointly, of the Sylphs, of the Fairies, of the Genii, and of the Gnomes. (PT, 870)

An allusion to Fonthill Abbey earlier in the story half prepares the reader for this architectural extravagance at its conclusion. Fonthill's notorious master, William Beckford, had died in 1844, two years after the publication of "The Landscape Garden" and two years before Poe expanded the tale into Arnheim's otherworldly domain. But Beckford's disastrously engineered mansion whose massive central tower had dramatically collapsed of its own weight in 1825, is (like Ermenonville) an index of what Arnheim is not. Ellison's Paradise begins in an actual city and concludes with a glimpse of a fantastically weightless one, a conflation of all the major religious visions with which Poe is likely to have been familiar from his eclectic reading, and a faint echo of key features occurring in each of his earlier vortex stories. In many senses, it is a conjoint place.

The intoxicating amphitheatre in the center of Ellison's garden is both a fulfillment of and an antidote to the vortex—not a direct depiction of nature's remorseless force, but an elaborate music box, or automaton, that takes for its subject the mysterious linkages among gravity, space, and time implicit in Poe's celestial geometry. The light of the setting sun presides over the first circular basin at the garden's heart, much as the full moon floods the ebony interior of the Norway maelstrom with its golden light. The gorgeous hues that carpet Arnheim's treeless hills—its polychromatic birds and meadows—recall the lurid colors that begin to glow on the heated dungeon walls of "The Pit and the Pendulum," just before they too begin to emit an eerie music as they collapse on the Inquisition's helpless victim. To create Ellison's masterwork, however, Poe purges these earlier vortices of their sublime terrors, reweaving the newly purified elements into Arnheim's gaudy tapestry. In each instance a spectacular and voracious form of time machine lends some of its elements to the extraordinary, jeweled watch that Ellison's fabulous wealth has permitted him to build.

Indeed, Arnheim is a mechanism disguised as a garden. Its structural architecture, like that of Poe's earlier vortices, suggests a rescaling of tools: the geognostical instruments of modern science expanded or recalibrated into uncanny fictional settings. Ellison's landscape design, in part at least, is an elaborately costumed version of a celebrated engineering enterprise of the day—a triumph of enlightened reason and political will over the intractable problems of urban waste and disease, one that Poe's recent move to New York City had given him ample opportunity to study.

Figure 3 Augustus Fay, "Croton Water Reservoir, New York City" (ca.1850). I. N. Phelps Stokes Collection, Miriam and Ira D. Wallach Division of Art, Prints and Photographs, The New York Public Library, Astor, Lenox, and Tilden Foundations.

Like all the cities of the eastern seaboard in Poe's lifetime, New York had struggled for decades to secure a reliable supply of clean water for its growing population. The 1832 cholera epidemic, in which 3,500 residents of the city had died, followed by a devastating fire in December 1835, gave impetus to these efforts. In May 1837 construction began on the great Croton Aqueduct, a masonry channel built to bring water from the Croton River in Westchester County, forty miles north of the city, first to a large storage reservoir near the center of Manhattan Island and then to a smaller, above-ground distribution reservoir at Murray Hill between 40th and 42nd streets. From there the water would flow through one hundred and sixty-five miles of underground iron pipes, weaving throughout lower Manhattan, furnishing the city's tallest buildings, its fire hydrants, and its public fountains with an abundant water supply.

Readers of the *Columbian Lady's and Gentleman's Magazine*, the New York periodical in which "The Domain of Arnheim" appeared, almost certainly followed the aqueduct's five-year construction saga very closely. Political wrangling, labor disputes, and the collapse of the first dam on the Croton River delayed the project's completion, but by June 1842 water began to flow south. A small boat, the *Croton Maid*, large enough to carry four passengers, traveled the length of the aqueduct to dramatize the achievement. With only two brief portages around short stretches of iron pipe, this ceremonial vessel was able to drift gracefully into the Yorkville reservoir on the site of what is now Central Park, the first of the two holding reservoirs that the aqueduct was designed to feed. On July 4, 1842 Croton water began to fill the Murray Hill Reservoir, an imposing stone edifice four-hundred-and-twenty feet square and nearly fifty feet tall, its thick walls gently flared at the base in imitation of Egyptian temples, topped with Egyptian-style cornices and equipped with a lofty promenade from which walkers could view the gleaming artificial lake at their feet, the Yorkville reservoir to the north, and the complete panorama of the city reaching south to the Battery. An official opening celebration for the Croton system took place the following October marked by parades, speeches, and spectacular new fountains throwing Croton water high into the air, but the entire project would not actually be finished until May 1848, when the High Bridge carrying water pipes over the Harlem River began service.

Poe published a handful of gossipy letters in the *Columbia Spy* in the spring of 1844, shortly after he and his family had moved to New York, which mentioned the beautiful view from the top of the Murray Hill Reservoir. The vista from its walls may have suggested the two aquatic amphitheaters at Arnheim's heart, sustaining the semi-Gothic pinnacles and minarets of its magic city. The sweet odors and vivid colors of Ellison's garden seem to signal the ecstatic experience of liberation from urban filth that the Croton project was designed to achieve by circulating its own "silver streamlets" through the elaborate network of pipes beneath New York's streets. Poe almost certainly anticipated that his local readers, at least, would quickly perceive the connection between their city's remarkable and costly new infrastructure—its fusion of the natural and the artificial—with Arnheim's fantastic design.

But unlike the city it mimics, Ellison's garden is a solitary place. Its enchanting melodies require no human musicians to produce them. Its boats are free of engines or sails, and free of any boatmen to steer them. Visitors (should there ever be any of an appropriately receptive class) receive assurances that the fates will see to their welfare, but no living speaker greets the first vessel in Poe's sketch when it arrives at the circular basin near the end of its day-long voyage—a pointed contrast to the celebratory public atmosphere accompanying the voyage of the *Croton Maid*. Despite Ellison's determination to locate his great work near a populous city, he is strangely indifferent to its civic value. No actual tourists appear to accompany the story's disembodied narrator on the mental visit that he makes to his late friend's meticulously executed domain. Arnheim has nothing in common with the therapeutic ambitions of Ermenonville or with the kind of genial rural influences that Auguste Dupin longs to find available to his fellow citizens on the outskirts of polluted Paris.

Ellison's eccentric construction is an unearthly zone posing as an earthly one: an inverse image of the Croton Aqueduct, like the perfectly inverted reflection of the story's first tour boat, conveying the reader's imagination away from the city rather than toward it, in conformity with much broader gravitational principles. Terrestrial gravity alone, not mechanical power, kept the Murray Hill Reservoir continually full with twenty million gallons of pure water, moving in steady streams through a network of iron distribution pipes beneath the city streets. These are practical but trivial achievements for a force that holds the earth in solar orbit, and keeps the sun revolving in turn around the center of its vast galaxy of companion stars. As the circular solar alignment at the heart of Arnheim implies, Ellison's design domesticates this celestial vista, miniaturizing its inconceivable scale and clothing it in an ambitious figurative costume.

During the long search for a suitable building site, Ellison had grown distrustful of vast, earthly panoramas. Natural grandeur clashed "with the sentiment and with the sense of seclusion" necessary for spiritual rejuvenation, Ellison declared: "The heart-sick avoid distant prospects as a pestilence" (PT, 865). Arnheim has been meticulously purged of this mental pestilence but not at the expense of the satisfactions to be derived by combining "vastness and definitiveness" in a single design. Grandiose comparisons to the engineering prowess of ancient Egypt or imperial Rome filled the New York press at the opening of the High Bridge over the Harlem River or the building of the Murray Hill Reservoir's "sphinx-like" walls. Poe undertook to redirect this civic self-glorification away from paltry themes, to float a weightless city rather than flush the gutters of an actual one. In "The Domain of Arnheim" he drifts effortlessly over the glistening surface of parochial vanities, gazing at the inverted heaven in their depths.

* * *

In July 1848—a few weeks after the High Bridge over the Harlem River opened its iron culverts to Croton water—Poe published *Eureka*, his last treatment of the vortex and by far the most elaborate hybrid artifact of his career. Part treatise and part lecture, *Eureka* is (according to Poe) a poem in prose and a "Book of Truths" aimed at illustrating a single emphatic proposition: *"In the Original Unity of the First Thing lies the Secondary Cause of All Things, with the Germ of their Inevitable Annihilation."* In order to give his sweeping idea the imaginative force of an "individual impression"—a *"oneness"* commensurate with the great unity that it describes—Poe begins with a futuristic hoax: a letter recovered from a bottle floating on the *Mare Tenebrarum* and purportedly written in the year 2848, testifying to a millennium of cultural progress and decay, germinal expansion and inevitable collapse, echoing the great truth of his treatise.

The author of this "impertinent epistle" is unnamed in *Eureka*, but when Poe publishes a modified version of the tale as "Mellonta Tauta" in *Godey's Lady's Book* early in 1849, the letter is signed "Pundita" and dated from on board the Skylark, a spectacular passenger balloon drifting at one hundred miles an hour on a month-long pleasure excursion above a planet ravaged by civil war and plague. Pundita has decided to cope with the boredom of her "odious voyage" by inflicting all of her trivial thoughts on her friends. Margaret Fuller had gone to Europe as a traveling correspondent for the New York *Tribune* in August 1846 and by the following summer had settled in Rome to begin her extraordinary series of letters on the birth and death of the Roman Republic. "Pundita" is almost certainly a sign of the mix of envy, mockery, and admiration with which Poe viewed Fuller's journalism in these eventful months. When "Mellonta Tauta" ultimately appeared in *Godey's*, it included a brief, dismissive preface associating it with the work of the Transcendentalists and other "divers for crotchets," but Poe clearly relished Pundita's peevish intelligence.

The dramatic speed of the "Skylark," she complains, is no more than a "jog trot": "Will *nobody* contrive a more expeditious mode of progress?" The six-thousand-ton magnetic ships on the ocean below are a nuisance to the balloon's long drag rope. From Pundita's lofty vantage point, war and pestilence seem beneficial events, the plague "doing its good work beautifully" by eliminating a "myriad" of surplus individuals from the populations of "Yurope and Ayesher." In the thousand years that separate her from Poe's readers, spelling has undergone some selective changes, but despite the corruption of several important names Pundita is able to offer a lucid and irreverent assessment of modern empiricism that Poe evidently shares. References to Neuclid, Cant, Aries Tottle, and Hog fill her letter, but the "Aristotelian" and "Baconian" roads to truth have retained their labels and their meaning, as have the names of Newton, Kepler, and Copernicus. Brutal futurist though she seems to be, Pundita is indignant at the obstacles to the advancement of knowledge imposed by scientific formalism:

> The ancient idea [of Baconian empiricism] confined investigation to *crawling*; and for hundreds of years so great was the infatuation about Hog especially, that a virtual end was put to all thinking properly so called. No man dared utter a truth for which he felt himself indebted to his *Soul* alone. It mattered not whether the truth was even *demonstrably* a truth, for the bullet-headed *savans* of the time regarded only *the road* by which he had attained it. They would not even *look* at the end. "Let us see the means," they cried, "the means!" If, upon investigation of the means, it was found to come neither under the category Aries (that is to say Ram) nor under the category Hog, why then the savans went no farther, but pronounced the "theorist" a fool, and would have nothing to do with him or his truth. (PT, 875)

The truth of gravitation—the "most important and most sublime" of the Baconian discoveries, Pundita concedes—derives from the work of Newton, a celebrated hoggish savan. But Newton's work, she declares, is built on Kepler's and Kepler worked by inspired guesses. He was a "theorist" in the best possible sense, a hero of the "ardent imagination," whose original insights, however marred by inconsistency, were avenues to absolute truth (PT, 878). This contrast between inductive crawling and the pneumatic flights of visionary science is a reassertion, in different terms, of Hans Pfaall's lunar adventure or of the delirious cognitive voyage that Poe inserts into the 1835 expansion of "Loss of Breath." Johannes Kepler's bi-part career, as empiricist and as visionary, links science to the soul, positioning both at the center of *Eureka*, which Poe was preparing to deliver in lecture form at the same time that he was writing Pundita's fantastic letter.

When he transcribes portions of "Mellonta Tauta" into his treatise he elaborates on the dramatic significance of Kepler's example to the cognitive scheme that underlies his fusion of science and the imagination:

> Yes!—these vital laws Kepler *guessed*—that is to say, he *imagined* them. Had he been asked to point out either the *de*ductive or *in*ductive route by which he attained them his reply might have been—"I know nothing about *routes*—but I *do* know the machinery of the Universe. Here it is. I grasped it with *my soul*!—I reached it through mere dint of *intuition*." Alas, poor ignorant old man! Could not any metaphysician have told him that what he called "intuition" was but the conviction resulting from *de*ductions or *in*ductions of which the processes were so shadowy as to have escaped his consciousness, eluded his reason, or bidden defiance to his capacity of expression? How great a pity it is that some 'moral philosopher' had not enlightened him about all this! How it would have comforted him on his death-bed to know that, instead of having gone intuitively and thus unbecomingly, he had, in fact, proceeded decorously and legitimately—that is to say Hog-ishly, or at least Ram-ishly—into the vast halls where lay gleaming, untended, and hitherto untouched by mortal hand—unseen by mortal eye—the imperishable and priceless secrets of the Universe! (PT, 1270)

David Brewster's popular *Martyrs of Science* (1842) describes Kepler's refreshing candor about the strange blend of enthusiasms that motivated him: his belief that the earth was sentient, an "enormous living animal" whose respiration was responsible for the movement of the tides; his lingering faith in astrology; his conviction that the orbits of the planets could be predicted by inscribing perfect spheres around and within a series of vast geometrical solids. Brewster cites, too, Kepler's extraordinary outburst of "sacred fury," in *Harmonice Mundi* (1619), where he introduced the last of the three laws of celestial motion that collectively transformed astronomy from an observational to a demonstrative science: "I have stolen the golden secret of the Egyptians,"

Kepler proclaimed, "I can afford to wait a century for readers when God himself has waited six thousand years for an observer."

Very early in *Eureka*'s pages, Poe signals his indebtedness to Brewster by transcribing Kepler's cry of triumph in a revised form that stresses the exultation of his investigative "theft" rather than the patience of God: the intuitive leap rather than the tedious inductive or deductive routes that Pundita scorns. Though *Eureka* may sometimes seem to crawl, particularly in contrast to the electrical vigor of Poe's fiction, it is also his most sustained effort to explain the broad significance of the vortex: its eradication of paltry individuality by the spectacle of universal energy enacting the master plot of material being. The figurative energies of the imagination become, for Poe, a crucial means of accelerating empirical investigation through the use of artistic intuition. The narrative path that he ultimately proposes to trace in *Eureka* is a familiar one from Unity to Multiplicity and back to Unity once again, in an apocalyptic return to creation's primordial state. But none of these evolutionary stages in the existence of matter is mythic or metaphorical, in Poe's account. The movement from a condition of Utmost Simplicity, at the instant of creation, to a condition of the utmost complexity or relatedness reflected in the scientific understanding of the universe begins (according to Poe) with a Divine pulsation, radiating matter outward from an "imparticulate" particle—a dimensionless point inhabiting a spaceless "space."

Radiation and diffusion, not explosion, are the initiating energies in Poe's cosmos. The movement of light is the closest analogy to the rhythms of sequential expansion that Poe describes—a successive, discontinuous, and ultimately finite series of creative acts, leaving the Universe full of concentric strata of equably diffused matter through which the forces of Attraction and Repulsion immediately begin to operate. Throughout *Eureka,* Poe prefers to use the "more definite expressions" of Attraction and Repulsion as replacements for the "equivocal" scientific analysis of gravitation and electricity. Along with the activity of the original Volition, Poe contends, these are the only forces in the Universe. Attraction is the body, he declares, Repulsion is the soul: "The one is the material; the other the spiritual, principle of the Universe. *No other Principles exist*" (PT, 1282). Matter itself is nothing more than a consequence of the perpetual interaction between these two forces. It "*exists* only as Attraction and Repulsion," Poe announces, not as some unique corporeal entity. Disembodied "desire" alone lies behind the veil of appearances that men consider to be the "physical" universe. In the bluntest possible sense, then, Poe declares that "Attraction and Repulsion *are* matter" (PT, 1283). He repeats and italicizes this critical doctrine three times in the space of a brief paragraph in order to fix it in the mind of his reader. From the outset, his universe is a bodiless choreography of force alone to which Poe nevertheless applies familiar scientific laws and a traditional physical vocabulary in order to fill out his account of its destiny.

The opening stages of that account require him to reformulate the Newtonian law of gravitation in order to embrace not just the primary celestial bodies of the solar system but *"every atom of every body."* Even these tiniest material particles attract every other particle of the Universe *"with a force which varies inversely as the squares of the distances between the attracted and the attracting atom"* (PT, 1284). Poe stresses these initial assertions so frequently, in *Eureka,* because from them he intends to extract "a flood of suggestion." The entire plot of his cosmogony, in fact, springs from the "unimaginable complexity of relation" created by this web of minute attractive influences set in motion by the "equable distribution" of particulate centers of Attraction throughout space. Equability, however, is the most fleeting of physical states in Poe's cosmos. It can scarcely be said to exist at all, once the Divine Volition has ceased its creative operations.

Instead once the material Universe radiates into being, it exists in a condition of perpetual and progressive agitation, produced by the minute and interlocking action of atomic sympathy:

> Had we discovered, simply, that each atom tends to some one point, a favorite with all—we should still have fallen upon a discovery which, in itself, would have sufficed to overwhelm the mind:—but what is it that we are actually called on to comprehend? That each atom attracts— sympathizes with the most delicate movements of every other atom, and with each and with all at the same time, and forever, and according to a determinate law of which the complexity, even considered by itself solely, is utterly beyond the grasp of the imagination. If I propose to ascertain the influence of one mote in a sunbeam on its neighboring mote, I cannot accomplish my purpose without first counting and weighing all the atoms in the Universe and defining the precise positions of all at one particular moment. If I venture to displace, by even the billionth part of an inch, the microscopical speck of dust which lies now on the point of my finger, what is the character of that act upon which I have adventured? I have done a deed which shakes the Moon in her path, which causes the Sun to be no longer the Sun, and which alters forever the

destiny of the multitudinous myriads of stars that roll and glow in the majestic presence of their Creator. (PT, 1286)

This hypothetical confession of responsibility for a momentous and terrible act—"I have done a deed which shakes the Moon"—recalls the extravagant assertions of individual guilt from the opening sentences of "William Wilson" or the vision of awful remorse that Dupin projects upon the murderer of Marie Rogêt, but Poe has adapted the language of moral culpability to an illustrative scientific act that stresses the mysteries of interconnection rather than the isolation imposed by guilt. These, he suggests, are the kinds of "soul-reveries" to which the vision of *Eureka* leads. Infinitely fine networks of mutual Attraction replace the old celestial hierarchy of gods or angels with a shimmering and constantly mutating fabric of energy, gradually accelerating toward the "general centre of radiation" from which the original creative impulse had begun. Matter's universal journey ends in the vortex.

Poe is in no hurry to arrive at this destination. *Eureka* seems at times like a rudderless vessel in its own right, drifting through a conceptual landscape far more uncanny than that of Arnheim, treating subject after subject with no discernable means of propulsion. Poe diagrams the geometric pattern of luminous diffusion responsible for the existence of the Universe and considers the various phases by which the condensing forces of Attraction would eventually produce large orbiting planets surrounding the much larger luminous and nonluminous suns that hold the galaxies and nebulae together. The findings of "the magnificent modern telescopes," he concedes, appear to have undermined many features of Laplace's Nebular Theory. But Poe undertakes a lengthy defense of the theory in part because Laplace offers what Poe believes to be the only coherent explanation for the observed complexity of the cosmos. Both Laplace and Kepler, are models of the intuitive investigator, capable of founding great discoveries upon the hybrid of fact and error that marks all human effort:

> His original idea seems to have been a compound of the true Epicurean atoms with the false nebulæ of his contemporaries; and thus his theory presents us with the singular anomaly of absolute truth deduced, as a mathematical result, from a hybrid datum of ancient imagination intertangled with modern inacumen. Laplace's real strength lay, in fact, in an almost miraculous mathematical instinct:—on this he relied; and in no instance did it fail or deceive him:—in the case of the Nebular Cosmogony, it led him, blindfolded, through a labyrinth of Error, into one of the most luminous and stupendous temples of Truth. (PT, 1322)

Like the old guide trapped in the Norway maelstrom, Laplace too is adrift on the wreckage of ancient imagination and modern science, making a rudderless voyage through a network of elaborate channels toward a brilliant but in many ways unforeseen result.

For Poe that ultimate result springs from the unlikely blend of miraculous instincts with unwavering faith—a combination of aptitudes to which even a scientific amateur might aspire. Turning to a passage that first appeared at the conclusion of "The Mystery of Marie Rogêt" six years earlier, he insists that "cowardice of thought" has no place in the study of God's design. The human observer who keeps this realization firmly in mind—"who, divesting himself of prejudice shall have the rare courage to think absolutely for himself"—must finally conclude that the plurality of separate physical "laws" deduced in painstaking detail by modern science must finally condense into "Law" alone: the interdependent outcome of the Divine Volition, infusing unimaginable complexity with an equally unimaginable Simplicity (PT, 1313). Despite its Emersonian ring, this language is not a version of Transcendentalism's compensatory moral Law. Poe's master principle is ethically indifferent; it is an architecture of dispassionate energy alone and not of morals.

Once the operations of Attraction and Repulsion, gravitation and electricity, Body and Soul have organized Poe's expansive Universe of Stars into a vast celestial community, he is ready to link the infinitely small with the infinitely large components of his cosmological amphitheater:

> Let us now, expanding our conceptions, look upon each of these [planetary] systems as in itself an atom; which in fact it is, when we consider it as but one of the countless myriads of systems which constitute the Universe. Regarding all, then, as but colossal atoms, each with the same ineradicable tendency to Unity which characterizes the actual atoms of which it consists—we enter at once a new order of aggregations. The smaller systems, in the vicinity of the larger one, would, inevitably, be drawn into still closer vicinity. A thousand would assemble here; a million there—perhaps here, again, even a billion—leaving, thus, unmeasurable vacancies in space. And if, now, it be demanded why, in the case of these systems—of these merely Titanic atoms—I speak, simply, of an "assemblage," and not, as in the case of the actual atoms, of a more or less consolidated agglomeration:—if it be asked, for instance, why I do not carry what I suggest to its legitimate conclusion, and describe, at once, these assemblages of system-atoms as rushing to consolidation in spheres—as each becoming condensed into one magnificent sun—my reply is that μελλοντα ταυτα—I am but pausing, for a moment, on the

awful threshold of *the Future*. For the present, calling these assemblages "clusters," we see them in the incipient stages of their consolidation. Their *absolute* consolidation is *to come*. (PT, 1324)

In this passage Poe associates the Greek phrase "mellonta tauta" ("these things are in the future") not with Pundita's flippant tone but with a sublime account of titanic atoms suspended in vacancy and a forecast of the destiny of the Universe: its consolidation into a species of unity that transcends physical law. "Matter without Attraction and without Repulsion," Poe will call this final state, "in other words, Matter without Matter—in other words, again, *Matter no more*," reinstating the "Material Nihility" that precedes "the Volition of God" (PT, 1355).

Poe delays the conclusion of his treatise—its own absolute consolidation—long enough to consider in detail the recent achievements of observational astronomy: the meticulous nebular catalogues of John and William Herschel; the visual discoveries of Lord Rosse's six-foot reflecting telescope, "whispering in our ears the secrets of *a million of ages* by-gone"; the contributions of von Mädler and von Humboldt to cosmological theory. "*Space and duration are one*," he declares, in accounting for the significance of the great interstellar voids produced as matter collects into larger and larger celestial bodies (PT, 1340). Emptiness and size are, in a sense, elaborate timepieces: astrophysical clocks that provide chronological scope for the story of the cosmos to unfold, much as they allow the text of *Eureka* to orbit its own conclusion in a series of digressive, scientific circles that draw almost imperceptibly closer to Poe's final insight.

The elaborate Universe that he describes is ultimately doomed to a climactic descent "amid unfathomable abysses" toward the fire of "unimaginable suns." It must eventually enter the maelstrom of Attraction and disappear, along with all the other elements of corporeal existence upon which the power of Attraction acts. The destiny of Conscious Intelligence, however, is quite different—like that of those particularizing minds that survive Poe's earthly vortices. "*Spirit individualized*," as Poe calls this special aptitude of consciousness, is able at certain "luminous" points of life to recognize that matter is only a means, not an end. The closing sentences of *Eureka* transcribe a reassuring message from "low voices" that persist throughout the lifetime of all thinking beings. The "Night of Time," these voices tell us, is no more than a transition zone, an infinity of "partial and pain-intertangled pleasures" moving slowly toward a transcendent change: the absorption of all animate and inanimate being into "the *Spirit Divine*." Even Poe's darkest stories contain glimpses of this latent possibility—a point of incandescent simplicity that no natural or artificial shadows can entirely extinguish.

CHAPTER 4

The Kingdom of Inorganization

A ttraction and Repulsion acquire a remarkable purity as they collaborate on the spectacular narrative scale of *Eureka*. The emotional and physical debris of the earthly maelstrom—the chaos of terror and wonder, the wreckage of ships and of people—drop from view when Poe focuses his attention on the great theater of space and duration. Neither the titanic nor the infinitesimal realms of being are designed to accommodate the intermediate sphere of human feeling. Atoms are free of the contagions of the flesh; they work out their story of expansion and contraction in an uninfected universe of force: the "kingdom of inorganization," Roderick Usher's childhood friend and visitor will call it, a sentient dimension only briefly visible to human organs.

Poe's fiction, by contrast, treats the definitive principles of his cosmology as they appear in the elaborate masquerades of bodily life. Conscious Intelligence floats free of gravity's vortex on an empty water cask, while corporeal fear disappears down the whirlpool's insatiable throat. "A Descent into the Maelström" is triumphantly candid about its figurative relationship to celestial force. In a much less simple formulation, "MS. Found in a Bottle" depicts a perilous equilibrium between self-command and terror: an interval just long enough to permit consciousness to preserve a fascinating narrative of annihilation sealed in a vessel that is less vulnerable than its author to the destructive power of nature. Attraction and Repulsion play vivid complementary roles in both of these terrestrial plots—absorbing some voices entirely but releasing others to reverberate through expanding circles of listeners and readers. A manuscript found in a bottle is a writer's, or a culture's, conventional fantasy of preservation. The stone base of Baltimore's Washington Monument contained commemorative texts and speeches, sealed in a glass bottle and cemented into the monument's masonry foundation—a refuge far less vulnerable than an external inscription to the inevitable defacements of time.

The writing, the bottle, and the monument form a nest of preservative vessels, constructed to survive indefinitely a host of earthly storms. But in the end they seem to anticipate a reader in the ruins: a form of Conscious Intelligence much like that which survives the fiery amalgamation of *Eureka,* deciphering the record of its imperfect predecessors. Poe's fiction repeatedly explores these parables of attraction, repulsion, and preservation. Inevitably they become parables of transmission as well, completing the interplay of vast energies that comprises the dense, dramatic rhythm of Poe's best stories. The entire figurative system appears with unusual clarity during the destruction of the *Jane Guy* in *The Narrative of Arthur Gordon Pym.* An unexpected pulse of energy that anticipates the cosmological panorama of *Eureka* abruptly extinguishes a violent struggle between the forces of attraction and repulsion evident in the racist fury that Poe's language captures. The result is a magical impetus for the story he has set out to tell.

Pym and Dirk Peters, the last surviving members of the *Jane Guy's* crew, witness the events from their hiding place on a nearby hill, as an army of natives from the mysterious island of Tsalal systematically loot the captured ship, "hammering with large stones, axes, and cannon balls at the bolts and other copper and iron work":

> They had already made a complete wreck of the vessel, and were now preparing to set her on fire. In a little while we saw the smoke ascending in huge volumes from her main-hatchway, and, shortly afterward, a dense mass of flame burst up from the forecastle. The rigging, masts, and what remained of the sails caught immediately. . . . On the beach, and in canoes and rafts, there were not less, altogether, in the immediate vicinity of the schooner, than ten thousand natives, besides the shoals of them who, laden with booty, were making their way inland and over to the neighbouring islands. We now anticipated a catastrophe, and were not disappointed. First of all there came a smart shock (which we felt distinctly where we were as if we had been slightly galvanized), but unattended with any visible signs of an explosion. The savages were evidently startled, and paused for an instant from their labours and yellings. They were upon the point of recommencing, when suddenly a mass of smoke puffed up from the decks, resembling a black and heavy thunder-cloud—then, as if from its bowels, arose a tall stream of vivid fire to the height, apparently, of a quarter of a mile—then there came a sudden circular expansion of the flame—then the whole atmosphere was magically crowded, in a single instant, with a wild chaos of wood, and metal, and

human limbs—and, lastly, came the concussion in its fullest fury, which hurled us impetuously from our feet, while the hills echoed and re-echoed the tumult, and a dense shower of the minutest fragments of the ruins tumbled headlong in every direction around us. (PT, 1160–1161)

The *Jane Guy* is the third of four vessels that Poe uses to convey the reader of his only completed novel from the comparatively familiar waters around Nantucket Island in the summer of 1827 to a tumultuously "enkindled" ocean deep in southern latitudes, nine months and many harrowing adventures later. None of Pym's other ships, however, meets a fate as remarkable as this one: a gripping physical tableau that seems to break out of the ship's bowels, symptom by symptom, like a terrible disease.

Curiosity and greed had brought the *Jane Guy* to this remote and savage place—forces of attraction insufficiently powerful to eclipse the racial repulsion evident in Pym's language. Greed and rage combine to draw the natives who are looting the ship into dangerous proximity to its volatile cargo, pounding on its metal fittings with a kind of industrial frenzy in the moments before a circular "expansion" of flame engulfs the ship. Even after the fiery concussion passes, "horror, rage, and intense curiosity" keep the survivors swarming through the wreckage, startled by the carcass of an exotic animal from the *Jane Guy*'s scientific collections hurled to the beach by the explosion. Amidst this furious disorder, Pym's language depicts the precisely parallel motives that shape the purposeful energy of the islanders as well as their victims among the ship's crew, enclosing them all in the same charmed but fatal circle. The powerful mix of magical expansion and sudden death that extinguishes the *Jane Guy* produces a nourishing and defiling shower of fragments out of which the next phase of Pym's story almost immediately begins to assemble itself.

Before abandoning the beach, the natives of Tsalal construct an impromptu wall between themselves and the strange animal thrown from the ship whose appearance both terrifies and fascinates them. Pym and Dirk Peters, despite the sheer cliffs that appear to isolate them from the rest of the island, manage to descend from their hill-top hiding place, seize a large canoe, and make their escape. An artificial barrier is hastily built while a natural one is overcome; one vessel is no sooner destroyed than a successor takes its place. Pym's story itself responds to underlying forces, like the powerful southerly current that quickly pulls his canoe deeper into the weirdly luminous waters at the bottom of the world. *The Narrative of Arthur Gordon Pym* (1838) is Poe's most ambitious, as well as his most sustained, attempt to create a fictional stage capable of encompassing the profound antagonism between chance and design, order and disorder, attraction and repulsion that constitutes "the mystery of our being in existence." This resonant phrase from the book's opening chapter, describing the outcome of an improbable boyish adventure, signals the full artistic scope of Poe's story: an attempt to penetrate the shimmering sensory veil that beckons at the end of the voyage, to enter the soundless "chaos of flitting and indistinct images" that Pym glimpses through the limitless cataract ahead.

* * *

As the events surrounding the destruction of the *Jane Guy* suggest, containment rather than disposal is the central preoccupation of *The Narrative of Arthur Gordon Pym*. The book's title page presents an elaborate inventory of highly explosive narrative contents, a manifest of adventures adequate to fill several lengthy memoirs rather than the single, slender volume at hand. Pym's tale is a modest vessel indeed for such a range of extreme experience: mutiny and butchery, famine and deliverance, exploration, massacre, and incredible discovery, much of which takes place deep in mysterious southern seas. Like Melville's book-loving Ishmael, Poe swims through libraries to collect the literary materials to carry off this performance, ransacking published accounts of nautical disaster and exploration wherever he could find them and packing the results into the disorderly stowage of Pym's story.

Moreover, Poe invites his reader at every turn to reflect on the problematic relationship between vessels and the heterogeneous cargo that they contain, between the mind and its imperfect resources of recollection or belief, between books and their contents, between words and the many layers of meaning that they evoke. All of these complex structures of containment cluster within one another in Pym's narrative, like the interlocking pattern of albatross and penguin nests in the great rookeries that he encounters during the *Jane Guy*'s voyage, or like the still more elaborate nest of his manuscript itself. Poe goes to some lengths to provide a provenance for Pym's story: a pre- and post-composition account of how the book comes to be packaged as it is. Encouraged by a friendly circle of gentlemen in Richmond, Virginia—a quartet of albatrosses around a solitary penguin—Pym first ventures to present his tale though the agency of "Mr. Poe," who writes down Pym's "facts" in Poe's words under Pym's name and publishes the partial results in the *Southern Literary Messenger*. Later Pym takes up the story on his own but retains Poe's contribution, like a cuckoo's egg beside a songbird's, confident that the reader will be able to tell the difference when the hatchlings ultimately emerge together in print.

After Pym disappears, along with the last few pages of his manuscript, in a fatal and mysterious accident, Mr. Poe steadfastly refuses "to fill the vacuum" or even to write a postscript for the incomplete tale, leaving that final task of textual stowage to a nameless mediator. This anonymous figure is eager to apply a bit of ancient learning to some enigmatic inscriptions that Pym had copied in his closing pages—marks that may or may not be a written script, preserved on a rock wall deep within what appears to be a still more monumental inscription, the last of the nested messages which Pym's story contains. The writing, the bottle, and the monument reappear, however strangely disguised, in these suggestive details. It should come as no surprise, then, that even a very gifted reader like Umberto Eco resorts to diagrams of nested boxes as he tries to describe the ornate narrative structure of Pym's pages or that John Irwin would take the origins of inscription itself as Poe's subject.

The innermost box of any story would seem to be the storyteller's body itself. But in Pym's account, the flesh proves to be the most baroque vessel of all, a container of containers that mingles the foulest with the most sublime contents. It is both a fecal, utterly lightless cavern and a luminous cognitive interior—resplendent and polluted, like glittering Venice presiding over its stagnant canals. The portrayal of these drastically opposed extremes begins with the opening episodes of Pym's tale, as he and his school companion Augustus Barnard convert themselves into vessels of adolescent excess, first with the wines and liquors that they consume during a party at Augustus's New Bedford home, and later with stories of nautical adventure that delude them into entertaining melodramatic fantasies "of shipwreck and famine; of death or captivity among barbarian hordes; of a lifetime dragged out in sorrow and tears, upon some gray and desolate rock, in an ocean unapproachable and unknown" (PT, 1018).

The consequence of their first drunken escapade—the wreck of Pym's small schooner, the *Ariel*—is hardly more plausible than a sailor's yarn. Pym's dramatic rescue when a projecting timber-bolt on a homeward-bound whaler snags him through the sinews of his neck seems little more than a mischievous reminder that (as Pym puts it) boys "can accomplish wonders in the way of deception." But the incident of the *Ariel* accomplishes much more than that. In his wry reminder that necks are a structural feature common to bodies and to bottles, Pym points directly to the corporeal "vessel" that underlies every artificial and natural body in the story, even the earth itself. Moreover Poe uses this sensational preamble to stage the first of several awakenings and reawakenings that the book explores: the reiterative movement from mental inertia to vivid emotional alertness, from stupor to the heights of excitement and back again, that structures the entire narrative.

Poe compresses four oscillating versions of intense wakefulness and near-paralytic sleep into the opening pages of Pym's tale: the explosive oath with which Augustus shakes off his drunken lethargy to propose a sailing "frolic" in a hurricane, followed by his equally sudden collapse into a "mere log" in the *Ariel*'s bilge; Pym's reciprocal ascent from the borders of sleep to an "intense agony of terror" before taking his own headlong plunge into insensibility; the double awakenings of outrage and of remorse among the officers and crew of the *Penguin*, the ship that ultimately rescues the two boys. Together these incidents comprise a sequence of rehearsals for the elaborate metempsychoses that follow: a zigzag exchange of cognitive states that is both repetitive and progressive as Pym approaches the geographic and spiritual extremes of his story.

The consequence of Pym's second, more profound variety of drunkenness—his fascination with nautical adventure and an attendant "desire" to experience terrible despair—is his decision to accompany Augustus as a stowaway when the Barnards embark on their next whaling voyage aboard an aging hulk called the *Grampus*. With the introduction of the second of the book's succession of sailing vessels, Poe's mental voyaging begins in earnest. Augustus manages to contrive an elaborate hideaway for his friend in the *Grampus*'s hold: a large packing crate filled with a variety of supplies including meat and sea biscuit, cordials and liqueurs, a jug of water, plenty of matches and candles along with "books, pen, ink, and paper," the storage vessels of mental rather than physical nourishment. Once Pym is shut away in his "little apartment"—an island of order in a "complete chaos" of ship furniture, crates, barrels, and bales—he quickly loses track of time. During the first of several extended episodes of deep sleep, his watch runs down, and his meat supply appears to rot with unnatural speed. "My limbs were greatly cramped," Pym notes, "and I was forced to relieve them by standing between the crates"—words that amount to Poe's genteel way of reminding his reader that Augustus has made no suitably tidy provision for Pym's waste. The longer he remains in the hold the more his snug retreat must come to resemble a privy rather than a gentleman's reading nook.

Such conditions soon produce what Poe's contemporaries, living in the polluted cities of the day, must have viewed as an entirely predictable result. Pym grows feverish and delirious, experiencing among other sensations an astonishing collection of hallucinatory dreams, which he gathers into a suggestive sequence of visions:

> My dreams were of the most terrific description. Every species of calamity and horror befell me. Among other miseries, I was smothered to death between huge pillows, by demons of the most ghastly and ferocious aspect. Immense serpents held me in their embrace, and looked earnestly in my face with their fearfully shining eyes. Then deserts, limitless, and of the most forlorn and awe-inspiring character, spread themselves out before me. Immensely tall trunks of trees, gray and leafless, rose up in endless succession as far as the eye could reach. Their roots were concealed in wide-spreading morasses, whose dreary water lay intensely black, still, and altogether terrible, beneath. And the strange trees seemed endowed with a human vitality, and, waving to and fro their skeleton arms, were crying to the silent waters for mercy, in the shrill and piercing accents of the most acute agony and despair. The scene changed; and I stood, naked and alone, amid the burning sand-plains of Zahara. At my feet lay crouched a fierce lion of the tropics. Suddenly his wild eyes opened and fell upon me. With a convulsive bound he sprang to his feet, and laid bare his horrible teeth. In another instant there burst from his red throat a roar like the thunder of the firmament, and I fell impetuously to the earth. (PT, 1026)

These provocative mental contents are far more interesting than the trite materials of romantic fantasy that Pym and Augustus had imbibed from their boyish reading. They reflect, at some points, a semilucid awareness of Pym's actual surroundings: the claustrophobic confinement of the ship's hold, its poisonous bilge, the "skeleton arms" of its masts "crying to the silent waters," the inexplicable appearance of Pym's dog, Tiger, who finally awakens him from his stupor. The lion's explosive roar foretells the terrible concussion from the *Jane Guy* near the end of the story, but it also suggests the culmination of a desperate struggle for wakefulness, a vocal explosion that finally breaks through the muffling and constricting images with which the dream sequence begins.

Mixed with these elements of half-conscious perception are scenes from a fantastic, cognitive underworld reminiscent of the dungeons of Toledo in "The Pit and the Pendulum." Immense serpents cradle Pym in their coils and study him with half parental, half menacing intensity. Then equally immense trees, in an endless forest, wave their limbs as if stricken by "the most acute agony and despair." Finally the barrier between unconscious and conscious life breaks down into paradox: Pym's dream self, in its nakedness, confronts a terrible image of awakening and falls "impetuously to the earth," a phrase that blends willfulness and passivity in a clash of mental extremes. Circumstances thrust Pym into a border region where reason has to grope toward an understanding of its plight through rich veils of illusion—a shimmering array of images that seems to carry him away from his sensory present into a sequence of profoundly archaic places: a deep reptilian past, a post-lapsarian world from which the formative (or punitive) waters have not yet quite withdrawn, a lion that suggests the agency of mythic or religious power, deployed with judgmental fury against a helpless (or perhaps a newborn) soul.

These visions have much more in common with Ovid, Dante, or Spenser than with the journalistic world of Daniel Defoe, evoking a much more complex interplay of thoughts than Poe's narrator had previously displayed, before the fumes of the *Grampus'* hold began to transform him from Augustus Barnard's deferential side-kick into a fully laden consciousness with its own engrossing story to tell. That story requires, at first, to be painstakingly pieced together out of the sensory jumble from which Pym is suffering, assisted by the scraps of a message from Augustus that Pym had impulsively torn to pieces under the mistaken impression that it was a blank piece of paper. He must reassemble these fragments in darkness so complete that he cannot tell one side of Augustus' note from another, like a blind man assembling a jigsaw puzzle. His second attempt to read the note takes place during the brief glow produced by simple friction from a few chips of phosphorous—all that Pym can salvage from the supply of candles and matches that Tiger has apparently eaten.

The partial message that he is finally able to read, through the eerie "brilliancy" of the phosphorus, conveys little information about what has been transpiring on the ship's deck: "*blood—your life depends upon lying close.*" This tantalizing verbal vessel is both empty and overflowing:

> Had I been able to ascertain the entire contents of the note—the full meaning of the admonition which my friend had thus attempted to convey, that admonition, even although it should have revealed a story of disaster the most unspeakable, could not, I am firmly convinced, have imbued my mind with one tithe of the harrowing and yet indefinable horror with which I was inspired by the fragmentary warning thus received. And "*blood*" too, that word of all words—so rife at all times with mystery, and suffering, and terror—how trebly full of import did it now appear—how chillily and heavily (disjointed, as it thus was, from any foregoing words to qualify or render it distinct) did its vague syllables

fall, amid the deep gloom of my prison, into the innermost recesses of my soul! (PT, 1035)

A great deal of blood has in fact been spilled during a mutiny on the *Grampus* that broke out during Pym's delirious sleep in the hold. Captain Barnard has been seriously wounded and twenty-two members of the crew cast overboard, after the ship's ruthless cook coolly split each victim's head with an ax. In the course of Pym's story, Poe neglects few opportunities to open the body's secretive containers. Pym himself knows nothing of these events at the time that he reads Augustus's enigmatic warning, but their gruesome import seems to pour into him, in any case, until he too is a vessel "rife" with fear and despair, a level of emotional intensity that neither he nor his story can sustain: "I threw myself again upon the mattress, where, for about the period of a day and night, I lay in a kind of stupor, relieved only by momentary intervals of reason and recollection" (PT, 1036).

Vivid phases of physical sickness, delirious sleep, and debilitating terror repeatedly succeed one another before Pym is able to achieve the visionary mental state with which his book concludes. He loses consciousness out of sheer terror when the *Ariel* disappears beneath the keel of a large whaling brig in the book's opening chapter. "Extreme horror and dismay" immediately follow his discovery that an immoveable coil of chain cable has sealed the trap door in the floor of Augustus's cabin, effectively burying him alive in the *Grampus'* hold. Near the end of his long ordeal, fear strikes him dumb when he first hears Augustus whisper his name. A profound appreciation for the power of fear lies behind the strikingly successful plan that Pym, Augustus, and Dirk Peters ultimately contrive for seizing the ship from the mutineers, but fear in itself is not central to Poe's interest in the story. Pym stresses, above all else, the peculiar mixture of physical paralysis and emotional intensity that extreme fear represents, a hybrid state of being nearly unique in its ability to immobilize the body while the spirit grows frantic for movement. That word of all words, blood, drops like a cake of Antarctic ice, "chillily and heavily," into the recesses of Pym's soul when he is finally able to read Augustus' note. Fear is the stupor from which one longs, most desperately, to awaken.

Exploiting the renegade sailors' drunkenness and superstition, Pym determines to disguise himself as the corpse of one of their companions whom the ringleader of the mutiny, the *Grampus'* mate, has apparently poisoned. Using as a costume the clothes stripped from this man's grotesquely bloated body and painting his own face with chalk and blood, both provided by the ingenious and increasingly essential Dirk Peters, Pym's imitation of a vengeful ghost, fitfully illuminated by "the uncertain and wavering light...of the cabin lantern," strikes the treacherous mate instantly dead from fear. His remaining accomplices are paralyzed with terror just long enough for Pym and his companions to gain a decisive advantage in the brutal fight that ensues. Pym emphasizes that the frenzied action of the battle all takes place "in far less time than I have taken to tell it" (PT, 1073). A measure of narrative paralysis is necessary in order to survey the psychological and circumstantial conditions that make this murderous blend of stillness and movement plausible. The mutineers all sat rooted to the cabin floor, Pym reports, rife with much the same complex of emotions that Pym himself had experienced in the hold. Out of the ten sailors who had been collected in the captain's cabin when Pym, Augustus, and Peters had launched their desperate plan, only one survives.

The four remaining men on board the ship quickly discover that the *Grampus* has become both their life raft and a tantalizingly inaccessible storehouse of supplies. A complete wreck after riding out a series of fierce storms, the hull is entirely full of water, making it impossible to retrieve any food or drink from the various compartments of the ship. Through great effort, Pym and Peters are able to bring up a number of objects from the flooded hold: a small jar of olives, a bottle of port that Pym's companions greedily drink and shatter during one of his repeated dives beneath the deck, another bottle and then a carboy of Madeira wine, a tortoise with a small reservoir of fresh water stored in its neck pouch. Poe fills this section of the book with a profound anxiety over the recovery and the contents of various corporeal vessels as the four voracious and thirsty men grow increasingly desperate to fill themselves out of a hodgepodge of lesser containers that the wreck reluctantly yields.

A brief explosion of feeling breaks this urgent filling and emptying cycle when a large brig suddenly comes into view and appears to be approaching the *Grampus*. In one of the book's most memorable episodes, this vessel proves to be a plague ship—a grotesque extension of Pym's terrible experience in the darkness and stench of the hold at the beginning of the voyage:

> The brig came on slowly, and now more steadily than before, and—I cannot speak calmly of this event—our hearts leaped up wildly within us, and we poured out our whole souls in shouts and thanksgiving to God for the complete, unexpected, and glorious deliverance that was so

palpably at hand. Of a sudden, and all at once, there came wafted over the ocean from the strange vessel (which was now close upon us) a smell, a stench, such as the whole world has no name for—no conception of—hellish—utterly suffocating—insufferable, inconceivable. I gasped for breath, and, turning to my companions, perceived that they were paler than marble. But we had now no time left for question or surmise—the brig was within fifty feet of us, and it seemed to be her intention to run under our counter, that we might board her without her putting out a boat. We rushed aft, when, suddenly a wide yaw threw her off full five or six points from the course she had been running, and, as she passed under our stern at the distance of about twenty feet, we had a full view of her decks. Shall I ever forget the triple horror of that spectacle? Twenty-five or thirty human bodies, among whom were several females, lay scattered about between the counter and the galley, in the last and most loathsome state of putrefaction! We plainly saw that not a soul lived in that fated vessel! Yet we could not help shouting to the dead for help! (PT, 1085–1086)

This passage is replete in every sense, from the soulful pouring forth of thanksgiving at its beginning, through Pym's overflowing disgust at the odor of death, to their irrational cries for help after Pym and his companions take a "full view" of the stranger's terrible decks. The four men spend the rest of the day in "a condition of stupid lethargy," watching the death-ship slowly disappear in the distance. The corpse that had appeared to be signaling from its bow proves to be a gruesome puppet. As the strange vessel draws closer Pym and his companions notice that the knees of the signaler are "lodged upon a stout rope," his palms extend outward over the ship's rail in an eerie, cruciform display, and his face is "turned from us so that we could not behold it" (PT, 1086). The calculated echo of the Psalms in this last phrase is an especially bitter feature of the passage.

On the corpse's back is a gull whose vigorous feeding had made the dead sailor appear to move. This creature is the harbinger of a number of momentous changes in Pym's story, the narrative tacks or yaws that mimic a sailing vessel's zigzag movement across the direction of the wind, or the abrupt shifts between aimless stupor and wakeful purpose that are the definitive condition of Pym's hallucinatory world. The morsel of human carrion that the gull drops on the *Grampus*' deck initially awakens in all four survivors the latent realization that cannibalism might enable some of them to endure their ordeal a bit longer. Richard Parker, the sole remaining mutineer, loses the fatal lottery that the men conduct; Pym, Peters, and Augustus quickly reduce him to a bodily vessel by removing his appendages, drinking his blood, and gradually devouring his flesh "during the four ever memorable days of the seventeenth, eighteenth, nineteenth, and twentieth of the month" (PT, 1099). Parker's death signals a shift to journal form that permits Pym to date precisely both the death of Augustus and the providential appearance of the *Jane Guy*. Cannibalism, and the subsequent recovery of more food from the wreck's flooded hold, come too late to save Augustus from gangrene and starvation, the feverish thirst and icy feet that signal impending death and make his body a gruesome model of the tropical and polar latitudes that the story ultimately explores.

The atavistic nightmare that comprises the first half of Pym's book is in many respects a grim nutritional carnival: a festival of the belly, beginning with the tempting cordials and meats in Pym's cozy wooden box, progressing through cold potatoes, junk beef and pudding in the *Grampus'* forecastle, through the four-day feast on Parker's torso, followed by a jumble of olives, wine, and tortoise meat that ends with the ceremonial disposal of Augustus' rotted corpse in a phosphorescent sea of feeding sharks. As if to complete the uncanny Lenten echo, the wreck finally capsizes once Augustus's body is gone, leaving Pym and Peters to scramble onto its keel and find that it too—like the swarming vermin that magically appeared in their precious supply of water—is replete with life, coated with large barnacles on which the two men conclude they might live for weeks. The resurrection, or reawakening, that follows this exhilarating discovery, however, celebrates the secular mysteries of commerce and science that the *Jane Guy* represents. She is on a voyage of trade and exploration when she rescues the last two members of the *Grampus'* crew, much like the voyage that Charles Darwin's *Beagle* was conducting in the same months that Poe was writing his book.

The second half of Pym's narrative rapidly becomes saturated with navigational terms and technicalities, with the correction of erroneous charts and the probing for possible routes through the southern ice pack. Though only a rescued castaway, Pym plays a strangely influential role in these activities, commenting in great detail on the information contained in the logs of earlier explorers and encouraging the *Jane Guy's* commander, Captain Guy, to sail as far to the south as he can, even to the point of ridiculing the captain's fears when he briefly expresses a desire to turn back. The incompetent stowaway who had begun this adventure abruptly awakens to assume the joint identities of ship's naturalist and captain's confidante. Pym repeatedly refers to Dirk Peters as a "hybrid," or as the "hybrid line manager" among the

Grampus's original whaling crew, but Pym himself is a hybrid of narrative attributes at least as ill-assorted as the thick, compact stature, the massive arms, and the startlingly permanent grin that comprise the grotesque physical peculiarities of his friend:

> This man was the son of an Indian squaw of the tribe of Upsarokas, who live among the fastnesses of the Black Hills near the source of the Missouri. His father was a fur-trader, I believe, or at least connected in some manner with the Indian trading-posts on Lewis river. Peters himself... was short in stature—not more than four feet eight inches high—but his limbs were of the most Herculean mould. His hands, especially, were so enormously thick and broad as hardly to retain a human shape. His arms, as well as legs, were bowed in the most singular manner, and appeared to possess no flexibility whatever. His head was equally deformed, being of immense size, with an indentation on the crown (like that on the head of most negroes), and entirely bald. To conceal this latter deficiency, which did not proceed from old age, he usually wore a wig formed of any hair-like material which presented itself—occasionally the skin of a Spanish dog or American grizzly bear.... The mouth extended nearly from ear to ear; the lips were thin, and seemed, like some other portions of his frame, to be devoid of natural pliancy, so that the ruling expression never varied under the influence of any emotion whatever. This ruling expression may be conceived when it is considered that the teeth were exceedingly long and protruding, and never even partially covered, in any instance, by the lips. To pass this man with a casual glance, one might imagine him to be convulsed with laughter—but a second look would induce a shuddering acknowledgment, that if such an expression were indicative of merriment, the merriment must be that of a demon. (PT, 1043–1044)

Unpromising though his appearance may be, Peters proves to be the chief means of carrying off Pym's adventure. His great physical strength is the decisive factor in defeating the mutineers. When the *Grampus* abruptly capsizes, throwing Peters and Pym among the sharks, Peters regains the ship's keel first and pulls his exhausted companion to safety. Much later he catches Pym in his arms when he nearly falls to his death while descending the sheer cliffs on Tsalal, the island where the *Jane Guy* is destroyed. During the cannibalism episode, when Pym cannot bear to look at the results of the fatal lottery, it is the superficially demonic hybrid who takes him gently by the hand and reassures him (PT, 1098).

This powerful and tender companion—half monster and half rag doll—withdraws into silence and a strange "apathy" as the two men approach the "gigantic curtain" of vapor that spans the southern horizon at the story's conclusion. "I can liken it to nothing but a limitless cataract, rolling silently into the sea from some immense and far-distant rampart in the heaven," Pym writes (PT, 1179). A forerunner of the silent, jeweled cataract in Arnheim, this uncanny vision marks the culmination of the cycles of emptiness and repletion, stupor and terror, that fill Pym's story. Earth is the book's last vessel, endlessly fed from an apparently limitless cascade of light that Pym describes in his final paragraphs as he draws closer and closer to its "embraces," shortly before an enigmatic "human figure" in a white shroud interposes to block the way. It is largely Peters' "ingenuity and resolution" (Pym concedes) that make the journey toward this climactic moment possible. Throughout most of the story—and even in the midst of its mysterious closing scenes—the silence maintained by Pym's grotesque but selfless companion suggests the inherent secrets of the human vessel: the absence of any direct correspondence between the corporeal envelope and its hidden contents.

Most readers quickly recognize Peters to be a literary convention, a descendant of Crusoe's Friday and a progenitor of Melville's Queequeg, a creature of books, or of the imagination alone, assembled out of the intractable disorder of historical contingency. Poe uses him to underscore the book's final shift in direction: a decisive tack in the narrative's course, away from the technical, scientific, or commercial details that impinge on earthly existence and toward the imaginative sphere of the rudderless voyage, a journey in the direction of unknown, luminous forms. As Pym sets out on his fourth voyage, the triumphant tools of modern culture remain behind, abandoned to a remarkable, destructive vortex on the island of Tsalal, the last of the book's evocative hybrid creations.

This complex place of all places in Poe's fictional geography is the uncharted archipelago of blackness where the *Jane Guy* originally expects to gather a lucrative cargo of sea cucumber, *biche de mer*, a valuable delicacy on the Chinese market. The simplest of all organic vessels—merely "an *absorbing* and an *excretory*" organ, joined by a fleshy tube—these creatures when properly prepared and dried are thought to have medicinal properties as an antidote for sensual excess. Captain Guy hires the apparently compliant inhabitants of Tsalal, through their leader Too-wit, to help collect the cargo. But Too-wit proves to be the representative of a wily and highly organized people—a parasitic culture, in some respects, barely subsisting upon the ruins of a lost civilization, living in tents of animal skin, huts of brush, or simply holes in the ground, but cautious, vindictive, and determined to acquire the tools and the materials they need to construct their own, far-ranging vessels of exploration, to cut their own cultural story into the world's primordial rock. These hidden but urgent purposes entail the murder of the *Jane Guy*'s crew, the scavenging of the ship itself for its cargo and its useful metal fittings, and finally its complete destruction.

As Poe was revising his novel during the second half of 1837 and early 1838, he was reading and reviewing (among many other books) John Lloyd Stephens's newly published *Incidents of Travel in Egypt, Arabia Petræa, and the Holy Land*, the best of many contemporary accounts of Holy Land travel that capture the uneasy mixture of fascination, prejudice, impatience, and horror which Europeans and Americans often felt as they journeyed through the ragged Arab communities inhabiting the Nile Valley, dependent all the while on the ingenuity, good faith, and resourcefulness of Arab boatmen and Arab interpreters to make their pilgrimages to the origins of civilization.

This region contained the monumental ruins of ancient empires—like the vast inscriptions in the black rock of Tsalal that Pym and Peters explore—but it was also the Egypt of Mehemet Ali, the ruthless and determined Albanian mercenary who ruled the country, along with much of the Arabian Peninsula, Palestine, and Syria, under the nominal authority of the Ottoman Turks, for over forty years, modernizing Egypt's army, transportation systems, and economy in order to make it a Mediterranean power capable of competing with the Europeans and the Russians for geopolitical influence. Eventually he even rebelled against his Turkish masters and nearly captured Constantinople itself.

Egypt in Poe's and Stephens's day seemed to display in especially compact form the complete cycle of civilization: the incomparable ruins of the pharoahs, the degradation of the Arab poor, and the resurgent ambition of Mehemet Ali, all spiraling through various changes of fortune and of cultural development in a vast and potentially endless chronological vortex. Poe incorporates this complex background directly into the portrait of Tsalal. With its furious but carefully harnessed multitudes of people, its colossal and enigmatic stone inscriptions, and its guileful leader, Poe's island is both the tomb and the breeding ground of civilizations—a cultural theater for the operations of Attraction and Repulsion on the broadest chronological scale.

The miraculous water of the island that the sailors from the *Jane Guy* at first refuse to drink incorporates all of these dramatic attributes—a hybrid of hybrids that (as Pym suggests) encircles Tsalal with its unsettling implications like a "vast chain" embracing its many mysteries. At once beautiful and repulsive, shimmering with the "hues of changeable silk," but suspiciously thick and apparently "polluted," the water on closer examination proves to be a compound of "distinct veins, each of a distinct hue"— a fusion of properties that simultaneously identifies it with solids, with liquids, and with the chromatic bands of light. Pym compares it to "a thick infusion of gum Arabic in common water," a recipe that Poe's contemporaries would quickly recognize as the basis of various inks, of watercolor paints, of certain herbal medicines and nutritional mixtures used to treat digestive diseases like diarrhea and dysentery. Gum arabic was a lucrative export from Sub-Saharan Africa via the Nile through Alexandria, where Egyptian merchants could convey it to European and American markets. It helped to underwrite the political ambitions of Mehemet Ali's regime at the same time that it sustained the literary life of the Western press and contributed to Western medicine. Tsalal's water is an extraordinarily rich container of hybrid meanings, an enigmatic and wonderful "solution" to its own riddles.

The direction that Pym and Peters take in their captured canoe breaks free of Tsalal's violent and endless encirclement, escaping in the final vessel of the book on a rudderless voyage toward "a region of novelty and wonder." The ocean's temperature increases, "wild flickerings" in the sky and "agitations" on the surface of the sea fill their surroundings with hints of barely suppressed energy, "a powerful current" seems to electrify the water. Drawn into this steadily augmenting system of force, Pym and Peters yield to a "dreaminess of sensation," free of terror, as they approach the nearly translucent curtain of a final theater, one which is on the point of losing its opacity and revealing the larger drama behind it. The "shrouded human figure," sheathed in flawless white, that blocks their way is an obstacle to this ultimate awakening, a final emissary of corporeal limits imposing an unbroken sleep on Pym's unfinished tale.

* * *

Over the year that followed the appearance of his novel, Poe published a series of stories that adapt vital elements of Pym's performance to a strikingly varied range of settings and narrators. "The Fall of the House of Usher" (1839), for instance, would seem to have little in common with the sensational contents listed on Pym's title page, but Usher's story too depicts the starkly contrasted fates of two boyhood companions in a crisis that revolves around the receipt of a momentous letter.

Augustus' bloody scrawl is a desperate expedient compared with Roderick Usher's "singular summons," but each epistolary message is charged with an energy that exceeds the limitations of its medium. Indeed Usher's "acute bodily illness" and "mental disorder" prompt a plea that Pym himself might easily have written from what he calls, at one point, the nautical "dungeon" of the *Grampus'* noxious hold. An extraordinary dungeon, sheathed in copper like a ship's hull, plays a critical role in the architecture of Roderick Usher's ancestral mansion, and both plots repeatedly evoke the paralytic impact of fear as an index of some deeper human dilemma.

In "William Wilson" (1839) the narrator's thirst for "soul-less dissipation" greatly exceeds the alcoholic experiments that mark the beginning of Pym's adventure on the *Ariel*. But like Pym, Wilson seems consumed by a perverse desire for the doom of an utter outcast, "a lifetime dragged out in sorrow and tears," as Pym puts it, "upon some gray and desolate rock, in an ocean unapproachable and unknown." Twice Wilson's uncanny namesake confronts him at dawn as if to underscore the imperfect awakenings that each visit produces. Twice more Wilson confronts his nemesis at night for unmaskings that lead ultimately "to the horror and the mystery of the wildest of all sublunary visions" (PT, 335)—language far more extreme than a simple fable of the admonitory conscience would seem to require, and far more applicable to the sublime spectacle that Pym briefly glimpses at the bottom of the globe.

In the first of this sequence of variant stories, "Ligeia" (1838), Poe's narrator bluntly announces his loyalty to the same transgressive urges that lead Pym to ridicule Captain Guy's timidity about pushing his ship still deeper into the Antarctic ice: "I was possessed with a passion to discover," he declares (PT, 264). Ligeia's husband makes this statement as he struggles to describe his wife's remarkable eyes, but it applies much more broadly to the entire instructive relationship between them. Before Ligeia's own protracted struggle to reawaken in another woman's body, she proves herself to be an incomparable agent of awakening:

> I have spoken of the learning of Ligeia: it was immense—such as I have never known in woman. In the classical tongues was she deeply proficient, and as far as my own acquaintance extended in regard to the modern dialects of Europe, I have never known her at fault...I said her knowledge was such as I have never known in woman—but where breathes the man who has traversed, and successfully, all the wide areas of moral, physical and mathematical science? I saw not then what I now clearly perceive, that the acquisitions of Ligeia were gigantic, were

astounding; yet I was sufficiently aware of her infinite supremacy to
resign myself, with a child-like confidence, to her guidance through the
chaotic world of metaphysical investigation at which I was most busily
occupied during the earlier years of our marriage. With how vast a triumph—with how vivid a delight—with how much of all that is ethereal
in hope—did I feel, as she bent over me in studies but little sought—but
less known—that delicious vista by slow degrees expanding before me,
down whose long, gorgeous, and all untrodden path, I might at length
pass onward to the goal of a wisdom too divinely precious not to be forbidden! (PT, 266)

A delicious vista of metaphysical possibility likewise flickers through
the gigantic polar "curtain" that Pym's canoe is never able to reach.
Catastrophic thresholds of enlightenment mark the narrative limits of
many of Poe's greatest stories, but the trajectory of this forbidden learning takes a unique form in "Ligeia."

Poe's most spectacular heroine concentrates in her person all the
antagonistic energy of attraction and repulsion that infuses Pym's
Antarctic latitudes. Ligeia's face is unequalled in its beauty, but her husband compares its impact to "the radiance of an opium dream," faultless
in its features yet pervaded by an impenetrable "strangeness." Her
appearance blends the same opposed intensities of blackness and white-
ness, light and dark, heat and cold that confront Pym on the final stage
of his uncanny journey, but the "sullen" darkness and "luminous" ocean
glare of Pym's last journal entries lose all their negative connotations in
the radiance of Ligeia's eyes: "The hue of the orbs was the most brilliant
of black, and, far over them, hung jetty lashes of great length" (PT,
264). The "hue of the skin" of the imposing shape that blocks Pym's
pathway south is perfectly white. The appearance of Ligeia's eyes echoes
and inverts the effect of Pym's forbidding incarnation. The icy fire of
her presence is an enticement to movement, to the investigation of limitless mental distances, not an embodied limit.

In tandem with her eyes, Ligeia's voice seems to capture the essence
of her significance, the striking opposites that she is able to contain:

An *intensity* in thought, action, or speech, was possibly, in her, a result,
or at least an index, of that gigantic volition which, during our long
intercourse, failed to give other and more immediate evidence of its existence. Of all the women whom I have ever known, she, the outwardly
calm, the ever-placid Ligeia, was the most violently a prey to the tumultuous vultures of stern passion. And of such passion I could form no
estimate, save by the miraculous expansion of those eyes which at once

so delighted and appalled me—by the almost magical melody, modulation, distinctness and placidity of her very low voice—and by the fierce energy (rendered doubly effective by contrast with her manner of utterance) of the wild words which she habitually uttered. (PT, 265–266)

A frenzied quietude marks Ligeia's speech throughout the first half of her story. Even as she wrestled with death, the narrator remembers, "Her voice grew more gentle—grew more low—yet I would not wish to dwell upon the wild meaning of the quietly uttered words. My brain reeled as I hearkened, entranced, to a melody more than mortal—to assumptions and aspirations which mortality had never before known" (PT, 267).

Ligeia's "wild desire for life" is hardly an unprecedented mortal aspiration. Like William Wilson's hyperbolic allusion to "the wildest of all sublunary visions," this language points beyond the conventional requirements of the tale in which it appears: a guilty soul's confrontation with conscience in Wilson's case; a passionate woman's bitter rebellion against death in Ligeia's. Her unforgettable intensity and "gigantic volition" reflect her own insatiable appetite for a species of transformation that seems indifferent to bodily boundaries, to the ordinary corporeal vessels a living spirit might inhabit. The narrator glimpses this transcendent hunger as he tries to characterize the expression in Ligeia's eyes and finds himself forced to draw on a "circle of analogies" that include an inventory of "the commonest objects of the universe," as well as some suggestively uncommon ones: a vine, a moth, a butterfly, a chrysalis, a flowing stream, a falling meteor, the ocean, and one particular star "of the sixth magnitude, double and changeable, to be found near the large star in Lyra" (PT, 265). Along with "certain sounds" of stringed instruments, certain passages from books, and the "glances of unusually aged people," this catalogue suggests the collective preoccupations of natural philosophy: a museum of curiosities for the biologist, the explorer, the moralist, or the astronomer to ponder, as well as an inventory of possible comparisons for Ligeia's expressive mysteries. The title of the magazine in which "Ligeia" first appeared, the Baltimore *American Museum*, must have made this analogy seem inevitable to the story's first readers as well as to Poe himself.

In fact the narrative is structured in architectural wings that suggest the design of a great museum, symmetrically divided by the extraordinary poem that Poe first added to the text in 1845 but which fits so perfectly that it is impossible to imagine the plot without it. A frequent resident (though not necessarily a citizen) of an "old, decaying city near the Rhine," Ligeia seems to haunt the origins of print itself, assembling the gigantic "acquisitions" of learning that enable her to guide the narrator's halting progress through abstruse studies that prove utterly opaque without her help. The curatorial power of Ligeia's presence evokes the narrator's wakeful intensity; her absence reduces him to a stupor. The alternating pattern replicates in compressed form the rhythms that govern the experience of Arthur Gordon Pym. Though Ligcia has no family name or personal history to act as a counterweight for her formidable intellectual powers, she is the fountainhead of memory: Mnemosyne herself, rather than some lesser deity, mired in an ordinary erotic genealogy. Though a master of all tongues and disciplines, she has no real need for the many figurative aids to reflection or understanding that her husband will desperately deploy in his attempt to recall her ineffable nature.

When the narrator eventually remarries after the death of this incomparable partner, the new wife he selects is conspicuous almost exclusively for the completeness of her mortal pedigree: Lady Rowena Trevannion, of Tremaine. "In a moment of mental alienation," he aligns himself with what proves to be a sterile human lineage in place of Ligeia's superhuman force and installs this pale successor in a wedding chamber that is itself a grotesque museum: a "capacious" pentagonal room in a renovated English abbey, decorated with Gothic, Druidic, and Sarcenic designs and objects, with furniture of "Eastern figure" and "Indian model" along with five, great sarcophagi from Luxor covered with Egyptian sculpture. This parody of Ligeia's vast mental vistas is a completely "embodied" museum, shrouded in pornographic tapestries that depict Norman superstition and the "guilty" dreams of monks. It is a chamber of delirious, vaguely erotic, sleep in which Lady Rowena falls mysteriously ill at the beginning of the second month of her marriage: the commencement of a fleshly "pregnancy" that will yield an uncanny birth.

A thread of verse running through the center of the story divides Ligeia's incorporeal museum from Rowena's corporeal one. Poe stresses this nearly hemispheric division of the plot—an odd echo of Pym's hemispheric voyage—by having his narrator recite Ligeia's provocative, untitled poem "at high noon of the night" of her death: a reference to time's peculiar symmetries that echoes the structural symmetries of the story itself, mixing the apogees of light and darkness in a single musical phrase. The verses themselves describe the staging of a terrifying fable before an audience of angels who identify its characters and its theme at the end of the performance. Though Ligeia is the poem's author, she asks her husband to repeat the lines:

> Lo! 'tis a gala night
>> Within the lonesome latter years!
> An angel throng, bewinged, bedight
>> In veils, and drowned in tears,
> Sit in a theatre, to see
>> A play of hopes and fears,
> While the orchestra breathes fitfully
>> The music of the spheres.

The stanzas open as the story itself does, with an evocation of "low musical language"— the phrase that the narrator uses in his first halting sentences to describe the enchanting effect of Ligeia's voice. As the poem's "motley drama" unfolds it proves to be a recapitulation of the theater of fear that Pym and his companions present to the *Grampus* mutineers in the flickering light of the captain's cabin: a confrontation with decay capturing Ligeia's anguish at the forced alliance between permanence and impermanence, memory and flesh, that the conditions of existence impose.

The blood red Conqueror Worm that dominates the angelic stage at the end of Ligeia's drama is a loathsome variation on the scavenger gull of Pym's plague ship, or the worm-life of the *biche-de-mer*, the sea-cucumber that tempts the greed of the *Jane Guy* in Tsalal. The poem's closing stanza reassembles the curtains, veils, lights, and rushing winds of Pym's polar ocean into a new configuration, one far more fatal and fixed in its conclusions than either the novel to which it alludes or the story in which it appears:

> Out—out are the lights—out all!
>> And over each quivering form,
> The curtain, a funeral pall,
>> Comes down with the rush of a storm,
> And the angels, all pallid and wan,
>> Uprising, unveiling, affirm
> That the play is the tragedy, "Man,"
>> And its hero the Conqueror Worm.
>>> (PT, 269)

In mimicry of the angels, Ligeia herself rises as the narrator finishes his recitation to express her bitter resistance to death. The "unveiling" at the close of the poem will repeat itself, in vivid form, at the end of the story, when Lady Rowena's funeral "cerements" finally drop away to liberate "into the rushing atmosphere of the chamber" Ligeia's streaming hair (PT, 277).

But why should the play's all-too-familiar plot be so harrowing to the supernatural viewers that the poem depicts? The tragedy "Man" might well disturb a human audience, even on repeated viewings, but a theater of angels would surely be immune to its corporeal menace. The poem's second stanza provides a partial explanation for the strange pallor that the performance induces when it introduces the human "mimes" upon which the Conqueror Worm will ultimately feed:

> Mimes, in the form of God on high,
>   Mutter and mumble low,
> And hither and thither fly—
>   Mere puppets they, who come and go
> At bidding of vast formless things
>   That shift the scenery to and fro,
> Flapping from out their Condor wings
>   Invisible Wo!
>   (PT, 268)

The fate of these puppets, formed in God's image, is anything but surprising. As far as Poe's orthodox contemporaries were concerned, their destiny was settled in the opening chapters of Genesis. But through momentary rents in the play's scenery, the angelic audience is able to glimpse something more ominous: formless power, winged like the gigantic birds that sail on the soundless winds of Pym's climactic polar vision, transmitting "invisible" woe. These terrible, incorporeal energies signal an end to the ceremonial visibility of "seraphic" as well as "mimic" embodiment. The angels glimpse their own death, not man's. No bodily or cultural vessel, however elaborately or crudely "bedight," exists in the kingdom of inorganization that lies behind the extraordinary veil of Ligeia's words.

                              *   *   *

It would be nearly a year before Poe returned to the dramatic potential of awakening that he puts to such startling use at the conclusion of "Ligeia," publishing in the interval a handful of burlesques that mock what one comic tale refers to as the "intensities" of metaphysical romance. By the late summer of 1839, however, Poe recasts these intensities as a narrative of schoolboy rivalry faintly reminiscent of the relationship between Augustus Barnard and Arthur Gordon Pym. William Wilson's perverse lifelong descent through a "vortex of thoughtless folly" is much less innocent than Pym's infatuation with the tragic experience of shipwreck and despair, and Wilson's nemesis ultimately tries to thwart his desires rather than abet them, but the two share "many points of strong congeniality," Wilson admits: "a motley and heterogeneous admixture" of animosity, esteem, respect, and curiosity that inevitably makes them "the most inseparable of companions" (PT, 343).

This companionship, however, like the marriage between the narrator of "Ligeia" and his remarkable muse, has an almost mythic scope, a sense of immeasurable chronological depth rooted in "wild, confused and thronging memories of a time when memory herself was yet unborn" (PT, 346). Enfeebled remembrance is the mark of the imperfectly awakened soul in William Wilson's long confession, as it is in the pages of "Ligeia," but a key distinction between the two stories is that the narrator of "William Wilson" tries to repudiate these thronging memories rather than embrace them, resentful even of the "meaning whispers" with which his companion quietly voices his criticism of Wilson's behavior or insinuates his unwanted advice. Once Poe's narrator is lodged at Eton, a few months after a furtive, midnight visit to his companion's bedchamber prompts his flight from the boy's school where the two had first met, his powers of recollection dramatically deteriorate, leaving only the "froth" rather than the substance of a past.

From this moment on the narrator of "William Wilson" moves through a range of very particular, very real locations in the course of presenting his fate, beginning with Dr. Bransby's school at Stoke Newington and continuing through Eton and Oxford, before concluding with a series of European capitals through which Wilson attempts to flee the "inscrutable tyranny" that stalks him: Paris, Vienna, Moscow, and Rome. In one sense "William Wilson" is among the most topical, and most political, of Poe's plots: the tale of a hero with a suggestive "constitutional malady" that leads him to devise the downfall of aristocratic foils; a commoner who cheats at écarté by stuffing his sleeves with "court cards" and "honors." Wilson resembles an extravagant version of William R. Taylor's anxiety-laden antebellum American: an "emergent Yankee" of fabulous wealth trying to move into higher social circles, or an embittered Cavalier from America's slaveholding elite, resentful of the enclaves of European nobility that are closed to him.

But these aspects of the story, like the punitive spectre of conscience that it seems to illustrate, remain an inadequate context for what Wilson terms "the wildest of all sublunary visions" at his story's end: the striking realization latent in the final words of his victim at a Roman carnival ball, "In me didst thou exist." It is not so much what is "double" in Wilson's nature—conscience and desire, the soul and the self, memory and imagination—that haunts Poe's narrator. He is relentlessly pursued by what is "singular," a word that insinuates itself repeatedly into a number of tales from this remarkable period. In "William Wilson" it is the "singular" whisper with which he speaks that is the defining attribute of Wilson's schoolboy rival. His "singular" auroral appearance at Eton after Wilson's night-long debauch drives the narrator into the next stage of his flight, but the same insistently "singular being" reappears yet again to thwart his Oxford gambling plot. The "marked and singular lineaments" of the blood-stained face that Wilson ultimately destroys in Rome belong to this same uncanny companion.

Each of these distinct confrontations entails a sharp change in fictive direction, a tack in the dramatic course that Wilson pursues, carrying him from the motley and evocative blend of feelings at the outset of this relationship to his explosive rage at its end. Wilson's rejected monitor and guide, like Ligeia, only grows quieter and ultimately sadder as he descends into the shadow, responding to Wilson's final violent assault with "a slight sigh" before drawing his sword. When Wilson pays his momentous midnight visit to the "closet" of his schoolboy rival, early in the tale, he must first part the curtains surrounding the bed before the rays of his lamp can illuminate the sleeper's countenance. This brief glimpse through a parted curtain triggers an "iciness of feeling" that marks the beginning of Wilson's descent into the frozen extremes of human vision: the same unattainable vista that neither Wilson nor his predecessor, Arthur Gordon Pym, can finally describe.

The geometrical pattern that lies beneath "William Wilson" is a variant of the zigzag course that Poe navigates through all of the major stories that he writes in the three years following the publication of Pym's seafaring adventure. The shape presents itself with unusual clarity in the repeated motifs of Wilson's boyhood schoolroom: its "pointed Gothic windows" and "terror-inspiring" angles, the lines of classroom desks "crossing and re-crossing in endless irregularity," their surfaces "beseamed" with carving that reflects the erratic mental voyaging of their boyish occupants. The building's winding stairways and interior passages are forever "returning in upon themselves" in a circle of futility that Wilson's life too ultimately emulates. This inescapable circularity derives directly from the bitter futility of Ligeia's poem:

> That motley drama!—oh, be sure
> It shall not be forgot!
> With its Phantom chased forevermore,
> By a crowd that seize it not,

Through a circle that ever returneth in
To the self-same spot,
And much of Madness and more of Sin,
And Horror the soul of the plot.

(PT, 268)

"The Man of the Crowd," a companion fable to "William Wilson," incorporates an even more vivid moral geometry, linking the restless movements of a troubled conscience to the repetitive tacking of a vessel at sea, as well as to the desperate circularity of human desire in a shadowy and contaminated urban world. Like "Ligeia" this remarkable tale too has a bi-part structure: a first half in which its narrator observes the swelling throng of people that surges through the street before his London coffee house window; a second half in which he ties a handkerchief over his mouth to fend off infection and plunges into the crowd in pursuit of a strange old man who has seized his attention.

This urban spectacle itself consists of "two dense and continuous tides of population" that the narrator never completely distinguishes from one another. The categories of people he observes in its midst likewise come in "divisions," or in contrasted scales like the "upper" and "junior" clerks he notes, or the gamblers who "seem to prey upon the public in two battalions." Even the prostitutes participate in this relentless dividing and subdividing of the human stream: from exquisite but inwardly filthy beauties in their prime through the "loathsome and utterly lost leper in rags," to old women "making a last effort" to sell themselves on the city streets. Peddlers, professional beggars, innocent working girls, drunkards, and tradesmen of all kinds fill out the vivid picture, heightened by the garish luster of street lamps. "All was dark yet splendid," the narrator concludes, like a beautifully cut gem.

Confident in the freshly "electrified" state of his intellect, as he convalesces from a bout of illness, the narrator lays claim to peculiar perceptive powers that enable him to read "the history of long years" with a single glance in a passing individual's face. Suddenly, however, his reading facility encounters a more resistant set of features:

With my brow to the glass, I was thus occupied in scrutinizing the mob, when suddenly there came into view a countenance (that of a decrepid old man, some sixty-five or seventy years of age,)—a countenance which at once arrested and absorbed my whole attention, on account of the absolute idiosyncracy of its expression. Any thing even remotely resembling that expression I had never seen before.... As I endeavored, during the brief minute of my original survey, to form some analysis of the meaning conveyed, there arose confusedly and paradoxically within my mind, the ideas of vast mental power, of caution, of penuriousness, of avarice, of coolness, of malice, of blood-thirstiness, of triumph, of merriment, of excessive terror, of intense—of supreme despair. I felt singularly aroused, startled, fascinated. "How wild a history," I said to myself, "is written within that bosom!" Then came a craving desire to keep the man in view—to know more of him. Hurriedly putting on an overcoat, and seizing my hat and cane, I made my way into the street, and pushed through the crowd in the direction which I had seen him take; for he had already disappeared. (PT, 392–393)

Startled into a singular state of wakefulness, the narrator embarks on a long and furious pursuit. The oblivious old man takes a zigzag course through the thoroughfares and alleys of the great city—its "noisome" and its prosperous districts, its plush theaters and gin palaces, its crowded and its deserted places—all the while enduring a "fierce" rain, and twice circling back to the street directly in front of the narrator's hotel coffee house, the self-same spot where the tale both begins and ends.

In the course of this apparently pointless journey, the narrator notices beneath a filthy, second-hand cloak that the old man wears some intriguing articles of dress: a linen shirt of "beautiful texture" followed by a glimpse "both of a diamond and of a dagger" just visible through a "rent" in his clothes (PT, 393). These objects do little more than arouse the narrator's prurient curiosity, but at the same time they readily align themselves with the insistent divisions, battalions, and scales of the first half of his story, as well as with the wild history of guilt and remorse that the narrator had expected to find written within the old man's bosom. The dagger and the diamond in particular seem external emblems of the "two continuous tides" that divide the stream of humanity flowing through the city's streets, as well as through each individual in its midst. They are a traditional romance code for attributes of the spirit.

In *The Secular Scripture* Northrup Frye describes an interplay between disguise and disclosure in Philip Sidney's *Arcadia* that anticipates Poe's use of these evocative objects. Pamela, one of two heroines in Sidney's elaborate plot, adopts a disguise at one point in the story through which the *Arcadia*'s narrator is still able to detect a symbolic jewel that hints at her true identity and attributes: a rich diamond set in "black horne" signaling the unsullied purity of her soul in the midst of a corrupt world. Poe's aged wanderer in "The Man of the Crowd" is poised between similar, emblematic alternatives that the story's narrator clumsily misreads as the "genius of deep crime." The jewel suggests little more to him than material wealth, while the dagger is the secretive weapon of a thief and a murderer. As emblems, however, the diamond and the dagger are at spiritual cross-purposes with one another: figures of incorruptible purity and of unbridled passion, of luminous beauty in conflict with selfish guile, the gem that grows more dazzling when it is cut as opposed to the assassin's mutilating blade.

Each of these richly suggestive objects is briefly visible through yet another of the provocatively rent curtains that serve Poe as vehicles of imperfect enlightenment: a filthy cloak that barely conceals the beautiful texture beneath. If deep crime does indeed lie below the tale's surface, as the narrator believes it does, then it is some unspoken atrocity that the old man strives to resist rather than one he strives to hide, like the wild sublunary vision that haunts William Wilson. Unbearable purity, not unbearable guilt, is the plight that drives the man of the crowd through London's human flood. The fate of Roderick Usher will prove to illustrate the same dark yet brilliant predicament of consciousness: its imperfect vision of veiled possibilities that fall outside the boundaries of bodily life. Instead of the traditional moral iconography of "The Man of the Crowd," however, Usher's story offers an expressionist picture of the inner life that is new in fiction—paintings of the soul's desire that dispense with the motley drama of all inherited forms.

*　*　*

During the summer of 1839, nearly a year after the publication of *The Narrative of Arthur Gordon Pym*, Poe turned his attention to weaving a story around a poem that he had written the preceding April for a periodical with one of the most eclectic names of the day, the *American Museum of Science, Literature, and the Arts*. "The Haunted Palace," the title of Poe's contribution to this inclusive literary museum, would appear a second time in the September 1839 issue of *Burton's Gentleman's Magazine* as one of Roderick Usher's musical *impromptus*: a rhapsodic performance conveying the mixture of morbidity and intense excitement that fills the atmosphere of "The Fall of the House of Usher." Coming roughly midway through the story, like Ligeia's deathbed verse, these lines too divide the surrounding narrative into architectural wings, signaling two dramatically different trajectories for Usher's formidable artistic gifts: their zigzag propensity to divide his spiritual domain like the "barely perceptible fissure" extending down the front of his house (PT, 320).

The poem itself is a nostalgic lament for a "feudal" cast of consciousness that can never return—an inherited architecture of artistic and
intellectual forms loosely resembling the "old cause-way" that conducts
the narrator of "The Fall of the House of Usher" across the ominous
black pool, the "sullen" tarn, lying before the ancestral mansion of the
title. The literal and the verbal paintings to which Usher's rhapsodies
finally yield, at the story's conclusion, depict a new order of aesthetic
and spiritual insight, struggling like the shrouded presence of Ligeia to
embody itself. Every feature of Poe's plot points toward this dual goal of
destruction and rebirth—the replacement of old causeways with new
causes—a variation on the narrative pattern that guides Pym's reiterative sequence of ships and voyages to the equally sullen Antarctic waters
that devour his story.

Unlike the frantic energy that propels the man of the crowd through
London's streets, or the explosive physical violence of William Wilson,
Roderick Usher's primary activity consists of waiting. Ligeia's husband
takes a similar passive approach toward the drama of resurrection that
he witnesses, but even he displays more agency than Usher, completely
redesigning rather than simply inheriting the elaborate abbey chamber
where the story's climax unfolds. By contrast, both the Usher domain
and its peculiar master present a paradoxical mix of utter depletion and
intense expectation: a fusion of outer lethargy and an "intolerable agitation of soul" (as Usher terms it) that the story's narrator vaguely detects
in the surrounding landscape from the moment that he first approaches
his old friend's home. Poe stretches his treatment of this initial scene
over several pages in order to develop the "singular impression" he hopes
to make, another addition to the fabric of insistent singularities that
haunt this family of tales:

> I know not how it was—but, with the first glimpse of the building, a
> sense of insufferable gloom pervaded my spirit. I say insufferable; for the
> feeling was unrelieved by any of that half-pleasurable, because poetic,
> sentiment, with which the mind usually receives even the sternest natu-
> ral images of the desolate or terrible.... What was it—I paused to
> think—what was it that so unnerved me in the contemplation of the
> House of Usher? It was a mystery all insoluble; nor could I grapple with
> the shadowy fancies that crowded upon me as I pondered.... And it
> might have been for this reason only, that, when I again uplifted my eyes
> to the house itself, from its image in the pool, there grew in my mind a
> strange fancy—a fancy so ridiculous, indeed, that I but mention it to
> show the vivid force of the sensations which oppressed me. I had so
> worked upon my imagination as really to believe that about the whole

mansion and domain there hung an atmosphere peculiar to themselves and their immediate vicinity—an atmosphere which had no affinity with the air of heaven, but which had reeked up from the decayed trees, and the gray wall, and the silent tarn—a pestilent and mystic vapor, dull, sluggish, faintly discernible, and leaden-hued. (PT, 317–319)

At first the narrator dismisses these oppressive sensations as childish or imaginary, but they reverberate through his account of Roderick Usher's striking cast of mind, his description of Madeline Usher's "singular" burial, and of the "wildly singular" storm that breaks out on the final night of the tale. The generic categories with which he strives to contain his feelings—his appeal to the ridiculous nature of childish superstitions, or to the well-known laws of terror—are at odds with the latent uniqueness of the story he is telling.

The vivid energy of "fancy" and a "sluggish" stupor clash in these opening impressions of the Usher domain. A similar "wild inconsistency" marks the fragile solidity of the house itself, as well as the behavior and the voice of its owner. The narrator addresses these details without appearing to notice that inconsistency is the deeper consistency of his tale. This perceptual fissure, in turn, points both to the flaw in the house's facade and to the peculiar vocal fractures in Roderick Usher's speech that seem to condense the overall impression he makes:

> In the manner of my friend I was at once struck with an incoherence—an inconsistency; and I soon found this to arise from a series of feeble and futile struggles to overcome an habitual trepidancy—an excessive nervous agitation. For something of this nature I had indeed been prepared, no less by his letter, than by reminiscences of certain boyish traits, and by conclusions deduced from his peculiar physical conformation and temperament. His action was alternately vivacious and sullen. His voice varied rapidly from a tremulous indecision (when the animal spirits seemed utterly in abeyance) to that species of energetic concision—that abrupt, weighty, unhurried, and hollow-sounding enunciation—that leaden, self-balanced and perfectly modulated guttural utterance, which may be observed in the lost drunkard, or the irreclaimable eater of opium, during the periods of his most intense excitement. (PT, 322)

The more the narrator strives for descriptive precision, in this passage, the less precise his words become. Usher's guttural phase is itself an incoherence within the larger inconsistency of his character, incorporating pairs of qualities that cancel one another out: the abrupt and the unhurried, the weighty and the hollow, leaden modulation and intense excitement. The lost drunkard and the opium eater may well descend into a vivid and frenetic dream world, but their outward appearance is cataleptic—a nearly inert stupor closely resembling the peculiar malady that appears to afflict Usher's sister, not Usher himself. When the reclusive lady Madeline drifts across the narrator's vision in a "remote portion of the apartment" where he and her brother are sitting, remoteness itself is her oddly contagious sickness: "A sensation of stupor oppressed me," the narrator recalls, "as my eyes followed her retreating steps" (PT, 323).

The form of paralysis into which Usher himself has fallen is paradoxically wakeful and restless. His senses are not dulled but intolerably acute. He anticipates with dread the impending time "when I must abandon life and reason together" in his struggle with fear, but he is indifferent to any particular source of danger and even in some degree to death itself. Abandonment is the outcome that unnerves him, not necessarily the cessation of physical being. Indeed the visual impression that Usher leaves upon the narrator is that of a spirit already in the process of abandoning its fleshly shell: his eyes are "large, liquid, and luminous beyond comparison," in stark opposition to the sullen tarn outside his door; "the regions above the temple" display "an inordinate expansion" of forehead or skull; and his web-like hair is already floating around Usher's face like a weightless aura. These changes suggest a mysterious cognitive transformation much more dramatic in scope than the parody of puberty that Usher's cracking voice calls to mind.

Poe's hero is on the brink of shattering his corporeal frame, an experience he tries both to foretell and to paint in the remarkable works of art that he produces. The most prominent of these, at least from a textual standpoint, is the nostalgic song that Usher composes in tribute to the "radiant" palace of the monarch "Thought," whose reign was a feast of color and music, wit and wisdom, until sorrow reduces it to a glimmering coal. The narrator transcribes Usher's verses from memory, adding a framework of stanzaic numerals to suggest his instinctive loyalty to the conventions of containment that break down as the song concludes:

V
But evil things, in robes of sorrow,
    Assailed the monarch's high estate;
(Ah, let us mourn, for never morrow
    Shall dawn upon him, desolate!)
And, round about his home, the glory
    That blushed and bloomed
Is but a dim-remembered story
    Of the old time entombed.

VI

And travellers now within that valley,
  Through the red-litten windows, see
Vast forms that move fantastically
  To a discordant melody;
While, like a rapid ghastly river,
  Through the pale door,
A hideous throng rush out forever,
  And laugh—but smile no more.

(PT, 327)

Thought's palace (as many readers have recognized) is the human head, with its multiple sensory avenues to the throne room of consciousness, but it is also a theater where the sorrowful pageant of "Man" first rendered in Ligeia's poem receives yet another artistic treatment. Vast forms dimly visible through the palace's "red-litten" eyes pour a throng of hideous sounds over its oral threshold that Usher's lines appear to associate with discordant, or incoherent, speech. But the sublime size of these new, mysterious tenants links them with the vast stage managers of Ligeia's pageant, not with the gruesome feeding of the Conqueror Worm. Their "discordant melody" is not identical to mere discord but to a perpetual flood of ghastly laughter that may signal an embittered wisdom as readily as madness.

Usher's poem depicts a mental landscape dramatically different from the one that marks the story's starting point: the "dull, dark, and soundless" autumn day, the dreary "tract" of desolate country, the "few white trunks of decayed trees" that prompt the narrator's "utter depression of soul" and "iciness" of heart as he enters the Usher domain. But even this forbidding and apparently lifeless picture is subject to strange metamorphic possibilities. A slight modification of its details (the narrator suspects) might even be able to "annihilate its capacity for sorrowful impression" (PT, 318). The scene is a subtle revision of the terrible and redemptive dreamscapes that haunt Arthur Gordon Pym during his stupor in the *Grampus'* hold. And like that sequence of visions, the soundless world outside Roderick Usher's house seems to be holding its breath in expectation, anticipating the sudden rejuvenation of spirit that Usher too seems waiting to experience.

Roderick Usher's most immediate struggles, however, appear to be with sound and light—physical phenomena that represent the chief sensory agents of instruction or expression and that complete Poe's depiction of the house itself as an ambitious cultural depository, an elaborate museum perfectly suited to the title of the periodical in which "The Haunted Palace" had originally appeared. Usher attempts to manage his spiritual plight through the weirdly minimalist music that he makes and the disturbing but engrossing pictures that he produces:

> From the paintings over which his elaborate fancy brooded, and which grew, touch by touch, into vaguenesses at which I shuddered the more thrillingly, because I shuddered knowing not why;—from these paintings (vivid as their images now are before me) I would in vain endeavor to educe more than a small portion which should lie within the compass of merely written words. By the utter simplicity, by the nakedness of his designs, he arrested and overawed attention. If ever mortal painted an idea, that mortal was Roderick Usher. For me at least—in the circumstances then surrounding me—there arose out of the pure abstractions which the hypochondriac contrived to throw upon his canvas, an intensity of intolerable awe, no shadow of which felt I ever yet in contemplation of the certainly glowing yet too concrete reveries of Fuseli. (PT, 324–325)

Usher's gallery, like his songs, must be reconstructed from memory—a liability that only underscores the abstract intensity of his images. They are canvases painted on the viewer's consciousness and as a result are inaccessible to reproduction. But the feelings they evoke are all the more vivid for being vague. One small picture in particular, the narrator believes, may be "shadowed forth" in words: a painting of "an immensely long and rectangular vault or tunnel" formed by low, white walls stretching "without interruption or device" through an indeterminate but "vast extent." The whole of this strange interior seems buried "at an exceeding depth below the surface of the earth" (PT, 325). Unlike the monkish fantasies of "The Pit and the Pendulum," this is an underworld of radiant emptiness offering neither source nor outlet for the flood of light that "bathed the whole in a ghastly and inappropriate splendor." Like Usher himself, his canvas is a physical anomaly: a desperate attempt to impose finite shape upon infinite spiritual energies, to build a frame for what cannot be contained. The burial place of his twin sister duplicates this attempt in different media: a damp and airless "vault" that is partly a feudal dungeon and partly a powder magazine, sheathed in copper and sealed by a door of "massive iron."

An obvious anticipation of this singular tomb, Usher's abstract canvas is also a storehouse for the atmospheric forces that erupt to encompass the house on the last night of the tale. Together these depictions of energy—the painting and the storm—capture the "daring character" of

Usher's metaphysical opinions, in themselves extensions of opinions that the narrator recognizes from earlier studies but completely reshaped by Usher's "disordered fancy" into a system of beliefs to which Usher clings with "earnest *abandon*." He is convinced that the vegetable world is "sentient," that the stones of his ancestral house are the work of this mysterious sentience, a "collocation" of matter drawn into a single "importunate" spiritual influence that pervades the entire family domain. Usher himself seems to have pored over a library of "rare and curious" volumes, in the deserted university that his house has come to resemble, framing ideas that "trespassed" on what the narrator terms "the kingdom of inorganization." "Such opinions need no comment, and I will make none," the narrator insists, but his reference to Usher's sacrilegious "trespasses" is comment enough (PT, 327). A "wild ritual" of forbidden thought has long sustained Usher's mental life. Abandonment itself has become his goal.

Like the young nobleman in "The Assignation," Usher grows increasingly immersed in a private world after his sister's death. The light in his eyes seems extinguished and his voice ceases to oscillate between opposite poles, retaining only its "tremulous quaver." "I beheld him gazing on vacancy for long hours," the narrator reports, "as if listening to some imaginary sound" (PT, 330). Gradually the "wild influences" of Usher's nature begin to infect the narrator's mind with his host's "impressive superstitions." As he sits listening to the sounds of a rising storm outside the house, seven or eight nights after Madeline Usher's burial, her brother abruptly appears in his bedchamber and leads him to a window. "And have you not seen it?" he urgently inquires as he throws open the casement: "you have not then seen it?—but, stay! you shall." These actions make explicit what the Usher family name has always implied: they are a fulfillment of the role of conductor, an escort across potentially magical thresholds that lead out of ordinary life toward the realm of heightened experience:

> The impetuous fury of the entering gust nearly lifted us from our feet. It was, indeed, a tempestuous yet sternly beautiful night, and one wildly singular in its terror and its beauty. A whirlwind had apparently collected its force in our vicinity; for there were frequent and violent alterations in the direction of the wind; and the exceeding density of the clouds (which hung so low as to press upon the turrets of the house) did not prevent our perceiving the life-like velocity with which they flew careering from all points against each other, without passing away into the distance. I say that even their exceeding density did not prevent our perceiving this—yet we had no glimpse of the moon or stars—nor was

there any flashing forth of the lightning. But the under surfaces of the
huge masses of agitated vapor, as well as all terrestrial objects immediately around us, were glowing in the unnatural light of a faintly luminous and distinctly visible gaseous exhalation which hung about and
enshrouded the mansion. (PT, 331)

Unlike the sublime geometry of the Norway maelstrom at its height,
this atmospheric whirlwind is a chaos of misdirection, the "careering"
clouds prefiguring the bodily collision that shortly brings the story to a
close. Usher will announce the presence of his sister outside the chamber door with a cry of "superhuman energy" that replicates the frantic
but beautiful vitality of the storm. The moon is temporarily hidden
behind the unnatural, gaseous glow of this nebular scene, but Poe will
soon supply the missing visual ingredients that he recasts two years later
into his great vortex tale.

For all its violence and menace, this whirlwind briefly succeeds in
freeing Usher from his prison of inexplicable fear—the anxieties of a
paltry humanity—by disclosing an outward turmoil that dwarfs the
cognitive energies of his inward one. Much like the narrator of "The
Man of the Crowd," however, Usher's guest is oblivious to the larger
forces on display in the night sky. Taking up an antique romance, for
the first time in the story the narrator strives to dictate events: "I will
read, and you shall listen," he declares, selecting an "uncouth and
unimaginative" tale as an antidote to Usher's frantic "ideality." This
nominally therapeutic instinct suggests the narrator's intuitive grasp of
the incipient wreckage surrounding him. Surely the specious totality of
an old book can restore the structural integrity of Usher's "house." But
Usher himself seems impervious to the efficacy of old books: murmur-
ing inaudibly as he faces the chamber door, rigidly alert, and rocking
"from side to side with a gentle yet constant and uniform sway" as if he
were chanting some ancient verse or reciting a prayer. This eerie yet
soothing posture is the last of Usher's pervasive incoherencies.

The destructive climax of the tale is an extraordinary pictorial fusion
of scientific and biblical myth:

The storm was still abroad in all its wrath as I found myself crossing the
old causeway. Suddenly there shot along the path a wild light, and
I turned to see whence a gleam so unusual could have issued; for the vast
house and its shadows were alone behind me. The radiance was that of
the full, setting, and blood-red moon, which now shone vividly through
that once barely-discernible fissure, of which I have before spoken as
extending from the roof of the building, in a zigzag direction, to the

base. While I gazed, this fissure rapidly widened—there came a fierce breath of the whirlwind—the entire orb of the satellite burst at once upon my sight—my brain reeled as I saw the mighty walls rushing asunder—there was a long tumultuous shouting sound like the voice of a thousand waters—and the deep and dank tarn at my feet closed sullenly and silently over the fragments of the *"House of Usher."* (PT, 335–336)

Like Roderick Usher, Poe too is an accomplished painter of ideas, but unlike the cognitive dungeon that his narrator had earlier described, wild rather than imprisoned light is the chief feature of this closing vision. Celestial and earthly physics form a potent blend of forces. The blood-red radiance of the setting moon pierces the widening fissure of the house and carries the eye upward in a scene that both foretells and inverts the serene spectacle of Earth's satellite illuminating the depths of the Norway maelstrom. The collapse of the House of Usher, too, is a shipwreck—a convulsion vaguely linked to a whirlwind of judgmental wrath but engineered by the last Usher heir, as he casts off the "old causeway" of thought and custom. Both a creative and a destructive flood break through the deceptively solid masonry of the mansion's facade, carrying Poe forward to the increasingly ambitious and elaborate vortices of his later fiction.

CHAPTER 5

The Infected World at Large

Figure 4   "The Island of the Fay" (engraved by John Sartain). *Graham's Magazine* 18 (June 1841). Courtesy of Hargrett Rare Book and Manuscript Library, University of Georgia Libraries.

Poe's interest in Roderick Usher's conception of universal sentience takes overt, scientific form two years later in "The Island of the Fay," a so-called plate article that he published in *Graham's Magazine* for June 1841, one month after "A Descent into the Maelström" and two months after "The Murders in the Rue Morgue" had appeared in the same periodical. "The Colloquy of Monos and Una" would follow its three predecessors into the pages of *Graham's* in August, presenting to the magazine's readers, over a period of five months, a compact anthology of Poe's artistic and philosophic interests. Nearly everything that he wrote both before and after this burst of activity in the spring and summer of 1841 could be classified under a heading identified with one of these four pieces—all pointing toward the linked interests in cosmology and consciousness that Poe systematically introduces, for the first time in his career, at the beginning of "The Island of the Fay."

Written to accompany the publication of a landscape engraving by John Sartain, this sketch would seem to be the least ambitious of the four contributions with which Poe marks the beginning of his editorship at *Graham's*. The text purports to describe a walk that its author takes through a peculiarly inward terrain of "writhing" rivers and "mountain locked within mountain" in search of the seclusion and happiness that he only experiences in contemplating natural scenery. During his ramble the narrator comes across the tiny island pictured in the Sartain engraving. Slight though it may seem, "The Island of the Fay" quickly proves to be an excursive encounter with speculative science and spiritual morbidity that begins with an extraordinary endorsement of loneliness:

> In truth, the man who would behold aright the glory of God upon earth must in solitude behold that glory. To me, at least, the presence—not of human life only—but of life in any other form than that of the green things which grow upon the soil and are voiceless—is a stain upon the landscape—is at war with the genius of the scene. I love, indeed, to regard the dark valleys, and the grey rocks, and the waters that silently smile, and the forests that sigh in uneasy slumbers, and the proud watchful mountains that look down upon all—I love to regard these as themselves but the colossal members of one vast animate and sentient whole—a whole whose form (that of the sphere) is the most perfect and the most inclusive; whose path is among associate planets; whose meek handmaiden is the moon; whose mediate sovereign is the sun; whose life is eternity; whose intelligence is that of a God; whose enjoyment is knowledge; whose destinies are lost in immensity; whose cognizance of ourselves is akin with our own cognizance of the animalculæ in crystal, or of those which infest the brain—a being which we, in consequence, regard as purely inanimate and material, much in the same manner as these animalculæ must thus regard us. (PT, 933–934)

This language briefly pictures the Earth as part of a vast organic design, comparable in scale to the vast atomic design of *Eureka*. Once purged of the stain of animal life, according to Poe's narrator, the landscape reveals itself as mysteriously "sentient," part of a godlike intelligence largely at peace with the universe but suffering from uneasy slumbers and an infestation of the mental parasite that is humanity.

These thoughts in themselves are not an original account of the troubled relationship between the Earth and its fallen human inhabitants. The excursionist of "The Island of the Fay," however, brings a scientific cast of mind to his misanthropic disgust, dismissing the "cant of the more ignorant of the priesthood" in favor of a naturalistic conception of the Divine. Telescopes and "mathematical investigations" draw his attention outward toward infinite space and grand scales of being, a universe filled with vast "cycles" of inconceivably massive stars that partly console him for the animal pettiness of the social world. But even his rejuvenating, lonely stroll ultimately produces an ambivalent picture of celestial movement that is the implicit subject of the Sartain engraving: an island in the middle of a woodland river with its small grove of shadowy trees eclipsing the setting sun. The appearance of "A Descent into the Maelström" in the preceding number of *Graham's Magazine* suggests that Poe is predisposed from the beginning of the sketch to view this little island as a miniature planet, exerting its gravitational influence over what soon proves to be a pastoral version of the old fisherman's orbital descent into the tidal vortex.

The analogy gradually takes hold as the narrator of "The Island of the Fay" slips into a doze in order to contemplate the woodland "phantasm" before him. The little river to which he first turns his attention seems drawn eastward, toward the viewer of the Sartain engraving, gradually disappearing into a forest "prison" behind him. To the west the landscape looks much different, though that is apparently the direction which the engraving itself partly conceals behind the island's dark silhouette. As Poe's narrator faces the setting sun, he discovers in his "dreamy vision" a magical cascade replenishing the valley from an unexpected source. Feeding this tiny stream, as it steadily disappears into the thirsty eastern shadow, is a flood of light that "poured down noiselessly and continuously into the valley, a rich, golden and crimson waterfall from the sun-set fountains of the sky" (PT, 936). To the mind's eye, at least, this fountain of color is part of an unbroken, and eerily silent fluid system. The verbal landscape—not the engraved one—constructs a surprisingly complete chromatic spectrum: passing from the golden and crimson mixtures of one extreme, through the verdant green of the forest, before disappearing into the encroaching darkness. This vivid ribbon seems to be unspooling before the narrator's eyes as he studies the small, circular island of the sketch's title, surrounded by a stream that resembles a flawless mirror.

The island itself replicates this larger chromatic contrast, as well as the blend of artificial and natural features that will take on such exaggerated scope in "The Domain of Arnheim." Its western end is a profusion of brilliantly colored flowers interspersed with trees that are covered in a "smooth, glossy, and particolored" bark, like the polished surface of marble columns. The butterflies whose "gentle sweepings" give the entire scene the appearance of movement are as varied and vivid as "tulips with wings." By contrast, the eastern end of the island is predictably funereal. The narrator imagines that the trees in that direction cast a malignant shade into the stream, "impregnating the depths of the element with darkness": "I fancied that each shadow, as the sun descended lower and lower, separated itself sullenly from the trunk that gave it birth, and thus became absorbed by the stream; while other shadows issued momently from the trees, taking the place of their predecessors entombed" (PT, 937). Under the spell of the scene, the narrator's half-shut eyes convert a piece of floating bark into a "fragile canoe" carrying what he imagines to be a lovely woman slowly around the little island, into and out of "the region of light," a last survivor from the "wreck of the race" of woodland fays.

Poe is reconstructing the image of the beautiful Marchesa di Mentoni from "The Assignation," poised above the corrupting waters of the Venetian canals. But he has also built a tiny model of the solar system, with the drifting "revolutions" of the Fay imitating those of the moon as it passes into and out of the rays of the sun, slowly orbiting the Earth. With the repeated circling of this minute canoe, the Fay's "elastic joy" gradually diminishes, her sorrows appear to increase, and the shadows acquire greater and greater force, until the vision completely disappears into "the ebony flood." The entire process purports to dramatize a displacement of old mythologies: the gradual encroachment of "dull realities" that the story's original epigraph—a reprinting of Poe's 1829 "Sonnet—To Science"—appears to lament:

> Science, true daughter of old Time thou art,
>   Who alterest all things with thy peering eyes!
> Why prey'st thou thus upon the poet's heart,
>   Vulture, whose wings are dull realities?
> How should he love thee, or how deem thee wise
>   Who wouldst not leave him, in his wandering,
> To seek for treasure in the jewelled skies,
>   Albeit he soared with an undaunted wing?
>   (PT, 933)

The narrator of "The Island of the Fay," however, effectively replies to this complaint on behalf of the scientific, rather than the poetic, wanderer. These pages introduce a final phase of the rudderless voyage that had engrossed Poe's attention since the beginning of his career, a journey through the universe of sentient matter that haunts Roderick Usher and that the tubercular visionary Vankirk will try to describe during the hypnotic, deathbed trance of "Mesmeric Revelation" three years later.

Only the delusions of human self-esteem—of what Vankirk will term "rudimentary life"—impede Poe's narrator from realizing a sublime scientific vision of soul's universal diffusion. On his long, meditative ramble in the mountains, before encountering the Fay's shadowy island, he indulges in the fantastic idea that the Earth, along with all other celestial bodies, has colossal powers of enjoyment that more than compensate for the loss of the mythic world which the speaker of Poe's sonnet seems to lament. Though the sketch employs a completely different figurative register, "The Island of the Fay" reports on an unexpectedly successful search "for treasure in the jeweled skies," a triumphant discovery, rather than a thwarted one, that the narrator readily superimposes on John Sartain's muted image.

The flaw in this expansive vision of life's endless concentric cycles, orbiting a "far-distant centre which is the Godhead," is the stain of animate life—the parasitic presence of men and animals that prevents consciousness from discerning its true nature. "The Colloquy of Monos and Una," the last in this series of early contributions to *Graham's Magazine*, exposes the consequences of this blindness and raises its cultural stakes from a simple incitement to melancholy to the level of a universal plague. The withering commentary on the human condition that Monos offers in Poe's long monologue presents modern industrial civilization as an epidemic, deforming "the fair face of nature" with a "loathsome disease":

> This the mass of mankind saw not, or, living lustily although unhappily, affected not to see. But, for myself, the Earth's records had taught me to look for widest ruin as the price of highest civilization. I had imbibed a prescience of our Fate from comparison of China the simple and enduring, with Assyria the architect, with Egypt the astrologer, with Nubia, more crafty than either, the turbulent mother of all Arts. In history of these regions I met with a ray from the Future. The individual artificialities of the three latter were local diseases of the Earth, and in their individual overthrows we had seen local remedies applied; but for the infected world at large I could anticipate no regeneration save in death. (PT, 452)

Monos himself dies before the collapse of the contaminated world that surrounds him. The bulk of the colloquy consists of his elaborate report on the eerie mental state that follows death, loosely derived from Mr. Lackobreath's visionary journey to the tomb in "Loss of Breath" but without the earlier tale's burlesque evasions. As his "intemporal soul" approaches "the threshold of temporal Eternity," Monos notices that his five earthly senses begin to fail, leaving behind only a vague "consciousness of entity" accompanied by a mysterious "sixth sense": "a mental pendulous pulsation . . . the moral embodiment of man's abstract idea of *Time*" (PT, 456). In this curious, metaphysical chrysalis, the colloquy ends.

Over the last major phase of his career, Poe repeatedly applies the local remedies of his fiction to the local diseases of the Earth, recognizing all the while the presence of comprehensive infections that defy art's regenerative powers. Convinced though he may be of the vitality of matter, the narrator of "The Island of the Fay" still surrenders to apocalyptic gloom as his sketch concludes. "Darkness fell over all things," he declares, as the Fay's "magical figure" disappears for the last time into "the region of the ebony flood." Like Monos, however, Poe himself has recourse to a sixth sense, an "abiding sentiment of duration" that converts the "corrosive hours" into allies rather than enemies. A miraculous latency—a state of waiting similar to the pervasive mental condition of Roderick Usher—brings many of Poe's most powerful late tales to a close. His plots find ways to synchronize themselves with time's omnipresent influence, to dramatize its role in the emergence of what the visionary seer in "Mesmeric Revelation" terms "ultimate life." His last major contribution to *Graham's Magazine*, "The Masque of the Red Death" in May 1842, is his most explicit variation on the theme of the infected Earth that haunts "The Island of the Fay." Beginning with "The Tell-Tale Heart" and "The Gold-Bug" in 1843 and ending with "Hop-Frog" in 1849, Poe continues to address, through a variety of memorable masques, the painful metamorphosis from rudimentary to complete experience.

*　*　*

The ominous clock that signals the end of Prince Prospero's masquerade ball with its twelve, melodramatic, midnight strokes ticks quietly beneath the surface of "The Masque of the Red Death" from the story's opening paragraph. Poe's narrator begins by describing the gruesome symptoms of a deadly plague that is ravaging the nameless principality where the tale's events are set: sharp pains, "sudden dizziness," and a "profuse bleeding at the pores" that stains the faces of the plague's victims with a "pest ban" of blood. Sympathy itself is a casualty of the epidemic, in part perhaps because the fatal course of infection is stunningly swift: "the whole seizure, progress, and termination of the disease," Poe's narrator remarks, "were the incidents of half an hour" (PT, 485). The Red Death literally overruns its victims, like a mysterious form of combustion. Between the publication of this brief tale and the terrible flames of "Hop-Frog" eight years later, Poe will embark on an extended exploration of the metaphorical possibilities of fire, along with its chief antagonist: the chill, fluid suppression of Montresor's vengeance in "The Cask of Amontillado."

The terse, clinical account with which "The Masque of the Red Death" begins is carefully phrased to link the stages of sickness with the stages of reading. The plague's pathology is composed of a sequence of "incidents" that have a recognizable narrative shape—the beginning, the middle, and the end of a carefully composed work of fiction. Poe gives the implicit analogy a gentle assist in his first two paragraphs by twice enclosing the "Red Death" in quotation marks, as if he were citing a title. His printed masque is itself a type of mortal seizure—a confrontation with the mix of physical and metaphysical dread that the prospect of an infected world inevitably entails. In the face of that prospect, Prince Prospero and his thousand companions—the "hale and light-hearted" knights and dames who fill his parodic ark—have sealed themselves away in a secluded abbey to pass the fury of the epidemic in safety, welding the abbey's iron gates shut with "furnaces and massy hammers" that seem particularly incongruous tools in the hands of Prospero's high-born courtiers.

Insulated by their prince's wealth, and indifferent to the suffering of the "external world," they seem attentive only to the dancers, buffoons, musicians and other "appliances of pleasure" (as the narrator puts it) provided for their diversion. By implication, perhaps, they are attentive to their own sexual potential as well. The clumsy nature of the narrator's euphemism is an index to the tale's sterile eroticism. Prospero's companions are more adept at shutting anatomical gates than at opening them. They are determined to close all avenues of "ingress or egress" from their isolated fortress—a surrogate for the hermetically sealed, but distinctly feverish, fortress of the flesh.

The international vogue for Fourierist communities had just begun to make an impact on American utopian thought as Poe described Prince Prospero's singular domestic program. It seems likely that he intended to ridicule the promiscuous reputation of communal experiments like Brook Farm when he designed "The Masque of the Red Death." But social satire is not the story's primary object. As quickly as he can, Poe's narrator turns away from the human participants in his tale—almost as quickly, in fact, as the abbey's self-indulgent occupants turn away from the fearful spectacle of the external world. What does intrigue the narrator is the elaborate setting that Prospero devises for his masked ball: its physical backdrop, its lighting, and its single conspicuous prop, the gigantic ebony clock that tolls the hours at the end of the "imperial suite" of seven, fancifully decorated rooms. The "assembly of phantasms" at the ball itself are simply the "moveable embellishments" of their location.

In conformity with his "love of the *bizarre*," Prospero's seven chambers are "irregularly disposed," configured as a zigzag line, rather than a stately vista, with "a sharp turn at every twenty or thirty yards, and at each turn a novel effect" (PT, 486). Each of the suite's rooms is decorated in a dominant color, enhanced by tinted Gothic windows in the side walls through which firelight streams from heavy tripod braziers in two halls that parallel the rooms. A "profusion of golden ornaments" fills each chamber, but no lamps or candelabra are present to provide interior light or to compete with the elaborate architectural appliance composed by the arrangement of the seven chambers themselves. The complete ensemble of the scene is a kind of verbal brazier: an incandescent vessel of different shapes, angles, and colors, intended to evoke the vitality of flame.

Poe's narrator is very specific about the chromatic sequence of the rooms:

> That at the eastern extremity was hung, for example, in blue—and vividly blue were its windows. The second chamber was purple in its ornaments and tapestries, and here the panes were purple. The third was green throughout, and so were the casements. The fourth was furnished and lighted with orange—the fifth with white—the sixth with violet. The seventh apartment was closely shrouded in black velvet tapestries that hung all over the ceiling and down the walls, falling in heavy folds upon a carpet of the same material and hue. But in this chamber only, the color of the windows failed to correspond with the decorations. The panes here were scarlet—a deep blood color . . . the effect of the fire-light that streamed upon the dark hangings through the blood-tinted panes, was ghastly in the extreme, and produced so wild a look on the countenances of those who entered, that there were few of the company bold enough to set foot within its precincts at all. (PT, 486)

At first the suite seems to echo the seven unique tones of the musical scale, but "disconcert" rather than harmony arises from its design whenever the gigantic ebony clock in the black apartment begins to strike. Confronted with this fatal sign of the "stricken" hour not even Prospero's orchestra can maintain its playing. The clock's note tolerates no competitor for human attention, much as the layout of the entire suite precludes a comprehensive survey of its extent.

Yet mixture is the implicit message of the colors that saturate the masque. The fiery rays from Prospero's braziers pick up tints from his Gothic windows as they pass into the suite's decorated interior. Purple, green, orange, and violet—the hues of the four central rooms—are all blended pigments, mixed on a painter's palette, for instance, in subtle gradations of intensity out of the three primary colors: red, yellow, and blue. These, in turn, are represented at either extreme of Prospero's architectural sequence: the blue room to the east and the blood-red windows of the black chamber to the west, with an enigmatic white room in the middle of the suite offering a neutral medium for the brazier's yellow flames.

Poe's optical interests in this tale are less arbitrary than they might seem. Goethe's *Theory of Colors*, a spirited challenge to the Newtonian physics of light, had been translated into English in 1840, nearly two years before "The Masque of the Red Death" appeared in *Graham's Magazine*. Unlike virtually every reputable scientist of the day, Goethe chose to analyze color as an attribute of matter rather than a component of light: an endlessly mutable wheel of six, rather than seven, essential hues, in a perpetual state of amalgamation and transmutation throughout the organic and inorganic worlds. Framed as a deliberate rejoinder to Newton's *Optics*, Goethe's book is based on painting, dyeing, metallurgy, physiology and associational psychology rather than on the cool abstractions of the prism. In his preface, Goethe disparages Newton's theories, comparing them to "an old castle" born out of the "youthful precipitation" of its creator but gradually adapted and refortified over the years by its scientific partisans, "in consequence of feuds and hostile demonstrations":

All damages, whether inflicted by the hand of the enemy or the power of time, were quickly made good. As occasion required, they deepened the moats, raised the walls, and took care there should be no lack of towers, battlements, and embrasures. . . . Its great duration, its costly construction, are still constantly spoken of. Pilgrims wend their way to it; hasty sketches of it are shown in all schools, and it is thus recommended to the reverence of susceptible youth. Meanwhile, the building itself is already abandoned; its only inmates are a few invalids, who in simple seriousness imagine that they are prepared for war.

War is what Goethe proposes to bring to this bastion of English physics, "to dismantle it from gable and roof downwards; that the sun may at last shine into the old nest of rats and owls." Prospero's abbey is a similar kind of bastion: a defensive expedient aimed at isolating one kind of blood from another, a barrier to life's ubiquitous mixtures. The vividly painted setting of his climactic masque, however, is a mockery of separation. Its rooms have already been invaded long before the appearance of the spectral "mummer" who brings the entertainment to a close.

Taken as a whole, Prospero's rich interiors ultimately reflect a careful adaptation to the seven sensory orifices of the human head: the avenues of ingress and egress through which consciousness engages with the external world, assembling the intellect's profusion of "golden ornaments." As the story unfolds, Poe carefully aligns the reader's senses with the design of the rooms in order to stress this process of inner and outer exchange, sometimes through direct appeals to sight and hearing, sometimes by the puns on "taste" and "touch" with which the narrator addresses the vexed question of Prospero's peculiar madness: the degree to which he is or is not mentally "touched." Smell alone seems absent from the masque's design, until the arrival of the Red Death introduces the reign of "Darkness and Decay," entities that suggest a gruesome organic progression of color from the vivid pest ban of blood at the beginning of the story through the desiccated blackness of a mummy at its end. Like the complete dissolution of the sensory architecture that Monos experiences in the limitless duration of the grave, Prospero's masque is a remorseless pageant of extinction.

But Monos' transformation is implicitly regenerative, a stage in his cognitive liberation. There is little sign in "The Masque of the Red Death" that time flies to any other end than absolute annihilation. Indeed, the story closes on a note of biblical finality that is unusual in Poe's work. The grim image of the fatal plague enters Prospero's suite "like a thief in the night," a traditional metaphor for the Second Coming, striking down "the revellers in the blood-bedewed halls of their revel." The abbey's doomed inhabitants lie frozen in various postures of despair like the contorted human casts at Pompeii: victims whose bodies disintegrated in volcanic fire, leaving behind only the spatial shadows of their brief agony. It is possible, too, that Poe hopes this picture will evoke the poignant visual "shadows" of the daguerreotype as well. The carefully draped black chamber at the end of Prince Prospero's suite, with its terrifying red light, bears a suggestive resemblance to a darkroom—another variety of death chamber, in Poe's day, since the metal daguerreotype plate was originally sensitized with iodine vapor and developed with mercury fumes, poisonous processes that took place inside special boxes designed to minimize the daguerreotypist's potentially fatal exposure.

The story's final sentences, however, address neither chemical poisons nor the biological toxins of disease. They turn away from the spectacle of "widest ruin" that Monos had detected in the history of civilization, and that the residents of Prospero's abbey refuge had originally hoped to escape, focusing instead on the rituals of a strange benediction:

> And now was acknowledged the presence of the Red Death. He had come like a thief in the night. And one by one dropped the revellers in the blood-bedewed halls of their revel, and died each in the despairing posture of his fall. And the life of the ebony clock went out with that of the last of the gay. And the flames of the tripods expired. And Darkness and Decay and the Red Death held illimitable dominion over all. (PT, 490)

The Red Death remains a lingering "presence" in this closing scene: a vivid coal amid the ashes. The dancers' frantic animation during the height of Prospero's ball invites comparison both to the writhing hunger of the conqueror worm in Ligeia's eerie poem and to the desperation of its human food, as if Poe meant to dramatize an attempt on the part of the lower life to clothe itself in the brilliant colors of its transcendent, adult form without enduring the pupa's invisible stage of change. The appearance of the Red Death puts an end to this delusive display, but the "dominion" that it initiates has emblematic scope: an "illimitable" condition suggesting timeless powers of dormancy or readiness as well as closure. Each masquer preserves "the despairing posture of his fall" precisely as individual letters might be fixed on a page, with the rapid flourish of a steel pen freshly dipped in ink, to await a future restoration of light and a future reading.

* * *

Over the months that Poe remains in Philadelphia after leaving *Graham's Magazine* in the spring of 1842, disease steadily makes its way into the fortress of consciousness that his tales repeatedly depict, dramatizing both the efficacy and the catastrophic failure of the mind's recuperative powers. For reasons that are both personal and cultural, his most ambitious stories from this period become subtle therapeutic studies in the self-healing and the self-destructive soul. To meet his living expenses and provide at least some minimal care for his wife during this period, Poe scattered work through a hodge-podge of magazines and gift annuals: *The Extra Sun*, Snowden's *Ladies' Companion*, the Boston *Pioneer*, the *Columbian Magazine*, *The Opal: A Pure Gift for the Holy Days*, *Godey's Lady's Book*, the *United States Saturday Post*. The Philadelphia *Saturday Courier*, where "Metzengerstein" had appeared in 1832, took one story. The Philadelphia *Dollar Newspaper* took three, including "The Gold-Bug," for which Poe received the windfall of a one-hundred dollar prize, one tenth of the annual salary that Rufus Griswold was offered when he succeeded Poe as the editor at *Graham's*.

Through various intermediaries, Poe hoped to get a job from the Tyler administration in the Philadelphia custom house, but a drunken binge during a visit to Washington, DC, in March 1843 may have ruined his chances. He tried to interest his affluent acquaintances and correspondents in helping him found his own magazine. He drew up a title page for an ambitious collection of stories that no publisher appeared interested in taking. One pamphlet of a projected series called *The Prose Romances of Edgar A. Poe* did appear in 1843, but the "Uniform Serial Edition" that Poe envisioned never materialized. After the comparative stability of his editorial work, Poe must have grown increasingly frantic as this hand-to-mouth existence fueled his anxieties. It became increasingly clear, too, during this period that Virginia Poe was doomed. "Our rudimental body," Vankirk would observe in "Mesmeric Revelation," is a cage of crude organs from which the higher being strives to escape. After the winter and spring of 1842, Poe's domestic life dramatized for him the anguish of this cage.

The extraordinary crescendo that brings to a close the brief confession of "The Tell-Tale Heart" draws together much of this emotional and artistic background. On first leaving *Graham's Magazine*, Poe threw himself into "The Mystery of Marie Rogêt," hoping to tap a vein of popular interest in a contemporary murder investigation. In the course of that story, Auguste Dupin reflects on the changes that occur in the psychological state of a killer who finds himself appalled by the body of his victim and overwhelmed by the magnitude of his crime: "The fury of his passion is over," Dupin begins, "and there is abundant room in his heart for the natural awe of the deed" (PT, 546). This passing observation becomes the core of "The Tell-Tale Heart," a story that appears, at first, to make Dupin's analysis the subject of a murderer's monologue. A number of the story's details, however, detach it from the journalistic background of Auguste Dupin's world and link it to the fabulous one of "The Masque of the Red Death."

A sequence of nights, rather than a sequence of rooms, gives scenic structure to "The Tell-Tale Heart." On seven successive midnights, the story's narrator repeats the same preliminary steps: stealthily opening the bedroom door of the old man who shares his house, slowly putting his head through the opening and shining a thin ray of light from a dark lantern directly upon the old man's "vulture eye," the physical feature that seems to provoke the narrator's inexplicable murderous feelings, except when it is closed in sleep. This repetitive, slow-motion process calls to mind the movement of carved figurines on an elaborate clock and parallels the sequence of hours that mark the progressive stages of Prince Prospero's fatal ball. At the same time, the narrator's ritualistic introduction of light into darkness, across the seven nights of the week, is a macabre parody of Genesis: an act of anticipatory revenge against the symbol of a dictatorial, paternal omniscience.

Each night, the narrator announces, "it was impossible to do the work," to kill the unoffending old man while his eyes were closed. When on the eighth night a slight noise awakens his victim, the narrator's fury breaks loose, triggered by the apparently diseased appearance of the eye itself—"a dull blue, with a hideous veil over it that chilled the very marrow in my bones." The ray of light from his lantern bridges the darkness of the room with uncanny precision: falling on this tiny planetary shape, much as an astronomer might calculate the exact location of an invisible object in the night sky before training his telescope on the space that he expects it to occupy. The sound of the old man's terrified heartbeat only intensifies the narrator's rage, "as the beating of a drum stimulates the soldier into courage (PT, 557). These initial passages of the story describe what amounts to a meticulous process of self-ignition, as the narrator organizes his passions for an assault on the inert aqueous medium of the old man's occluded sight.

After the murder, he dismembers and conceals the body. All these events the narrator outlines for the benefit of an unnamed listener to whom the story is directed, the first of two audiences that he is striving to convince of his sanity:

> If still you think me mad, you will think so no longer when I describe the wise precautions I took for the concealment of the body. The night

waned, and I worked hastily, but in silence. First of all I dismembered the corpse. I cut off the head and the arms and the legs.

I then took up three planks from the flooring of the chamber, and deposited all between the scantlings. I then replaced the boards so cleverly, so cunningly, that no human eye—not even *his*—could have detected any thing wrong. There was nothing to wash out—no stain of any kind—no blood-spot whatever. I had been too wary for that. A tub had caught all—ha! ha! (PT, 558)

"The Tell-Tale Heart" is in fact a tale of a tub, a miniaturized version of the cultural landscape that Jonathan Swift had surveyed, a century earlier, when he cast the history of the Protestant Reformation as a fable of madness, initiated when a dying father bequeaths three symbolic coats standing for the great divisions of the Christian religion as legacies to his three sons and charges his heirs to live happily together in one house. Like Swift's book, "The Tell-Tale Heart," too, begins by introducing an enigmatic old man whose accumulations of wisdom (in Poe's story) take the form of golden "treasures" and an eye turned figuratively inward by the film of age and experience. These obvious surrogates for a fabulous mental estate under the care of a blind guardian, coupled with the narrator's instinctive hostility to "vision," suggests Poe's adaptation of Swift's parable to depict the imagination's furious rebellion against the tyranny of reason and memory.

Imagination, Swift observes in *A Tale of a Tub*, is the inexhaustible womb of things, while memory is their grave. The second is the storehouse of experience and reason, while the first is the birthplace of fiction and of happiness, an enviable state of mind that Swift facetiously defines as the "perpetual possession of being well deceived." At first the narrator of "The Tell-Tale Heart" is, in fact, well deceived by his criminal tactics. His own "loud yell" of rage and the old man's single cry of fear are (he believes) the only hints to the outside world that the house of consciousness has changed masters. But when three "suave" officers of the police appear at his door (descendants of the three sons in Swift's story), he cannot resist the temptation to perform: to dramatize the imagination's powers of self expression and self command by leading his visitors on a tour of the house, pointing out the undisturbed possessions of his predecessor, and seating himself over the spot where he had hidden his victim's remains "in the wild audacity of my perfect triumph" (PT, 559).

His bland, authoritative audience, however, simply sat and "chatted of familiar things," oblivious to the magnitude of the narrator's accomplishment. No trace of inner intensity appears to affect them, and in a desperate effort to drown out, or to voice, the dark energies of his mental life, the narrator grows increasingly fervent. The insistent heart beat that fills his ears drives him to dramatic extremes:

> No doubt I now grew *very* pale;—but I talked more fluently, and with a heightened voice. Yet the sound increased—and what could I do? It was *a low, dull, quick sound—much such a sound as a watch makes when enveloped in cotton.* I gasped for breath—and yet the officers heard it not. I talked more quickly—more vehemently; but the noise steadily increased. I arose and argued about trifles, in a high key and with violent gesticulations; but the noise steadily increased. Why *would* they not be gone? I paced the floor to and fro with heavy strides, as if excited to fury by the observations of the men—but the noise steadily increased. Oh God! What *could* I do? I foamed—I raved—I swore! I swung the chair upon which I had been sitting, and grated it upon the boards, but the noise arose over all and continually increased. It grew louder—louder—*louder*! And still the men chatted pleasantly, and smiled. (PT, 559)

Poe calibrates this splendid verbal escalation with great care. At first the narrator addresses his visitors "cheerily" as he leads them through the house, "singularly at ease" in his dramatic mastery. But this serene confidence is short lived. As his performance grows increasingly extreme, he becomes an extension of his creator: an artist and a critic who responds to an uncomprehending or indifferent public with a crescendo of outlandish expressive tactics, desperate efforts to penetrate sensibilities that seem far more thickly insulated than one's own. The tale ends with a second, spectacular ignition as the narrator confesses his crime.

For Poe the unshackled imagination is above all a "teller," one who listens to otherwise undetectable messages from remote regions of space or consciousness and strives to convey their meaning to the inhabitants of the rudimental world: "True!—nervous—very, very dreadfully nervous I had been and am," the narrator of "The Tell-Tale Heart" begins, "but why *will* you say that I am mad":

> The disease had sharpened my senses—not destroyed—not dulled them. Above all was the sense of hearing acute. I heard all things in the heaven and in the earth. I heard many things in hell. How, then, am I mad? Hearken! and observe how healthily—how calmly I can tell you the whole story. (PT, 555)

The narrator of "The Masque of the Red Death" makes a similar claim on our attention, as if acute infection and acute perception were necessary complements of one another. "It was a voluptuous scene, that masquerade, "he begins: "But first let me tell of the rooms in which it was held" (PT, 485). After the summer of 1841, the impetus to "tell," to count and then to recount the impact of momentous insight, acquires particular urgency in Poe's fiction. It takes its most ambitious form in what would prove to be the most significant commercial success of his career. William Legrand summons the narrator of "The Gold-Bug" back to his woodland hut with an appeal that is nearly identical to the mad confession of the narrator of "The Tell-Tale Heart": "Since I saw you I have had great cause for anxiety," Legrand writes his Charleston friend in the early stages of Poe's famous story: "I have something to tell you, yet scarcely know how to tell it, or whether I should tell it at all" (PT, 566). When Emily Dickinson echoes this strange remark in the opening line of an early poem—"I never told the buried gold"—she is responding to the prominence of telling rather than treasure in the consciousness of the story's most fascinating character.

The theme of buried riches is an extraordinarily flexible one in "The Gold-Bug," a form of irregular inheritance capable of adaptation to a variety of intangible as well as tangible rewards. But Legrand's curious anxiety is of central interest to Poe and to his reader long before any actual digging takes place. It echoes the struggle between nervousness and calm that marks the opening of "The Tell-Tale Heart" and points toward an inner process of excavation—a kind of mining—unrelated to the precious contents of a pirate chest. By the end of "The Gold-Bug" Legrand makes what appears to be a full disclosure of his secret, but initially at least Poe seems to share Legrand's ambivalence. He arranges the story's plot around a sequence of distinct "tellings," explanatory acts that center on the recovery of a fabulous treasure but end with an enigmatic and elliptical question that raises once more the issue of narrative, rather than material, burdens. In the last words that Legrand addresses to his anonymous Charleston friend, he reintroduces the anxieties of his original summons: "Who shall tell?" he asks, as he considers the mysterious fate of the two men whose skeletons lay in a jumbled mass just above the accumulated gold and jewels that they had helped to bury.

From a practical standpoint, the initial answer to this question is the convivial Charleston gentleman who has accidentally "contracted an intimacy" with William Legrand, the impoverished descendent of "ancient" wealth now living in the dense, myrtle groves of Sullivan's Island, a few miles from the city. This unnamed intermediary, much like Auguste Dupin's faithful Paris companion, sets out to describe the strange events that flowed from a casual visit to his misanthropic friend on a chilly October day. Only the garrison at Fort Moultrie and the summer fugitives "from Charleston dust and fever" impinge on Legrand's solitude, though at long intervals the story's narrator makes unannounced visits to his isolated hut, out of the vague "interest and esteem" that Legrand's character has aroused. Once the story's events get underway, a second teller emerges, a manumitted slave, who at two different points in the plot is able to garble, in a delightfully manipulative way, the information that his two white companions try to extract from him.

Legrand himself is the third and most crucial teller, one with "unusual powers of mind," who deliberately chooses two strikingly different methods for reporting a remarkable discovery and explaining its consequences: one involving a pantomime of madness, in order to punish the story's narrator for his private doubts concerning Legrand's sanity, and the other an orderly reconstruction of the deductive processes on which the whole plot turns. Like the narrator of "The Tell-Tale Heart," Legrand suffers under the suspicion of lunacy. The freed slave who shares his exile is in fact a personal "keeper" more than a servant, charged with the discipline as well as the comfort of his irascible patient. For these reasons, Legrand finds himself confronted with an uncomprehending audience when the time finally arrives to unfold the story's secrets. His Charleston friend is especially obtuse when it comes to appreciating even the simplest features of Captain Kidd's "enigma," the coded message that ultimately discloses the location of his hoard.

Making generous allowance for his friend's limitations, Legrand patiently explains how he deftly converts a century-old cipher into a list of instructions guiding its reader to what Legrand calls, at first, a "deposit of value," one of the more peculiar euphemisms in a story that ultimately concerns itself with indexes rather than explanations: with meaningful verbal gestures rather than with meaning itself. By the time that Legrand alludes to this "deposit," however, it is clear that he is hunting pirate loot. Why should such an inherently appealing tale of splendid recovery be so difficult to tell? What is the elusive "something" that Legrand hints at in his letter which calls for such circumspect explanation? The story's narrator describes his friend as a man "infected with misanthropy, and subject to perverse moods of alternate enthusiasm and melancholy," but for a misanthrope Legrand seems oddly hospitable to the occasional drop-in guest, and his chief mood seems to be one of uncertainty regarding his ability to make clear his story's elaborate sequence of "indices," of which "gold" is only one of several referential terms.

Through the second half of the tale, Legrand carefully recounts the steps that slowly led him to the location of Captain Kidd's treasure chest. Beginning with a scrap of old parchment, a faint image of a skull, and an intuitive sense of hidden possibilities, he gradually teases out the secret significance in the odd array of typographic characters that form the text of Kidd's encrypted message. With comparative ease, Legrand breaks the code, interprets its telegraphic instructions, and fits them neatly to the landscape immediately adjacent to Sullivan's Island, a nearly impenetrable tangle of brambles that he and his companions are ultimately forced to cut their way through with a scythe. A great deal of good luck is involved in this wonderful discovery. To begin with there is the "rare and happy accident" of chilly October weather and a blazing fire on the evening that the tale's events begin, conditions that combine with Legrand's unusually affectionate dog to induce the accidental appearance of Kidd's invisible ink. Rarer still is the coincidence that leads Legrand's black servant, Jupiter, to wrap a remarkable beetle specimen in a handy piece of old parchment half-buried in sand, or the chance encounter with an officer at nearby Fort Moultrie, to whom Legrand briefly loans the beetle while absent-mindedly keeping the parchment scrap in which he had carried it.

Once Kidd's cryptic message is deciphered, Legrand is fortunate enough to meet with an old slave woman on a mainland plantation who is able to interpret an obscure place name in the pirate's instructions and leads Legrand to the high rock from which he is able to discern a great tulip tree with a bleached skull carefully positioned among its branches. This "insulated and artificial" vantage point, coupled with meticulous coded instructions for leveling a telescope, bring the skull into view. This object is the last of Kidd's long series of signposts, miraculously visible despite more than a century of presumptive growth in the surrounding vegetation, a natural measure of change responsible for the thick brambles through which the treasure-seekers must cut their way but which seems to have left the careful alignment of tree and rock unchanged. Selected features of Poe's fictional landscape are impervious to naturalistic time.

The outcome of this nearly magical blend of ingenuity, precision, and chance is a deeply satisfying inventory of Captain Kidd's treasure, another elaborate "telling" that is itself a suggestive compound of layered messages. The various objects in the chest appear to have been "heaped in promiscuously," Poe's narrator notes, not unlike the apparent promiscuity characterizing the mix of symbols and numbers in Kidd's original code. But this lucrative material disorder immediately invites a careful sorting. The numerous coins that Legrand and his companions find are all "gold of antique date and of great variety," a heterogeneous collection which they attempt to assess by appealing to "the tables of the period," converting the jumble of French, German, Spanish, and English coinage before them to a common scale of contemporary value. These monetary tables too are a concise index of information, like the tables that Legrand draws up for himself as he sorts through Kidd's cipher, all of which seem to be projected and magnified in the great natural "table" of land on which Legrand and his companions describe various lines and circles as they follow Kidd's meticulous geometric directions for determining where to dig.

This effort to affix value is at least partly thwarted by some enigmatic "counters" among Kidd's coins: metal blanks "of which we had never seen specimens before" (PT, 579). Like beetles, coins have a collector's taxonomy that links them, however loosely, to the richly minted world of living things. An unmarked counter is a blank page that no accidental exposure to heat will magically coax into revealing the hidden indices of its worth. Other than its shape, its weight, and its color, it offers little for the classifying intelligence to grasp. Some of the most remarkable coins in the collection—"several very large and heavy" specimens, not unlike Legrand's unusually dense bug—are so defaced that no readable inscriptions remain on their surfaces. They are messages that even the most exemplary patience and powers of linguistic analysis will not be able to decipher. "There was no American money," the narrator tersely notes; Kidd's coinage is uniformly old.

A great number of loose jewels are scattered in the treasure chest, deliberately separated from their metal settings, all of which "appeared to have been beaten up with hammers, as if to prevent identification." The pirates prudently sought to accelerate the natural processes of wear that had already so effectively obliterated the identifying marks on the oldest coins. But Poe's narrator carefully groups and tallies each class of gems. They are counters of a kind in which any lover of earthly treasure and beauty is bound to take considerable interest: a hundred and ten diamonds, three hundred and ten emeralds, eighteen rubies, twenty-one sapphires, and a single opal that suggests a mineral equivalent for Jupiter's dark but singularly luminous presence among the story's characters. Unlike minted metal, gems have timeless value, resembling that of the emblematic diamond glittering beneath the filthy cloak of the Man of the Crowd. "The Gold-Bug" replicates and multiplies the iconic objects from the earlier story: pirate violence extends the implications of the old urban wanderer's dagger; a chest of jewels springs from a single evocative stone. The "massive finger and ear rings" that the treasure chest contains resemble golden shackles for the senses, far too heavy for the purposes of human ornament. The dazzling gold-bug itself, as Jupiter threads it through the eye socket of the skull and drops it through the limbs of the tulip tree, suggests an inert substitute for living vision—a delusion rather than a fabulous emblem of good fortune. Gold is less meaningful in itself than it is suggestive as an index of consciousness: an emblem for knowledge of a particularly momentous kind that is buried within the speaker or the self. The "golden treasures" of the pitiable old man who is brutally dismembered in "The Tell-Tale Heart" play the same figurative role, as does the profusion of golden ornaments in Prince Prospero's eerie rooms. Legrand's mind is the site for this interior treasure hunt in "The Gold-Bug," a process that replaces acts of dismemberment with those of remembrance: a painstaking recreation of links and connections, the assembly of "a great chain" (as Legrand calls it) beginning with a few, tentative mental steps and ending with Legrand's prospective reinstatement in what he calls his "family possessions."

Legrand describes the first stages of this complex recovery with some care. He is on the point of destroying, in a fit of frustration, his drawing of the exotic insect that he and Jupiter had captured when he glances at the scrap of dirty parchment in his hand and notices "the figure of a death's head" that had thrown the story's narrator into innocent confusion. What follows is a more subtle kindling process than the one that had exposed Captain Kidd's invisible script, an introduction of heat and light that are the ingredients of Legrand's own heightened powers of awareness:

> For a moment I was too much amazed to think with accuracy. I knew that my design was very different in detail from this—although there was a certain similarity in general outline. Presently I took a candle, and seating myself at the other end of the room, proceeded to scrutinize the parchment more closely. Upon turning it over, I saw my own sketch upon the reverse, just as I had made it. My first idea, now, was mere surprise at the really remarkable similarity of outline—at the singular coincidence involved in the fact, that unknown to me, there should have been a skull upon the other side of the parchment, immediately beneath my figure of the *scarabæus*, and that this skull, not only in outline, but in size, should so closely resemble my drawing...I began distinctly, positively, to remember that there had been no drawing on the parchment when I made my sketch of the *scarabæus*. I became perfectly certain of

this; for I recollected turning up first one side and then the other, in search of the cleanest spot. Had the skull been then there, of course I could not have failed to notice it. Here was indeed a mystery which I felt it impossible to explain; but, even at that early moment, there seemed to glimmer, faintly within the most remote and secret chambers of my intellect, a glow-worm-like conception of that truth which last night's adventure brought to so magnificent a demonstration. I arose at once, and putting the parchment securely away, dismissed all farther reflection until I should be alone. (PT, 581–582)

Legrand is startled and puzzled by a remarkable graphic coincidence: not simply the presence of two sketches on the parchment scrap, but their perfect conformity in size and their exact superimposition on opposite sides of the sheet. In drawing the bug, he has created a visual equivalent of the bivalves that he also collects as he combs the beaches of Sullivan's Island, with a Death's Head forming one half of the "shell" and the outline of the *scarabæus* the other.

The matched images in Legrand's hand resemble a kind of oyster, enclosing "a glow-worm-like conception" that will mature into a magnificent pearl, but the faculty that ultimately produces Legrand's pearl out of this conceptual seed is memory. This first phase of his mental awakening is the prelude to several acts of recollection that he carefully recreates for the benefit of the story's narrator. To begin with the fragility of memory is responsible for the existence of Kidd's original, clumsily coded "memorandum" in the first place. Memory's tenacity is responsible for its triumphant interpretation—not Legrand's mental tenacity alone, but also that of the old slave woman on Bessop's plantation who is able to recall, from "time out of mind," the location of "Bessop's Castle," site of the "Devil's seat" in Kidd's message. Jupiter's memory too is critical. He cannot be relied on for the sort of trivial knowledge that distinguishes his right hand from his left, but he possesses a much more vital resource than this, a fruit of long-stored experience. "Yes, massa," Jupiter answers when Legrand asks him if he thinks that he can climb the magnificent tulip tree that holds the treasure's key: "Jup climb any tree he ebber see in he life" (PT, 570).

The tree itself is a blend of incompatible indices: part natural and part artificial, a living thing and a memorial column like Baltimore's Washington monument, homage to yet another American forester:

In youth, the tulip-tree, or *Liriodendron Tulipiferum*, the most magnificent of American foresters, has a trunk peculiarly smooth, and often rises to a great height without lateral branches; but, in its riper age, the bark becomes gnarled and uneven, while many short limbs make their appearance on the stem. Thus the difficulty of ascension, in the present case, lay more in semblance than in reality. Embracing the huge cylinder, as closely as possible, with his arms and knees, seizing with his hands some projections, and resting his naked toes upon others, Jupiter, after one or two narrow escapes from falling, at length wriggled himself into the first great fork, and seemed to consider the whole business as virtually accomplished. The *risk* of the achievement was, in fact, now over, although the climber was some sixty or seventy feet from the ground. (PT, 571)

Jupiter's achievement, in fact, never loses its element of risk. His cautious but ultimately successful act of "ascension" echoes Legrand's progress at decoding Kidd's message—a business that Legrand too regards as virtually accomplished once its characters become visible. Like his agile servant, he can solve any cipher he ever saw.

Kidd's treasure itself is a figure of human memory—half crippled by time and by the determination of the pirates to break apart the metal matrices that might identify the stolen gems. But some inscriptions on the old coins remain readable. Some of the heavy crucifixes are intact. Few of the nearly two hundred gold watches that the narrator counts still work, "but all were richly jewelled and in cases of great worth," enticements to and symbols of "keeping." Among the miscellaneous articles heaped in the chest, the narrator singles out two "exquisitely embossed" sword handles without their menacing blades and "a prodigious golden punch-bowl." The sword handles imply yet another variation on the old romance emblem from "The Man of the Crowd": a material embodiment of the distinction between imperishable and perishable states, the aptitude to make and the instinct to destroy. The punch bowl suggests the famous incitement to remembrance that begins Ecclesiastes XII, where the golden bowl is a figure for grateful recollection. Jupiter, at least, is moved to gratitude as he plunges his arms into Captain Kidd's golden bath and pronounces a heartfelt apology to the gold bug whose influence he had maligned through most of the story. Legrand himself is momentarily "stupified" by the spectacle.

By far the most shallow response to the great discovery is the narrator's officious concern with "the expediency of removing the treasure": "It was growing late, and it behooved us to make exertion, that we might get everything housed before daylight" (PT, 579). These are the sentiments of a pirate or a banker, a "teller" capable of only the most rudimentary forms of counting. But Legrand's initial, cryptic letter of invitation suggests that other sorts of telling are far more critical to the outcome of his story—a narrative of integration and recovery that points to immaterial forms of wealth. The extraordinary weight of Captain Kidd's gold, in its densely mineralized chest, is an inverse index of the treasure's actual value as a catalyst for Legrand's latent mental powers and his repossession of the buried legacy of consciousness.

* * *

Within a year of publishing "The Gold-Bug," Poe attempts much less tangible forms of repossession in "Mesmeric Revelation." This story falls in the midst of an unusually fertile period of his career, appearing in the August 1844 *Columbian Magazine*, roughly halfway between Poe's move to New York the previous spring and the appearance of "The Raven" in the New York *Evening Mirror* in January 1845. It purports to record an interview between its author, who goes by the initial "P," and a Mr. Vankirk, one of the author's favorite mesmeric subjects who happens also to be dying of consumption. In what prove to be his final moments of life, Vankirk submits to being mesmerized in the hope that P. will be able to elicit from him some convincing evidence for the immortality of the soul. The proofs of logic and philosophy, Vankirk insists, "take no hold upon the mind." But in a state of "mesmeric exaltation" a different form of reason holds sway, one that might well produce a revolutionary set of answers from the mesmerized consciousness, in response to the proper "catechism."

What Vankirk wishes to become is an inspired teller of truths that he recognizes are unusually "difficult to tell," even after the impeding influence of the ordinary sense organs has been put to sleep. Like Legrand with his "glow-worm-like conception" of hidden significance in Kidd's cipher, Vankirk is visited with what he calls "psychal impressions" hinting at revelations inaccessible to the ordinary wakeful mind: disclosures that he hopes may produce a complete conviction of the soul's immortality. Once P. succeeds in placing him in a sufficiently deep trance, however, Vankirk begins to outline a theory of God's unparticled materiality that apparently has very little to do with his personal anxieties. Like many of Poe's fables of "telling," this one too overflows its narrative occasion, once the initial barriers to disclosure break down. It is not Vankirk's troubled spirit but the narrator's blindness that finally requires the medicinal revelations of fiction.

At first, P. has some difficulty following the thread of his mesmeric subject's thoughts. How can matter exist without particles? "Is there nothing of irreverence," he wonders, in Vankirk's extraordinary claim that God and matter are one in the same? The answers to these objections carry an implicit political undertone that Charles Baudelaire must have found especially intriguing when he chose this story to be the first of his translations of Poe's work, during the tumultuous European spring and summer of 1848. "Destroy the idea of the atomic constitution," Vankirk explains in answer to P's anxious question, and "mass inevitably glides into what we conceive of spirit" (PT, 721). The revolutionary fervor of Vankirk's words invites cultural applications that alarm the story's narrator and entice its translator, though the mesmerized visionary himself is largely indifferent to both responses. Motion and thought will exchange places in the new cognitive hierarchy that Vankirk describes, replacing the old aristocracy of intellect. The motion of unparticled matter, he insists, "not only permeates all things but impels all things—and thus *is* all things within itself. This matter is God. What men attempt to embody in the word 'thought,' is this matter in motion" (PT, 720).

It follows, Vankirk continues, that matter is as worthy of reverence as mind, and that motion is the progenitor of thinking rather than the other way around. In the last phase of his trance, he shifts from comparatively abstract, if metaphorically suggestive, considerations of space and mass to a discussion of man's two bodies, "the rudimental and the complete; corresponding with the two conditions of the worm and the butterfly":

> What we call "death," [Vankirk explains] is but the painful metamorphosis. Our present incarnation is progressive, preparatory, temporary. Our future is perfected, ultimate, immortal. The ultimate life is the full design.
>
> *P.* But of the worm's metamorphosis we are palpably cognizant.
>
> *V. We*, certainly—but not the worm. The matter of which our rudimental body is composed, is within the ken of the organs of that body; or, more distinctly, our rudimental organs are adapted to the matter of which is formed the rudimental body; but not to that of which the ultimate is composed. The ultimate body thus escapes our rudimental senses, and we perceive only the shell which falls, in decaying, from the inner form; not that inner form itself; but this inner form, as well as the shell, is appreciable by those who have already acquired the ultimate life. (PT, 723–724)

Many of the original readers of "Mesmeric Revelation" recognized in these observations precisely the kind of spiritual reassurance that mesmerism strove to provide its nineteenth-century devotees: a pseudoscientific confirmation of conventional beliefs regarding the relationship between the body and the soul, as well as tactical access to an omnipresent spirit realm. Poe's mimicry was so perfect that a number of editors who reprinted the tale took it for a genuine interview rather than a fiction, a conclusion that Poe encourages by having Vankirk confirm the most familiar religious aphorism of the day: "The pain of the primitive life of Earth," he declares, "is the sole basis of the bliss of the ultimate life in Heaven" (PT, 726). "No cross, no crown," is the form that this pious adage takes in what Barton St. Armand terms the Sentimental Love Religion of Victorian culture. Poe never wrote a more conventional sentence.

"Unorganized life" is the term that Vankirk uses to describe the liberated consciousness after it escapes the cage of the flesh: a state of being completely free of the idiosyncratic physical "organs" that sustain the human worm. Moreover, he continues, following Roderick Usher's speculative journey through the Kingdom of Inorganization, all matter throughout the Universe is infused with "rudimental, thinking creatures" equally engaged with man in the same metamorphic journey toward a condition of bodiless movement, an incorporeal vibration that "swallows up the star-shadows" (PT, 725). Space is the "truest substantiality," Vankirk suggests in what are nearly his last words. Emptiness is full. This rarified elaboration on the cosmology of "The Island of the Fay" is more a treatise than a story. Vankirk and P. are locked in a static dialogue, rich with metaphysical suggestion but almost completely lacking in narrative energy—a contrast that corresponds very closely to the distinction that Vankirk draws, at one point, between the "negative happiness" of inorganic life and the "positive pain" experienced by organic beings. "Law inviolate," Vankirk suggests, results in complete contentment, a condition of changeless "right." By contrast, "Law violate," a network of impediments and wrongs, is the necessary dramatic forerunner of the ultimate, perfected life.

Within a month of the publication of "Mesmeric Revelation," Poe lends these abstract distinctions concrete form in one of his most celebrated tales. "The Purloined Letter" offers a remarkable dramatic complement to Vankirk's reflections: a fable depicting the predicament of beings immersed in the "law violate" and utterly blind to its metamorphic possibilities. Auguste Dupin's Paris is an ideal stage for a final effort at the fictional transformation of sordid materials into sublime ones: of coarse matter into incorporeal bliss. The last Dupin mystery appears in September 1844 as part of a commemorative holiday annual titled *The Gift: A Christmas, New Year, and Birthday Present* only a few weeks after "Mesmeric Revelation" had appeared in the August *Columbian Magazine*. This proximity in publication points to more substantive grounds for considering the stories in relation to one another. Like "Mesmeric Revelation" (and like "The Gold-Bug" for that matter), "The Purloined Letter" is a tale of disclosures, passed on from a gifted teller to a less perceptive but friendly listener, who records and preserves what he hears. Each narrator is literally a man of letters in the service of an informant whose intuitive spiritual aptitudes far exceed his own. This familiar duality—letter and spirit—lies behind nearly every feature of Dupin's final performance, a duality that readers of *The Gift* might have been predisposed to discern in the contents of their holiday volume.

The story's epigraph underscores these metaphysical ambitions. It is a spurious Latin aphorism purportedly from Seneca: *Nil sapientiae odiousius acumine nimio*, Wisdom hates nothing more than cleverness. The petty fraud of the false citation is a wry and wonderful enactment of its meaning. Poe imbeds both dualities—letter and spirit, cleverness and wisdom—directly into his setting: a "little back library, or book-closet," a shrine of the letter, in which Dupin and the narrator are meditating in "profound silence" when the story begins. Not even the abrupt appearance of Prefect G—— in his customary state of needy perplexity can prompt Dupin to light a lamp. Darkness, he observes, provides a more favorable atmosphere for reflection, as the Prefect introduces his dilemma: the recovery of an apparently compromising letter coolly filched from "the royal apartments," in the presence of their "exalted" occupants, by the lynx-eyed Minister D——. A number of the plot's features are immediately puzzling. What accounts for the privileged access that the thief apparently enjoys to the royal *boudoir* where the letter lay so strangely exposed? And why, for that matter, should a simple letter be so difficult to hide?

Minister D——, in fact, will elect not to hide his stolen goods at all when he wishes to thwart the police. But the royal personage most threatened by the letter's detection tries in vain "to thrust it in a drawer" when her husband suddenly appears. When Minister D—— enters the room, the letter sits open on a table, just as it will remain openly exposed later in the story in the apartments of Minister D—— himself, "turned, as a glove, inside out" and presumably only too readable, when Dupin contrives to retrieve it. Of all the characters concerned in the secrecy of this letter, only Dupin succeeds in concealing it, a ploy that he uses to manipulate Prefect G—— into naming a splendid reward for the letter's return and to heighten the policeman's surprise and financial chagrin when Dupin abruptly produces it from a drawer.

This dramatic gesture of disclosure is an index of Dupin's command over the story's plot, not an indication of the desirability, or even the possibility, of concealment. Poe repeatedly hints that this letter cannot be hidden. It can be "purloined," or set at a distance from its owners for some period of time, but it cannot be misappropriated or stolen. "A certain document of the last importance," as Prefect G—— provocatively terms it, the letter remains invitingly accessible throughout the tale, but few seem able to read its contents. Though Prefect G—— apparently pours over the letter's words when Dupin finally presents it to him, he originally identifies it by its material form and appearance only in a ludicrous effort to preserve its secrecy. "The Prefect was fond of the cant of diplomacy," Poe's narrator drily observes. Ultimately he is obsessed with the "letter" alone, as a thing rather than as a message. By contrast, Poe repeatedly presents the inner urgency of the tale in spiritual terms.

Things "of the last importance" are precisely those vital questions of the soul's immortality and of the ultimate emptiness or fullness of celestial space that deeply engage Vankirk on the threshold of death: a confrontation with the greatest as well as the last concerns of earthly existence. Biblical revelation, along with all other resources of the "letter," are not adequate to convert mere "psychal impressions" into the sort of deep reassurance and intellectual conviction that Vankirk requires, as he lies "suffering with acute pain in the region of the heart" and (like Virginia Poe) waiting to die. Through mesmerism, he hopes for an unmediated glimpse of the immaterial future. Dupin is a similar sort of mental prisoner. His two previous triumphs of detection are set in a sordid, urban world that he seems merely to visit rather than inhabit, as he moves through the dimly lit city streets steeping himself in the infinite resources of his mind. Like Vankirk, too, he falls into trance-like states when he hopes to draw on the powers of insight associated with the bi-part soul.

No trance is necessary, however, in "The Purloined Letter." With this third appearance in Poe's work, Dupin has broken almost completely free of the mind's rudimentary limits. He is perfectly indifferent to the fate of a seemingly precious document that Prefect G—— takes from him in "a perfect agony of joy" that suggests the recovery of a sacred object or relic rather than a textual pawn in a worldly intrigue (PT, 688). He is equally indifferent to the meticulous methods of investigation that had so engaged his energy in earlier stories. All the modern forensic science of the Paris police amounts in Dupin's view to little more than organized principles of guessing. Like algebra and differential calculus, the Prefect's microscopes and needle probes aim only at the material world of "form and quantity," Dupin scoffs, and not at the immaterial region to which his own intelligence turns. Dupin illuminates the comparison with a simple analogy:

> "There is a game of puzzles," he resumed, "which is played upon a map. One party playing requires another to find a given word—the name of a town, river, state or empire—any word, in short, upon the motley and perplexed surface of the chart. A novice in the game generally seeks to embarrass his opponents by giving them the most minutely lettered names; but the adept selects such words as stretch, in large characters, from one end of the chart to the other. These, like the over-largely lettered signs and placards of the street, escape observation by dint of being excessively obvious; and here the physical oversight is precisely analogous with the moral inapprehension by which the intellect suffers to pass unnoticed those considerations which are too obtrusively and too palpably self-evident. But this is a point, it appears, somewhat above or beneath the understanding of the Prefect. He never once thought it probable, or possible, that the Minister had deposited the letter immediately beneath the nose of the whole world, by way of best preventing any portion of that world from perceiving it. (PT, 694–695)

Minutely lettered names are ultimately a diversion: a cloud of deceitful detail. Unlike the rudimentary analyst Prefect G——, Dupin never relinquishes his focus on the largest possible characters, those that completely encompass both visible and invisible space.

By implication Poe invites readers of *The Gift* to enlarge the scope of their understanding as well: to detach the illustrious but victimized royal couple from the trivial puzzle of political intrigue and to grant them emblematic status, linked much like Adam and Eve by the transmission of fatal knowledge from one partner to the other. The "letter" in turn suggests a message from the invisible author of created being: a "revelation" so conspicuous that it requires no mesmeric medium to read. The multitalented Minister D—— recognizes as readily as Dupin the profound misperceptions of rudimental life: the moral inapprehension that confuses what Poe terms the crude "ascendancy" of blackmail with the visionary heights necessary for a transcendent grasp of the chart's riddle. That is why he sees no necessity to hide the stolen letter. He is a demonic adept at the game of puzzles from which the imprisoned soul strives to free itself: a poet as well as a mathematician, a courtier, and a "bold *intriguant*," but one who has chosen to play for rudimental rather than ultimate stakes. An unprincipled man of genius, Dupin concludes as he explains the crude trick that led to the letter's recovery, is a *monstrum horrendum*, a corruption of incomparable human gifts. "In the present instance," he observes, "I have no sympathy—at least no pity—for him who descends" (PT, 697).

*   *   *

In two of his most vivid, late tales, "The Cask of Amontillado" and "Hop-Frog," Poe addresses himself to the figure of the *monstrum horrendum* with particular intensity. Each plot becomes a complex drama of self-liberation that involves violent retaliation against the flesh: the final fragment of earthly ballast that restrains the mind from attaining its pneumatic dream. The central characters in each story blend powers of ascent and descent that express Poe's grasp of the terrible ambivalence of human life. The first of these, "The Cask of Amontillado," appeared in *Godey's Magazine and Lady's Book* for November 1846, the last work of fiction that Poe would complete before his wife's death the following January. This famous account of aristocratic revenge revisits in a much darker mode the triumph of memory that he had composed in "The Gold-Bug." Montresor's decision to bury alive his nemesis Fortunato behind a wall in his family vault is a figurative act of storage as well as a murder: the cellaring of a powerful vintage.

Judging from the skill with which Montresor tells his story, he has many linguistic gifts, but the primary ornament of his consciousness is memory. Memory, in fact, is the ancient heritage of his house. For centuries the Montresors have hoarded their dead, as the old man in "The Tell-Tale Heart" is a hoarder of private treasure, or as Prospero attempts to hoard the pleasures of organic life in his castellated abbey refuge. The catacombs beneath the Montresor family palace are lined with bones, the skeletons of Montresor's ancestors mingling with the bottles, casks, and puncheons of wine that resemble catacombs within catacombs—the residue of vineyards and of living harvests set aside long ago to age on the mould of Montresor's cellar. The story begins with a cool act of "telling" that reflects the defining feature of its narrator's temperament: his meticulous attention to mental records, as well as his determination to monopolize the power of recollection by closing off any possibility that his own actions might eventually be remembered to his disadvantage:

> The thousand injuries of Fortunato I had borne as I best could; but when he ventured upon insult, I vowed revenge. You, who so well know the nature of my soul, will not suppose, however, that I gave utterance to a

threat. *At length* I would be avenged; this was a point definitively settled—but the very definitiveness with which it was resolved, precluded the idea of risk. I must not only punish, but punish with impunity. A wrong is unredressed when retribution overtakes its redresser. It is equally unredressed when the avenger fails to make himself felt as such to him who has done the wrong.

It must be understood, that neither by word nor deed had I given Fortunato cause to doubt my good will. I continued, as was my wont, to smile in his face, and he did not perceive that my smile *now* was at the thought of his immolation. (PT, 848)

Sensations do not exist for Montresor unless they exist "at length": unless they subsist across formidable spans of time and meet specific criteria for closure. He is equally meticulous in withholding the nourishment of memory from others, the words or deeds that might rankle in another's mind.

A ceremonial sacrifice is what Montresor covets: an immolation, not an outburst of murderous rage, that will have the double advantage of satisfying his vow of revenge and of lending itself to an annual step-by-step recapitulation, much like the commemorative stages of the carnival season in which the murder takes place. The story itself is just such a recapitulation, expertly told in part because Montresor has had half a century—a jubilee of years—to polish it, to relive its features in memory, to mature the vintage. But Montresor's crime has none of the larger, sacramental implications of Lent. The many injuries and the crowning insult that he claims to have suffered at Fortunato's hands play no role in the development of the story, except as items entered on a long-accumulating list. They are hoarded knowledge, like the bones of Montresor's ancestors, an indiscriminate heap of generic wrongs in which the narrator himself takes little interest.

A long record of grievances is simply the necessary accessory of the Montresor family motto: *Nemo me impune lacessit*, No one insults me with impunity. The words imply an implacable devotion to old accounts—a mental discipline that is, in effect, the treasure to which the family name alludes. "I forget your arms," Fortunato comments, as he and his mortal enemy begin to wend their way through the damp tunnels of the Montresor vaults. In some respects, forgetfulness itself is what Montresor plots to destroy—first by imitating it in the feigned warmth that he expresses for his victim when he greets him in his carnival motley, and then by mocking it when he distracts Fortunato from his own inexplicable words and behavior by mentioning an equivocal pipe of wine that his palette is not adequate to assess.

Fortunato's name seems little more than a direct reference to his symbolic importance as an emblem for the worldly prosperity and happiness that Montresor claims to have lost. In fact his nature is more complex than this crude tag suggests. Though he dresses in cap and bells for the carnival, Fortunato is by no means a fool. "He was a man to be respected and even feared," Montresor concedes, despite the vanity and self-assurance that make him vulnerable to Montresor's plot. It is Fortunato who steers the two men unerringly to Montresor's palace to inspect the dubious pipe of amontillado, and Fortunato who virtually smacks his lips with appreciation over the design of the Montresor arms: "The wine sparkled in his eyes and the bells jingled," Montresor recalls, as Fortunato expressed approval for the vindictive spirit of his companion's family motto and for the figure of the "serpent rampant" that symbolizes the Montresor appetite for revenge. Fortunato's instinctive sympathies too lie with arcane signs or gestures, like the Masonic pantomime that he uses to signal his membership in the "brotherhood." But he is almost completely blind to the overt menace represented by Montresor's trowel, or by the equally deadly atmosphere of the vaults.

Neither of these material threats, however, is an indispensable forerunner to Fortunato's fate. He is already twice doomed, when he enters the Montresor catacombs, by the internal fires of the two forms of disease that afflict him. Fortunato is clearly destroying himself with drink, at the same time that his vicious cough signals an advanced stage of consumption: a drowning and a burning that echo the paradoxical oppositions of Fortunato's nature as the formidable fool. Ever eager to keep accurate records, Montresor savagely inquires after his companion's health: "How long have you had that cough?" The only answer to this question is a brutal series of noises: "Ugh!, ugh! ugh!—ugh! ugh! ugh!—ugh! ugh! ugh!" Poe reproduces the syllables, in groups of three, fifteen times without allowing even a fragment of speech to interrupt the count—recording five successive, wracking spasms of the kind that must have tortured his own ears during the final weeks of Virginia Poe's life. Fortunato's body combines both of the sicknesses afflicting Poe's family at the time he is composing Montresor's story, as if Poe were groping for a fictive means of burying disease itself, along with the mad devotion to an artistic calling that had brought him only death. "The Cask of Amontillado" appears to reverse the mental succession that Poe depicts in "The Tell-Tale Heart." Memory imprisons, and perhaps even destroys, the diseased fertility of the imagination in Montresor's calculated act of retribution against a self-destructive portion of his own consciousness.

In a second outburst of mindless noise at the story's climactic moment—a parallel to the painful coughing that cuts off the voices of both men a page or two earlier—Poe exposes the nature of the echo chamber that he has constructed. Fortunato gradually falls silent as the wall of stone with which Montresor is systematically enclosing him in the crypt grows higher. Only "the furious vibration of the chain" that binds him to the granite wall marks his presence in the shadows. When Montresor throws "a few feeble rays" of light into the dark recess, hoping to catch a glimpse of his victim's despair, Fortunato suddenly shrieks in agony. After a brief instant of panic Montresor answers in kind, and the two voices combine in a terrible, inarticulate duet:

> A succession of loud and shrill screams, bursting suddenly from the throat of the chained form, seemed to thrust me violently back. For a brief moment I hesitated—I trembled. Unsheathing my rapier, I began to grope with it about the recess: but the thought of an instant reassured me. I placed my hand upon the solid fabric of the catacombs, and felt satisfied. I reapproached the wall. I replied to the yells of him who clamored. I re-echoed—I aided—I surpassed them in volume and in strength. I did this, and the clamorer grew still. (PT, 853)

The solid fabric of the catacombs suggests the unbreakable matrices of memory, the grave of things, to which Montresor's vows have bound him. It is an architecture equally indifferent to Fortunato's coughing and to his screams but remorseless in its grip on his existence. The last sound to emerge from his tomb is a jingling of bells, the unvoiced presence of a mental vibration that can be silenced but not destroyed as long as its hiding place in memory remains. "I did this," Montresor repeats, in the last of ten instances with which the first person singular reverberates through the brief passage above, a pattern that underscores the excruciating inward collaboration the scene depicts.

Both "Mesmeric Revelation" and "The Purloined Letter" picture the opposition between rudimental and ultimate life as a clash between characters. In each story a gifted teller—Vankirk or Dupin—attempts to enlighten listeners who remain trapped by the moral incomprehension of rudimental existence. The configuration is far less straightforward in "The Cask of Amontillado." Though a gifted teller, Montresor remains as tightly shackled to the stones of his family catacomb as his victim. Though he is buried in memory's vaults, Fortunato pervades the thoughts of his enemy. The two are perfectly counterpoised weights in a single mental system—an emblematic image that Poe depicts with ruthless clarity in "Hop-Frog," the last of his extraordinary masquerades of consciousness.

The story appeared in *The Flag of Our Union*, a Boston periodical, on March 17, 1849, St. Patrick's Day, seven months before Poe's death. The deformed jester for whom it is named—a captive in the court of a modern king with a fondness for archaic customs—twice grinds his teeth in suppressed fury during the course of the tale, primordial sounds like Fortunato's wracking cough or terrible screams. The first time these noises occur the jester's barely contained rage is provoked when the king contemptuously strikes the diminutive court dancer, Trippetta, throwing a goblet of wine in her face. The startlingly "harsh and protracted *grating*" that results on that occasion recurs at the story's climax, when Hop-Frog (like Montresor) is on the point of performing his own, savage act of immolation. This story too incorporates several layers of costumes that seem almost simultaneously visible as Poe's plot unfolds.

Hop-Frog's disproportionate revenge for the king's rough treatment of Trippetta is to incinerate his callous master, along with the seven chief ministers of his court, as they hang helplessly from a chandelier hook, disguised as ourang-outangs for a costume ball. The ruse takes place in a great circular saloon with a single skylight in the center of the ceiling from which Hop-Frog contrives to suspend his victims. The king and his ministers, coated in tar and flax and joined together, at Hop-Frog's direction, by a circular chain, find themselves suddenly drawn into the air, thirty feet above the ballroom floor, by the action of the chandelier's invisible counterweight. Suspended in space like a human wick at the center of a ceremonial lamp, the men are as helpless as Fortunato chained to the stones of Montresor's vault or as Prince Prospero's guests before the implacable presence of the Red Death.

Once again "a low, harsh, *grating* sound" from Hop-Frog's "fang-like teeth" fills the room. Under the thin pretense of studying these captive "beasts," Hop-Frog selects a flambeau from "some fifty or sixty" ringing the grand saloon, like second marks, and ignites their bodies:

> In less than half a minute the whole eight ourang-outangs were blazing fiercely, amid the shrieks of the multitude who gazed at them from below, horror-stricken, and without the power to render them the slightest assistance.
>
> At length the flames, suddenly increasing in virulence, forced the jester to climb higher up the chain, to be out of their reach; and as he

made this movement, the crowd again sank, for a brief instant, into silence. The dwarf seized his opportunity, and once more spoke:

"I now see *distinctly*," he said, "what manner of people these maskers are. They are a great king and his seven privy-councillors—a king who does not scruple to strike a defenceless girl, and his seven councillors who abet him in the outrage. As for myself, I am simply Hop-Frog, the jester—and *this is my last jest.*" (PT, 907–908)

A final counterweight to his persecutors, Hop-Frog slowly climbs the chain and disappears through the skylight, presumably to join Trippetta, his accomplice in this grotesque assassination. We are "eight to a fraction," the king had cried with pleasure when Hop-Frog first described to him and to his ministers the sensational costume of the Eight Chained Ourang-Outangs with which he proposed to disguise them at the royal masquerade. This spuriously precise balance is the forerunner to the vengeful imbalance at the story's end: a grotesque retribution for the painful indignity that Trippetta had suffered at the king's hand.

To an embittered Irish exile in Boston, this scene might make compelling St. Patrick's Day reading. Re-costumed as a political fable, Hop-Frog's extravagant assassination might seem far less out of scale. The two court dwarves suggest caricatures of captive Ireland: a delicate fay or faerie and a coarse bog-trotter, with the "large, powerful, and very repulsive teeth" that signal his subhuman nature. Each in effect is a fraction of a person, in the eyes of the court, "two little captives" who had become sworn friends in a world governed by length, breadth, and weight, by density and by mass. In another sense, perhaps, they depict the diminutive Virginia Poe and her embittered husband, hostages in the household of a complacent reading public and its editorial courtiers, an institutional monarch indifferent both to their physical suffering and their rare gifts. The story's narrator observes at the beginning of the tale that Hop-Frog combined a number of attributes that fitted him particularly well for his role at court. He was a jester and a cripple as well as a dwarf, "a triplicate treasure in one person" (PT, 900). The same can be said of Poe's tale itself. It is a masquerade with more than one theme.

Prominent among these figurative purposes is a final grim attack on the rudimental life. The king and his seven ministers are all "large, corpulent, oily men," the narrator notes, human worms ripe for pupation. Encased in their fatal suits and hardened in fire, they swing from the saloon ceiling in "a fetid, blackened, hideous, and indistinguishable mass," a sensory atrocity in startling contrast to the fastidious madness that marks the other tales of retaliation Poe writes in the last years of his life. The torch that Montresor drops "through the remaining aperture" in Fortunato's tomb ignites nothing but the sound of bells. The concentric circles that enclose the scene of Hop-Frog's revenge—the skylight, the chain, and the ballroom itself—are an aperture of another sort. They invite comparison to the ritualistic braziers of Prospero's abbey apartments, or to the lamps that play conspicuous roles on the phantom ship from "MS. Found in a Bottle," in "Ligeia," or in "The Tell-Tale Heart," appliances of artistic exploration rather than pleasure. Like the visionary court that Roderick Usher celebrates in his eerie poem, Hop-Frog's climb up the chandelier chain leaving the ballast of his eight victims behind suggests a final, bitter picture of Poe's own haunted palace: the complex vessel of consciousness, abandoning its sensory and erotic shell, on the point of attempting an ascent toward ultimate life. Like many of Poe's tales, "Hop-Frog" too remembers its predecessors, multiplying its own artistic impact in a series of harmonic echoes that lend a fragile beauty to the dark design.

CONCLUSION

Pictures of Ascent

Figure 5 J. M. W. Turner, "Long Ship's Lighthouse, Land's End" (1835). Courtesy of The J. Paul Getty Museum, Los Angeles, California.

In an introductory note to Poe's last brief tale, "The Light-House," T. O. Mabbott includes a detailed physical description of the untitled manuscript. Poe never published the story and may never have intended to do so, at least in conventional form. Some of the manuscript's features, however, suggest that he may have meant to exhibit it as another variety of plate article, similar to the meditative ramble he composed in "The Island of the Fay." "The Light-House" resembles a carefully prepared textual caption for a miniature seascape, perhaps a study similar to one of J. M. W. Turner's superb, and frequently very small, expressionist paintings from the early nineteenth century. "Longships Lighthouse, Land's End" (1834–1835) drew particular praise from John Ruskin in *Modern Painters* for its extraordinary depiction of atmospheric energy. Like the thrilling pictorial "vaguenesses" of Roderick Usher, it too is a painting of ideas. Only nature and Turner, Ruskin thought, could make such scenes, though Poe had long been interested in the resources of the verbal canvas as a means of depicting the immaterial energy of consciousness.

At first Poe's last curious sketch appears to have little in common with Roderick Usher's Kingdom of Inorganization. Unlike Turner's swirling curtain of pictorial force, "The Light-House" seems a childish exercise, written in a meticulously neat, schoolboy's hand on four strips of ruled blue paper, each one just a fraction under four inches wide. The strips vary in length from slightly less than ten inches to roughly twelve and one half inches long and have glue residue on their edges, indicating that at some point they were joined together in a single strip, perhaps forty-five inches long once the overlapping ends were fastened together. Fully assembled, "The Light-House" would have a top and a bottom, as well as a beginning and an end, and might be rolled into a scroll or hung on a wall, a four by forty-five-inch column of paper containing Poe's last work of fiction.

The top of the first strip of manuscript has a large blank area preceding the initial dated entry in the narrator's light-house journal, January 1, 1796. Mabbott assumed that this space was where Poe intended the title and the author's name to appear. But despite the obviously high finish and clean transcription that Poe gave to the story's words, he never titled these pages. Once they were glued together from top to bottom, the blank space would appear to fall where the lantern does in an actual lighthouse, allowing room for an engraver like John Sartain or a gifted miniaturist to depict some form of light at the beginning of Poe's story. An artist with expressive tastes shaped by Turner's example could make this small oblong of paper appear to contain infinite depths. Not words but pure illumination, a blend of line and color, belongs at the top of Poe's written column, as a beautiful illuminated capital letter signals the beginning of a medieval Book of Hours.

Poe's story, though, is a book of days, covering just the first three entries in a diary that the narrator keeps in order to fulfill the terms of his appointment as the sole manager of a remote lighthouse nearly two hundred miles at sea. The record is too brief to contain much personal information. The narrator refers to himself only as "a noble of the realm," though which realm he doesn't specify. A political patron of the sort that Poe had repeatedly failed to secure in his own life obtained the lighthouse post for him from "the Consistory," a mysterious institution whose authority might be secular, sacred, or both. A friend named Orndoff had apparently hoped to join with the narrator in his duties, but he succeeds in avoiding this unwelcome companionship: "It never would have done to let Orndoff accompany me. I never should have made any way with my book as long as he was within reach of me, with his intolerable gossip—not to mention that everlasting meerschaum" (PT, 924). Poe's narrator is apparently embarked on an intellectual or artistic journey that requires complete solitude. The reader learns the name of his gossip-loving friend and of his faithful dog, Neptune, but not the name of the narrator himself.

The diary consists of only three paragraphs, one for each of the first three days of January 1796. The heading for January 4 is followed by a blank space at the bottom of Poe's paper column. Each paragraph in the preceding entries is repeatedly interrupted by ellipses of varying lengths that divide the successive layers of narrative accumulation. Sometimes only a brief interval for reflection seems to account for the break. At other points some hours appear to have lapsed. The narrator puts down his pen to climb the lighthouse stairs for "a good look around," or picks it up again to record a turn in the weather. He remarks on the dimensions of the building—160 feet "from the low water mark to the top of the lantern"—a climb made still more "interminable" by the fact that the actual floor of the shaft is twenty feet below sea level, making the total distance to the top "180 feet at least." Despite some doubts he has concerning the stability of this submerged floor, the narrator expresses faith in the structure's safety. Its sheer mass is reassuring: "At 50 feet from high-water mark," he reports, its "iron-riveted wall...is four feet thick, if an inch," a formidable vessel of containment and resistance in which the narrator shields himself like a crustacean in its protective shell. "The basis on which the structure rests seems to me to be chalk," the narrator concludes in his final sentence, the cornerstone of the textual column that comprises his vertical strip of manuscript.

With this enigmatic gesture, Poe has completed his whimsical picture. There is no need to assume the onset of an apocalyptic storm in which the narrator frantically stuffs his scrap of diary into a sealed bottle shortly before a wave overwhelms him. The story's verbal structure rises from "chalk" at the bottom to luminous space at the top, taking the measure of the lighthouse itself along the way as its own spiral staircase of sentences climbs, or descends, through a piece of writing that is brief enough to allow the reader many trips up and down its length. On these repeated journeys, a proud native of Baltimore might notice that the lighthouse has almost precisely replicated the dimensions of the city's splendid monument to George Washington: a Doric column of stone, one-hundred-and-sixty feet high, topped by an eighteen foot bronze statue, positioned where a lighthouse lantern would sit, but proportioned to correspond very closely to the dimensions of the subsurface foundation in Poe's story. One-hundred-and-eighty feet is the estimate Poe's narrator offers for the total height of his lighthouse. One-hundred-and-seventy-eight feet is the total height of Washington's marble outpost in Baltimore.

The association may be purposeful. George Washington personally commissioned the construction of many lighthouses along the eastern seaboard and took a direct interest in the appointment of keepers, an early form of government patronage. The beautiful lighthouse on Montauk Point at the tip of Long Island—one of those that Washington established—celebrated its fiftieth anniversary on November 5, 1846, a time when Poe and his family were living in Fordham, a few miles north of the Harlem River, during the last weeks of Virginia Poe's life. As a respite from the emotional pressures of their tiny cottage, Poe would take walks along the nearby Croton Aqueduct or visit some rocks in the neighborhood that gave him a view of Long Island Sound and the distant glimmer of Montauk Light. Of this particular realm, Poe himself was an unrecognized "noble," a grandson of General David Poe, who had been publicly praised by Lafayette for his service during the Revolution. More importantly, perhaps, Poe belonged to the nation's literary nobility: keepers of another sort of solitary beacon on another kind of perilous coast. For many reasons, Poe might have identified his own plight with that of the narrator in his last slender sketch and with the complex pictures of ascent that this final exercise in emblematic architecture and narrative design implies.

The chalk foundation on which Poe's lighthouse rests is composed of a material that had acquired special geophysical significance during his adult life. Alexander von Humboldt's colleague, Christian Gottfried Ehrenberg, beginning in the late 1830s had systematically demonstrated the biological basis of many sedimentary rock strata. A single cubic inch of polishing slate, Ehrenberg had shown, was composed of "40,000 million silicious shells," as Humboldt reported in the pages of *Cosmos*, the skeletal remains of ancient microorganisms deposited over an incalculable interval of time in what would ultimately become massive layers of stone. Chalk was formed by similar microscopic shell deposits—catacombs far more vast than the endless labyrinths of the Montresor family, laid down in sheets many hundreds of feet thick, one of which stretched from the celebrated white cliffs of the British Isles across much of northern Europe. Only the stars, Humboldt wrote, could suggest a scale of cumulative sublimity comparable to the chronological and mathematical vistas revealed in Ehrenberg's work or provoke a similar measure of "barren astonishment" in the overwhelmed human observer.

Everywhere Ehrenberg turned his microscope he found vast populations of living "infusoria" leaving their traces in rock, in water, even on the polar ice cap: minute creatures so numerous as to color entire square miles of open ocean with the faint pigments in their bodies, so charged with life that their phosphorescent energy (in Humboldt's words) could "convert every wave into a foaming band of flashing light," so ethereal that they were capable of traveling in windblown dust clouds from one continent to another. All these phenomena Charles Darwin confirmed in what Humboldt calls his "agreeable narrative" of the *Beagle*'s voyage, published the year after Arthur Gordon Pym's account of his spectacular adventure in the southern seas. Even oceanic beds of seaweed off the barren tip of South America, Darwin noted, proved to be submerged forests more vast and more populous with life than their terrestrial counterparts. When the narrator of "The Light-House" aims his telescope at the horizon and finds there only emptiness—a dead calm, a glassy sea, a few seaweeds "but besides them absolutely *nothing*"—he is a victim of immature perception rather than of loneliness. A different set of lenses, a different kind of glass (Poe knew) would tell a very different story.

Very early in his career Poe had recognized that the chief preoccupation of his work would prove to be what the narrator of "The Gold-Bug" calls "the difficulty of ascension." Despite the lofty intellectual goals and physical agility that characterize the narrator of "The Light-House," he too grapples with this difficulty. The mind's vertical aspiration—its insatiable pneumatic hunger—repeatedly seizes the attention of Poe's narrators and molds the language of his tales. Hans Pfaall's unparalleled balloon voyage and Hop-Frog's successful flight through a skylight are masquerade roles that have much in common. "The Murders in the Rue Morgue" compels its readers to pass up and down flights of stairs similar to those that fill Poe's fictional lighthouse: to ascend and descend a slender lightning rod, to examine a narrow chimney flue, reconstructing the uneven movement from confusion to clarity, from fear to reason, from lower to higher planes of intelligence that lies behind the mysterious circumstances of an urban tragedy. These actual and imaginary activities are all indices of one another, as well as of their physical settings. The glistening wall of the Norway maelstrom pulls one brother to his death on the ocean floor but releases another into a state of freedom so remarkable that he swings his legs fearlessly over a sheer abyss, as he tells his story, studying the distant sea.

The slender paper ribbon of Poe's last tale acknowledges this implicit imaginative allure. It positions a narrator handicapped by imperfect cognitive powers in a vertical architecture that rises from the inconceivable accretions of preconscious life in the chalk beds beneath his feet up a steep scale of awareness toward unmediated light—an ascent that the narrator himself fails to recognize, even as he inscribes it in the fragmentary record he leaves behind. These circumstances subtly extend and quietly revise the final entries in Arthur Gordon Pym's incomplete diary, reducing its vast polar seascape—its milky ocean and silent cataract of luminous vapor—to a chalk foundation and a lantern, isolated in endless space. The imaginative topography of "The Light-House," like so many of the fictive environments that Poe creates over his extraordinarily brief career, is a literal and a figurative picture of ascent: a scale model of the mind's irresistible determination to reach outward toward the walls of the universe.

Sources

Preface and Introduction

The first epigraph to this book comes from a letter that Kepler wrote to his daughter's fiancé in 1628, cited in David Park's recent cultural history of optics, *The Fire within the Eye: A Historical Essay on the Nature and Meaning of Light* (Princeton: Princeton Univ. Press, 1997), p. 171. Italo Calvino's provocative but incomplete Norton lectures offer grounds for an unusually fruitful approach to Poe's work. A reader intrigued by the quick summary of "Lightness" provided in these pages will enjoy all of *Six Memos for the Next Millennium*, trans. Patrick Creagh (Cambridge, MA: Harvard Univ. Press, 1988). Richard Wilbur's classic essay, "The House of Poe," has been reprinted many times but it first appeared in *Anniversary Lectures, 1959* (Washington, DC: Library of Congress, 1959).

Throughout the introduction, I have quoted Baudelaire from the useful collection of his commentaries on Poe's life and work prepared by Lois Hyslop and Francis E. Hyslop, Jr.: *Baudelaire on Poe: Critical Papers* (State College, PA: Bald Eagle Press, 1952). The long extract from "William Wilson" takes up pages 43–46 of the Hyslop edition; Baudelaire's reference to the "heavy vegetables" of critical opinion, also from his 1852 essay, is on page 61. Poe's appropriation of Coleridge's words in his 1831 preface invites comparison to similar instances of appropriation in *Biographia Literaria* itself. Richard Holmes addresses the issue in *Coleridge: Darker Reflections, 1804–1834* (New York: Pantheon, 1998), pp. 378–412. Louis Masur's concise national portrait, *1831: Year of Eclipse* (New York: Hill and Wang, 2001) helps identify the many intersections between Poe's private experience and the formative events of his day. Michel Foucault's use of paintings as conceptual tools in *Madness and Civilization: A History of Insanity in the Age of Reason* has interesting implications for the appreciation of Poe's highly pictorial style, both in "The Sphinx" and many other, more famous tales. The iconographic bestiary that Foucault cites appears on p. 21 of the Vintage edition in Richard Howard's translation (New York: Random House, 1988). Mary Oliver offers her brief comments on the ubiquity of madness in Poe's fiction in "The Bright Eyes of Eleonora— Poe's Dream of Recapturing the Impossible," *Ohio Review* 58 (1998).

The entomological details that lie behind "The Sphinx" are quite likely to have interested Poe. He may have helped one of his acquaintances, Thomas Wyatt, translate and abridge the work of the French naturalist Pierre Charles Lemonnier for use as a school textbook in Wyatt's *A Synopsis of Natural History* (Philadelphia: Thomas Wardle, 1839). Any American school child who read Wyatt's book, however, and immediately rushed outdoors searching for the remarkable sphinx moth that it describes was in for a disappointment. Lemonnier, along with the other French naturalists whose work Wyatt used, felt no need to discuss the habitation range and unusual size of an insect already familiar to European readers. Moses Harris' 1766 plate depicting the metamorphosis of the "bee tiger" or Death's Head sphinx moth was reproduced in an 1840 edition of *The Aurelian*, Harris' celebrated study of English moths and butterflies.

1 Problems of Disposal

The single indispensable study of nineteenth-century cholera epidemics in the United States is Charles E. Rosenberg's *The Cholera Years: The United States in 1832, 1849, and 1866* (Chicago: Univ. of Chicago Press, 1962). R. J. Morris, in *Cholera 1832: The Social Response to an Epidemic* (New York: Holmes & Meier, 1976), discusses the outbreak in England. François Delaporte does the same for France in *Disease and Civilization: The Cholera in Paris, 1832* (Cambridge, MA: MIT Press, 1986). William H. McNeill's vivid description of cholera's symptoms is from *Plagues and Peoples* (1977, rpt. New York: Doubleday, 1989), p. 267. Alan Bewell's *Romanticism and Colonial Disease* (Baltimore: Johns Hopkins Univ. Press, 1999) links cholera with early-nineteenth-century British life; Catherine J. Kudlick does the same for France in *Cholera in Post-Revolutionary Paris: A Cultural History* (Berkeley: Univ. of California Press, 1996). For the Baltimore epidemic of 1832, Sherry H. Olsen's general history *Baltimore: The Building of an American City* (Baltimore: Johns Hopkins Univ. Press, 1980) offers the best brief description.

It is worth noting that public records of cholera deaths in nineteenth-century American seaports are subject to question on several grounds. Local authorities and newspapers sometimes delayed announcing, or misreported entirely, the first cholera fatalities in any given outbreak out of concern that quarantine measures would drive shipping to other ports that did not have (or did not acknowledge having) the disease. Since cholera's symptoms resemble those of other serious forms of gastroenteritis, contemporary physicians sometimes used generic categories of sickness to identify the cause of death in cases where they could not be certain about the presence of cholera. For these reasons, and because early nineteenth-century health records in general are likely to be incomplete at best, the scope of the 1832 cholera outbreak in American cities is probably greater than the available numbers suggest.

Darwin mentions being turned away from Tenerife by quarantine authorities in the first paragraph of *The Voyage of the Beagle*. Janet Browne's account of this formative field experience in *Charles Darwin: Voyaging* (Princeton: Princeton Univ. Press, 1995) is an illuminating commentary on Darwin's intellectual growth both during the voyage and after returning home. Frederick Douglass's description of the atmosphere of Baltimore early in 1832 is from *My Bondage and My Freedom,* Chapter XII. John Ostrom's revised checklist of Poe's correspondence published in *Studies in the American Renaissance* (1981) records no surviving letters by Poe for the eighteen-month period beginning in late December 1831 and ending in April 1833. For most of that time, he was living with his aunt in Baltimore. Between mid-October and the end of December 1831, however, Poe wrote five times to John Allan, a rapid fire series of appeals that makes the long break in the checklist all the more conspicuous. The letter describing "Eleven Tales of the Arabesque" is dated May 4, 1833 and appears in John Ostrom's first volume of *The Letters of Edgar Allan Poe* (New York: Gordian Press, 1966), 1.53.

Michael J. S. Williams in *A World of Words: Language and Displacement in the Fiction of Edgar Allan Poe* (Durham, NC, and London: Duke Univ. Press, 1988) and David Halliburton in *Edgar Allan Poe: A Phenomenological View* (Princeton: Princeton Univ. Press, 1973) offer detailed and interesting treatments of "Berenice" and "Morella." Jonathan Elmer's discussion of both tales as instances of "stalled mourning" suggests a provocative link between Poe's work and the contemporary cult of sentimental fiction. See *Reading at the Social Limit: Affect, Mass Culture, and Edgar Allan Poe* (Stanford: Stanford Univ. Press, 1995), pp. 93–125. *Niles' Weekly Register* for November 28, 1829 reports on "the vast multitude of gratified spectators" who attended the raising of the last piece of George Washington's statue to the top of the Baltimore monument on the previous November 25. Poe was living in the city with his aunt at the time, hoping to hear favorable news about an appointment to West Point, and had many opportunities for visiting the monument site and examining the statue's large portrait head at close range (much as the Demon seems to do in "Silence—A Fable") before it was hoisted to the top of its marble column.

2 A Pneumatics of Mind

In *Fables of Mind: An Inquiry into Poe's Fiction* (New York: Oxford Univ. Press, 1987), Joan Dayan views the excised portions of "Loss of Breath" quite differently than I do here. She sees them as evidence of the "erosion" of meaning in much of Poe's work. The ancient trope of shipwreck that Poe frequently invokes in these and other passages is part of the intriguing figurative complex that Hans Blumenberg explores in *Shipwreck with Spectator: Paradigm of a Metaphor for Existence*, trans. Steven Rendall (1979, rpt.Cambridge, MA: MIT Press, 1997). J. Gerald Kennedy includes an informative discussion of contemporary anxieties about premature burial in *Poe, Death, and the Life of Writing* (New Haven: Yale Univ. Press, 1987), pp. 32–50.

contemporary anxieties about premature burial in *Poe, Death, and the Life of Writing* (New Haven: Yale Univ. Press, 1987), pp. 32–50. Though Paul John Eakin does not mention "Loss of Breath" in his examination of Poe's attraction to what he calls the "Lazarus plot," his article discussing Poe's fascination with experience "on the verge" is an illuminating assessment of this critical feature in Poe's imaginative life. See "Poe's Sense of an Ending," *American Literature* 45 (1973–1974): 1–22.

The comments from *The North American Review* (April 1835) on the character of Prefect Gisquet are part of the editors' sharp criticism of official repression in the aftermath of the Larmarque funeral riots (pp. 281–282). Catherine Kudlick discusses Gisquet's career in *Cholera in Post-Revolutionary Paris: A Cultural History,* pp. 176–183. Two recent articles take up "The Mystery of Marie Rogêt" in some detail: Laura Saltz, " '(Horrible to Relate!)': Recovering the Body of Marie Rogêt" in *The American Face of Edgar Allan Poe,* eds. Shawn Rosenheim and Steven Rachman (Baltimore: Johns Hopkins Univ. Press, 1995) and Mark Seltzer, "The Crime System" in *Critical Inquiry* (Spring 2004): 557–583. John Walsh, in *Poe the Detective: The Curious Circumstances behind the Mystery of Marie Rogêt* (New Brunswick: Rutgers Univ. Press, 1967), and Amy Gilman Srebnick, in *The Mysterious Death of Mary Rogers: Sex and Culture in Nineteenth-Century New York* (New York: Oxford Univ. Press, 1995), treat the story's historical and cultural context.

In *The Mystery to a Solution: Poe, Borges, and the Analytic Detective Story* (Baltimore: Johns Hopkins Univ. Press, 1994), pp. 318–356, John Irwin explores the role of mathematics in "The Mystery of Marie Rogêt" and links contemporary French politics to the events of the Dupin series as a whole. Lawrence Frank's elaborate account of the importance of Laplace to the intellectual ambitions of "The Murders in the Rue Morgue" touches on a daunting but stimulating array of sources, including Darwin's journals and the lectures of John Pringle Nichol, that add significant weight to Poe's tale. His pages are an instructive complement to Irwin's work. See *Victorian Detective Fiction and the Nature of Evidence: The Scientific Investigations of Poe, Dickens, and Doyle* (New York: Palgrave Macmillan, 2003), pp. 29–43. Shawn Rosenheim's treatment of the "Rue Morgue" plot as a psychoanalytic cryptogram is an illuminating complement to the discussion I try to offer. See *The Cryptographic Imagination* (Baltimore: Johns Hopkins Univ. Press, 1997), pp. 65–86.

Louis Braille's stenographic system of printing for the blind would not be widely known and adopted before the end of the nineteenth century. But a long and engrossing essay that appeared in *The North American Review* in 1833, "Education of the Blind," would have informed Poe about the pioneering work of the Institution for the Blind in Paris, the source of Dupin's reference to the value of interpreting prominences above the plane of the ordinary: "Persons who have witnessed exhibitions at the institutions for the blind have been surprised at the ease and fluency with which they can read books printed in raised letters, by passing the fingers rapidly over them." See *The North American Review* 80 (July 1833): 20–59.

David Halliburton's examination of Poe's strikingly self-absorbed narrators in "Berenice," "Ligeia," "Morella," and "Eleonora" is an important touchstone for any admirer of this group of tales. See *Edgar Allan Poe: A Phenomenological View*, pp. 223–228. Meredith McGill treats the enigmatic voices and vague settings that characterize stories like "Berenice" or "Eleonora" as tactical adaptations to the magazine culture of reprinting. A narrator completely cut off from external circumstances, McGill suggests, inhabits a generic rather than a geographic world—one that lends itself to the ubiquitous commercial practice of recirculating tales through as many different periodical outlets as possible. See *American Literature and the Culture of Reprinting, 1843–1853* (Philadelphia: Univ. of Pennsylvania Press, 2003).

3 The Gravity of Things

In *Victorian Sensation: The Extraordinary Publication, Reception, and Secret Authorship of Vestiges of the Natural History of Creation* (Chicago: Univ. of Chicago Press, 2000), James A. Secord describes the impact of Robert Chambers' book, as well as the complicated relations that existed between Chambers and John Pringle Nichol, who taught astronomy at Glasgow and lectured widely on contemporary science in England and in the United States. The public lecture that evolved into *Eureka* represents Poe's attempt to emulate the success that Nichol enjoyed when he published *Views of the Architecture of the Heavens* in 1837. Secord's recent edition of the *Vestiges* (Chicago, 1994) is the source for the quotations from Chambers' book at the beginning of this chapter. For a sense of how closely Chambers followed Nichol, compare his description of the small dimples and whirlpools in a stream cited in the text (*Vestiges*, p. 19) to the following passage from *Views of the Architecture of the Heavens* published seven years earlier:

> Have you ever walked in a mood of tranquil thought along the side of a quiet river, whose waving banks reflect a thousand currents, by the intermingling of which, numerous dimples or whirlpools are produced—their easy glide only marking the river's stillness? Have you seen these dimples follow and pursue each other as if in gambol, or watched the phenomenon of the near approach of two or three? Then have you witnessed the secret of the mystery of the double and triple stars! (*Views of the Architecture of the Heavens*, p. 172)

If Nichol had shared Poe's appetite for accusations of plagiarism, he would have been justified in lodging one here against the publisher of *Vestiges*. The extraordinary penetrating power of Lord Rosse's six-foot reflecting telescope, built on his estate outside Dublin, gave further contemporary impetus to the interest in nebular theory, the suggestive design of spiral galaxies, and their earthly replicas that Chambers, Nichol, Von Humboldt, and many others address during the years that Poe's stories appeared.

Planetary bodies and vortices served as the "islands" and the "whirlpools" of extraterrestrial space in the same years that Poe was exploring the vortex in fiction. David Halliburton notes the inherently "equivocal" nature of the vortex as a kinetic experience in his intriguing discussion of "MS. Found in a Bottle." See *Edgar Allan Poe: A Phenomenological View*, pp. 245–256. Terence Whalen's chapter "Subtle Barbarians" in *Edgar Allan Poe and the Masses: The Political Economy of Literature in Antebellum America* (Princeton: Princeton Univ. Press, 1999) is an informative discussion of the generic expectations that Poe was exploiting in his voyage and vortex stories. J. Gerald Kennedy treats "MS. Found in a Bottle" as a "metaphor for the project of writing," an approach that Halliburton's discussion partly anticipates, but Kennedy expands his discussion to reflect the opening stages of Poe's career-long inquiry into the links between writing and death. See *Poe, Death and the Life of Writing*, pp. 23–31.

Poe's detailed knowledge of telescopes and his familiarity with the findings of contemporary astronomy are evident as early as the elaborate technical notes that he attaches to "The Unparalleled Adventure of One Hans Pfaall" in 1835. The suggestive instrumental structure he gives to the Norway maelstrom falls midway between this early sign of his interest and his references, thirteen years later, to Lord Rosse's startling findings in the closing pages of *Eureka*. Von Humboldt's survey of the scientific utility of the pendulum, as well as a brief allusion to Galileo's legendary epiphany while observing the movements of a cathedral chandelier, come from *Cosmos*. For the passage in which Humboldt describes how to find the mean density of the Earth, and dismisses popular fantasies of a subterranean world, see the edition of Volume 1 recently issued by the Johns Hopkins University Press (1997), pp. 169–171. Poe also read explanations of Galileo's work with pendulums in a number of scientific biographies of the time. John Limon offers a wide-ranging discussion of Poe's engagement with works of contemporary natural philosophy in *The Place of Fiction in the Time of Science: A Disciplinary History of American Writing* (Cambridge and London: Cambridge Univ. Press, 1990).

On the Croton water project, see Nelson M. Blake, *Water for the Cities: A History of the Urban Water Problem in the United States* (Syracuse, NY: Syracuse Univ. Press, 1956). Poe wrote about the beautiful view from the top of the Murray Hill Reservoir in "Doings of Gotham" Letter III, from *The Columbia Spy* (June 1, 1844), and (as Kenneth Silverman recounts) took walks along the causeway covering the Croton Aqueduct after his family moved to Fordham in 1846. Evan Carton treats Ellison's construction of Arnheim as an allusion to the ideals of the Emersonian bard. See *The Rhetoric of American Romance: Dialectic and Identity in Emerson, Dickinson, Poe and Hawthorne* (Baltimore:

Johns Hopkins Univ. Press, 1985). A brief description of the Ermenonville gardens containing Rousseau's tomb is in Simon Schama's *Citizens: A Chronicle of the French Revolution* (New York: Random House, 1989), pp. 156–159. Like the fictional Ellison, Rousseau "foreshadows" the late-eighteenth-century figures of Turgôt and Condorcêt.

Joan Dayan's chapter on *Eureka* in *Fables of Mind* (pp. 19–79) is the most ambitious investigation of the book's philosophical roots, preparing a context for her thoughtful discussion of "The Domain of Arnheim" (pp. 83–104). David Halliburton is particularly perceptive in his consideration of the complex rhetorical life of "force" in *Eureka*. See *Edgar Allan Poe: A Phenomenological View*, pp. 392–412. John Irwin calls attention to Poe's interest in the work of David Brewster in *American Hieroglyphics*, with particular emphasis on Brewster's *Letters on Natural Magic* (1832). Brewster's biographies of Galileo, Tycho Brahe, and Kepler are in *The Martyrs of Science* (New York: Harper and Brothers, 1841).

4 The Kingdom of Inorganization

A sealed glass bottle containing a portrait of Washington, a copy of his valedictory address on leaving the Presidency, several contemporary Baltimore newspapers, and a selection of United States coins was deposited, along with a copper plaque, inside the cornerstone of the Washington Monument's base during a ceremony marking the beginning of construction in 1815. The entire event, including an inventory of the time capsule's contents, is described at some length in *Niles' Weekly Register* (Saturday, July 8, 1815): 329–333.

John Irwin recognizes the evocative nature of Pym's reference to "the mystery of our being in existence" in *American Hieroglyphics*, though the mysteries of language rather than of sheer being are Irwin's overriding interest. Burton Pollin's edition of *The Imaginary Voyages* (Boston: G. K. Hall, 1981) contains an exhaustive record of Poe's sources in *The Narrative of Arthur Gordon Pym*. Three book-length reviews of the scholarship devoted to Pym's narrative have been published within the last decade: *Poe's Pym: Critical Explorations*, ed. Richard Kopley (Durham, NC, and London: Duke Univ. Press, 1992), J. Gerald Kennedy, *The Narrative of Arthur Gordon Pym and the Abyss of Interpretation* (New York: Twayne, 1995), and Ronald C. Harvey, *The Critical History of Edgar Allan Poe's The Narrative of Arthur Gordon Pym: "A Dialogue with Unreason"* (New York: Garland, 1998). This interpretive avalanche shows no signs of stopping.

Umberto Eco's nested boxes depicting the multilayered structure of Pym's story appear in *Six Walks in the Fictional Woods* (Cambridge, MA: Harvard Univ. Press, 1994). Poe's interest in figures of containment throughout the book is usually treated as an adjunct of various psychological themes, beginning with the womb as an idealized refuge. Paul Rosenzweig examines the narrative from this point of view in "The Search for Identity: The Enclosure Motif" in *The Narrative of Arthur Gordon Pym ESQ* 26 (1980).

John Lloyd Stephens describes his audience with Mehemet Ali in Chapter III of *Incidents of Travel in Egypt, Arabia Petræa, and the Holy Land*, a book that Poe admired. Stephens's journey on the Nile provided him with a number of opportunities to remark on what he considered the stark contrast between ancient and modern cultures on display in this unique region. See for instance his account of a moonlight visit to the ruins of Edfu at the end of Chapter IX. When Mehemet Ali conquered the Sudan in 1821 he acquired control of the world's primary source of gum arabic, an extract of the acacia tree. Poe's reference to this substance in connection with Tsalal helps establish the link between its people and those of Mehemet Ali's resurgent Egypt.

Northrup Frye's observations about the romance assumptions on which Poe often draws, including his account of the symbolic objects beneath Pamela's disguise in the *Arcadia*, are in *The Secular Scripture: A Study of Romance* (Cambridge, MA: Harvard Univ. Press, 1976). William Taylor makes use of Poe as barometer of contemporary anxieties when he identifies Roderick Usher as an introverted "cavalier" figure in his study of nineteenth-century American literary and political culture, but the terms of Taylor's discussion cast a more searching light on "William Wilson." See *Cavalier and Yankee: The Old South and American National Character* (Cambridge, MA: Harvard Univ. Press, 1979).

5   The Infected World at Large

The most extensive, recent treatment of Poe's plate articles, including "The Island of the Fay," is Louis Renza's chapter in *The American Face of Edgar Allan Poe*, but Patrick Quinn's discussion of "The Island of the Fay," "The Oval Portrait," and "The Fall of the House of Usher" in the last chapter of *The French Face of Edgar Poe* (pp. 257–275) is the best starting point for an appreciation of Poe's ambitions in this unusual romantic excursion. Quinn cites Baudelaire's perceptive grouping of his translations as the starting point for his own reflections. Lawrence Buell gives a concise and elegant summary of the conventions of the romantic ramble in *Literary Transcendentalism* (Ithaca, NY: Cornell Univ. Press, 1974).

T. O. Mabbott cites the 1832 letters from France that N. P. Willis sent to the *New York Mirror* reporting the mockery of cholera during the year's Lenten masquerades in *Collected Works of Edgar Allan Poe*, 2.667–668. Heinrich Heine's account of the outbreak of the disease at a masquerade ball is cited in François Delaporte's book *Disease and Civilization: The Cholera in Paris, 1832* (Cambridge, MA: MIT Press, 1986). Poe clearly drew on this proverbial link between epidemics and masked balls in "The Masque of the Red Death." The Fourierest "phalanx" was only one of several kinds of nineteenth-century utopian experiments that incorporated elements of what Fourier called, in *The Theory of the Four Movements*, "amorous liberty." "Industrial attraction" is the term that Fourier used for the erotic bonds that he believed would hold his social idealists together. The phrase may help explain the furnaces and massy hammers that Prospero's courtiers take up in order to seal the abbey gates in Poe's tale. Fourier's book is the source that Hawthorne has his narrator, Miles Coverdale, consult in *The Blithedale Romance*, a fictionalized treatment of the Brook Farm setting, where Hawthorne briefly lived in 1841.

The elaborate setting of "The Masque of the Red Death"—particularly its flaming braziers—suggests aspects of an alchemical laboratory as well as a musical or a sensory architecture. Poe's acquaintance with alchemy was established nearly forty years ago by Barton St. Armand in a pair of articles in *Poe Studies* that shed a particularly useful light on "The Gold-Bug." John Irwin develops much of the same material in the early chapters of *The Mystery to a Solution*. Gaston Bachelard's reflections in *The Psychoanalysis of Fire* spring, in part, from his own earlier work on the alchemist's sexual "reverie," but they are equally illuminating for the broader, cognitive fires represented in the sequence of tales that this chapter discusses.

Goethe's *Theory of Colours* first appeared in German in 1810. Charles Lock Eastlake's translation was published in London in 1840. The quotation from Goethe's preface in this chapter comes from a facsimile of the Eastlake translation published by the MIT Press (1970). The daguerreotype process was only announced to the public in 1839, two years before the publication of "The Masque of the Red Death," but its popularity was immediate and widespread. Darkrooms in Poe's day used a variety of colored tissue papers to filter the light by which the daguerreotypist worked: orange, yellow, or red. The daguerreotype plate was sensitive to light in the blue range of the spectrum only, so it was important to exclude only blue light from the room where the plates would be sensitized and developed.

Swift's *A Tale of a Tub* caught Joan Dayan's eye as the basis for portions of *Eureka* (see *Fables of Mind*, p. 29), "The Murders in the Rue Morgue," and "Loss of Breath." Poe's attempt to highlight the pertinence of Swift's title to "The Tell-Tale Heart" has not attracted much attention, perhaps because it is hidden in plain sight. The passages that Poe draws on are from Section IX "A Digression concerning the Original, the Use, and Improvement of Madness in a Commonwealth" and Section XI, where Swift presents a diatribe against vision as a "scantling" (a sample) of the great wisdom of one of his heroes.

Recent critical considerations of "The Gold-Bug" have tended to be highly contextual in nature: those by Marc Shell in *Money, Language and Thought: Literary and Philosophical Economies from the Medieval to the Modern Era* (Berkeley: Univ. of California Press, 1982) and by Terence Whalen in *Edgar Allan Poe and the Masses* are good examples. Modern students are often embarrassed by the story's treatment of Jupiter, one of the few black characters in Poe's fiction. But he is a far more intriguing and more vital figure, in the unfolding story, than our contemporary discomfort with stereotypes usually permits us to recognize. Lilane Weissberg offers a detailed consideration of the complex racial undercurrents in "The Gold-Bug" in her chapter, "Black, White, and Gold" from *Romancing the Shadow: Poe and Race*, eds. J. Gerald Kennedy and Lilane Weissberg (New York: Oxford Univ. Press, 2001), pp. 127–156. Shawn Rosenheim's ingenious account of "Secret Writing as Alchemy" in *The Cryptographic Imagination* (Baltimore: Johns Hopkins Univ. Press, 1997), pp. 42–64 is the most recent adaptation of alchemical symbolism to Legrand's quest.

Baudelaire's translation of "Mesmeric Revelation," "Révélation magné-tique," appeared in *La Liberté de Penser* on July 15, 1848, more than two weeks after the notorious "June Days" in which Cavaignac's troops attacked the radical citizen-militias of Paris and seized control of the city. Karl Marx's long account of the events leading up to and following Cavaignac's assault, "The Eighteenth Brumaire of Louis Napoleon," is the classic treatment of these events. Barton St. Armand's discussion of the nineteenth-century cult that he calls "Sentimental Love Religion" is in *Emily Dickinson and Her Culture*. "The Purloined Letter" has provoked such an outpouring of sophisticated commentary in recent years that John Irwin half-whimsically, half-wistfully refers to the story itself as "that much-crumpled thing" in the opening chapter of *The Mystery to a Solution*. My own comments try to minimize any additional crumpling.

Conclusion   Pictures of Ascent

Thomas Mabbott quotes W. H. Bond's detailed description of Poe's manuscript copy of "The Light-House," part of which is currently held in the Berg Collection of the New York Public Library and part in Harvard's Houghton Library. The *Collected Works* also reproduces a facsimile of "The Light-House" manuscript at the end of volume 3. Poe's hand is so clear that the text reads just as easily from the facsimiles as from type. Ruskin's comments on "Longship's Lighthouse" are from the first American edition of *Modern Painters* (New York: John Wiley, 1847), pp. 250–252. The watercolor itself is one of 120 projected paintings that Turner agreed to do for an ambitious series of engravings, *Picturesque Views in England and Wales* (1825–1838). Only 96 paintings were ultimately engraved. For background, see Andrew Wilton, *J. M. W. Turner: His Life and Art* (New York: Rizzoli, 1979), pp. 175–190.

Kenneth Silverman describes Poe's Fordham walks in *Edgar A. Poe: Mournful and Never-ending Remembrance*, p. 302. Humboldt's discussion of Ehrenberg's micro-paleontology is scattered through various sections of the first volume of *Cosmos* (pp. 150, 309–310, 342–344), but Poe might have acquired his appreciation for Ehrenberg's work from any number of sources, including Robert Chambers' discussion of the composition of chalk in *Vestiges of the Natural History of Creation* (London, 1844), and two reviews of Ehrenberg's findings in *Scientific American*. The second of these reviews quotes Edward Young's "Night Thoughts" as an index of the imaginative impact of Ehrenberg's startling disclosures about the skeletal nature of sedimentary stone: "Where is the dust that has not been alive?" See *Scientific American* 4 (October 28, 1848), p. 46. Humboldt's reference to Darwin's *Voyage of the Beagle* in connection with the phenomena that Ehrenberg's work documents is in *Cosmos*, p. 309.

Index